It

The riders horses were blowing, and steam rose from the animals' hides in the chill air. Mr. Halston threw himself off his mount and caught Chastity's bridle, then he reached up to take hold of her waist. Chastity was laughing as she slid into Mr. Halston's arms. Her eyes sparkled and high color flew in her cheeks. "That was magnificent, Jeffrey!" she exclaimed.

He had been laughing, too. But as he looked at her, his arms still around her, a sudden shuttering came down over his face. He dropped his arms and stepped back. "It was indeed a grand ride, Miss Cummings. We must do it again someday." He bowed and walked away.

Chastity stared after him, her laughter caught in her throat. She rather thought she would do better to stay far clear of Mr. Halston. He was upsetting to her equilibrium in more ways than one. . . .

The Chester Charade

Gayle Buck

A SIGNET BOOK

SIGNET
Published by the Penguin Group
Penguin Putnam Inc., 375 Hudson Street,
New York, New York 10014, U.S.A.
Penguin Books Ltd, 27 Wrights Lane,
London W8 5TZ, England
Penguin Books Australia Ltd,
Ringwood, Victoria, Australia
Penguin Books Canada Ltd, 10 Alcorn Avenue,
Toronto, Ontario, Canada M4V 3B2
Penguin Books (N.Z.) Ltd, 182–190 Wairau Road,
Auckland 10, New Zealand

Penguin Books Ltd, Registered Offices:
Harmondsworth, Middlesex, England

First published by Signet, an imprint of Dutton NAL,
a member of Penguin Putnam Inc.

First Printing, May, 1999
10 9 8 7 6 5 4 3 2 1

Chapter One

Miss Chastity Cummings pulled on the bell rope to summon the housekeeper. It would be well to consult with Mrs. Timms concerning the west wing, which had been closed for a considerable length of time. In fact, it had not been open since before her brother had come into the title three years before.

Their father, the old Lord Cummings, had become progressively more reclusive after the death of his wife. He had shunned the society of London, preferring to entertain a small select group of friends that would periodically come out to his estate of Chester. During that time, much of the manor had been closed off, and the furniture in the unused rooms was swathed with holland covers.

The new Lord Cummings, Henry Alphonse, had had no intention of burying himself in the country as had his father, and he had chosen to maintain a house in London. During the autumn and winter months, of course, his lordship and Chastity left town and entertained at Chester.

When the housekeeper came into the drawing room, Chastity relayed his lordship's recent decision that the west wing was to be opened. Mrs. Timms greeted the news with approval. "That will make things go easier and no mistake, miss," she said.

"Yes, and we shall want the state room for Mr. and Mrs. Cummings. I know that I may rely on you to see to everything," said Chastity, a wealth of meaning in her words.

Mrs. Timms understood immediately and nodded. "That you may, miss. There will be no cause for complaint," she said, pursing her lips.

Since her sister-in-law's caprices were well known to the household, Chastity was not at all surprised by the housekeeper's grim promise.

"I think that will be all for now, Mrs. Timms," said Chastity. "Mr. and Mrs. Cummings will arrive within the week, so I authorize you to do whatever you must to ready the west wing in time. I know it is short notice."

"Be that as it may, miss, I shall see that it is done," said Mrs. Timms. The housekeeper bustled away, armed with her new commission and filled with zeal to see it carried out.

The housekeeper's exit was followed almost at once by the butler's entrance. Formally, he announced, "Lady Peters has arrived, ma'am. Shall I show her in?"

"Lady Peters! Here!" exclaimed Chastity. "Of course you may show her in."

The butler bowed and effaced himself. In a very few moments, Lady Merrill Peters swept into the drawing room. Her ladyship rushed forward, holding out slender kid-gloved hands to her hostess. Eau de rose wafted gently through the air with her passage. "Chastity!"

Lady Peters wore a fashionable olive pelisse, detailed with frogging on the cuffs and bodice and buttoned up to the throat with mother-of-pearl. A delightful velvet hat covered her hair, and a black feather curled over its brim to brush her cheek. As she reached her friend, she exclaimed, "My dear! How glad I am to find you at home."

Chastity laughed and exchanged an affectionate hug with her visitor. "Merrill, what a wonderful surprise! I thought you were firmly fixed in Dorcester for a few more weeks yet." With a gesture she invited her friend to join her on the silk-striped settee.

"Oh, it was so dreary that there was no bearing it any longer," said Merrill, sitting down beside Chastity on the cushions and beginning to draw off her gloves. "Charles would not be separated from his cows and his sheep. So I decided to come up early. I knew that you would not mind."

"No, of course not. But what of Charles?" asked Chastity.

"Oh, he said that I was to convey his apologies. He will come next year," said Merrill. Then with a pout, "Cows and sheep! It is all Charles will talk about."

Chastity chuckled. "How droll for you, Merrill!"

Merrill looked at her friend indignantly. "Yes, you may laugh, Chastity. But it is not you who must listen as the breeding line of this or that ewe is hotly debated over the dinner plates!"

"Oh, no! It cannot be as bad as all that," said Chastity with swift sympathy.

"It is worse," said Merrill firmly. "Take a word of advice from me, dear Chastity. Never, never allow Henry to dabble in agriculture. It simply ruins the man of fashion. Why, when I last saw him, Charles was striding across a muddy field to inspect a new calf, and never a thought for his white uppers! It was simply too provoking!"

"How very shocking! I can scarcely credit that our dapper dandy sacrifices his glossy top boots to such a bucolic cause," said Chastity. She was genuinely astonished at her friend's report, but also much amused.

"Charles is simply not the same gentleman that he was before he inherited his uncle's estate. If I had known what would come of it, I would not have been in the least happy for Charles. No, indeed!" Merrill shook her head in a mournful way. "I have been terribly, horridly disillusioned, and so I told him."

"But what does Charles have to say for himself?" asked Chastity curiously.

"He simply laughed. He promised, however, that after Christmas we shall go up to London," said Merrill, her expression brightening considerably at the prospect.

"We must hope that once he is returned to London that he will suffer a violent reversal of feeling toward agricultural pursuits," said Chastity.

"Oh, I do hope so! It will be so dull to have a husband who thinks more about a herd of cows than he does about the Season," said Merrill earnestly. "But enough of such dreary things! Tell me whom you and Henry have invited for your house party? I hope not your aunt, the one with those horrid little dogs."

Chastity laughed. "Yes, we have, indeed. Or rather, our aunt Webster has invited herself, and we have graciously accepted. And she is bringing her pugs. Oh, Merrill, I must tell you about Henry's wicked suggestion. We have discovered there are dead rats in the walls of the spare rooms. You may imagine the smell."

Merrill shuddered and acknowledged that she could.

"Well, Henry has proposed, quite tongue-in-cheek, of course, that since our aunt hasn't really got any sense of smell that she should be housed there with her dogs. Henry says that will keep the dogs so busy, trying to dig out the rats, that we shall all be spared their company."

"No!" Merrill stared. "What a terrible thing to suggest." Then she began to laugh. "But how utterly delicious, too! Only Henry could think of such an outrageous thing. Oh, Chastity, do it! If those nasty creatures keep your aunt up with their scratching and whining, she might take a pet and go home and you will be spared even the sight of those animals."

"That is just what Henry said, too, in the most reasonable tone imaginable," said Chastity, shaking her head and smiling. "But really, Merrill, I could not do it. It would be so mean-spirited."

"Oh, I cannot agree. It is far more mean-spirited for your aunt to expect you and Henry to put up with her dogs as you do every time she comes to visit."

"I am almost sorry that I told you," said Chastity.

"That is only because you are beginning to entertain the notion," said Merrill shrewdly.

"You *are* horrid," said Chastity cordially.

Merrill laughed, then said, "My dear! Before I left Dorcester, I had a letter from my brother. Imagine my astonishment when I read that he and *Jeffrey Halston* will be at your house party."

"Oh, yes. Henry invited them when he was last in town. He said that he was delighted to see Gabriel again," said Chastity.

"Chastity, surely you cannot be so blasé about it as you appear. Will it not be horridly uncomfortable for you?"

"I have not the least notion why," said Chastity, shaking her head.

"But Chastity—the Honorable Jeffrey Halston! And he is a widower now!" exclaimed Merrill, expectantly awaiting her friend's reaction.

But Chastity took the news with disappointing calmness. "Yes, so I had heard. It must have been difficult for Jeffrey, losing his wife so suddenly in childbirth."

"Chastity, I could just shake you!" exclaimed Merrill. "How can you speak of Jeffrey Halston in that cool fashion?"

Chastity smiled at her friend's indignant expression. "But how should I speak of him, Merrill? We are mere acquaintances, after all."

"Pooh! Jeffrey Halston was once head over heels for you, Chastity. You cannot convince me that he was not, nor that you were completely indifferent to him," said Merrill impatiently. "Surely, that history must count for something."

"It seems such a long time ago," said Chastity, shaking her head. A reminiscent smile tugged at her lips. "Jeffrey Halston was so devoted and so exceedingly obliging. I do believe that at one time he would have undertaken to walk across a bed of burning coals if I had but said the word."

"And you never would," said Merrill crossly. At Chastity's amused, inquiring look, she said, "You refused Jeffrey's offer. You never confided it to me, but I knew it all the same."

"But you see, I was never that deeply devoted to Jeffrey," explained Chastity.

"And so he turned around and married Mirabelle Sweeney. Mirabelle!" Merrill's tone was one of disgust. "What a waste. Mirabelle had more hair than wit and a dumpy figure besides. I have always thought that Jeffrey deliberately chose someone as completely opposite to you as he possibly could because he was secretly nursing a broken heart."

"Nonsense! Mirabelle did very well for Jeffrey. Once he had gotten over his infatuation for me, he was finally able to see it," said Chastity.

"For my part, I wish he had never met Mirabelle Sweeney,"

said Merrill roundly. "I doubt that he would ever have noticed her if some busybody had not introduced them, for she was such a wallflower."

"I was that busybody," said Chastity. "Mirabelle was instantly smitten, but Jeffrey took a bit longer. Then it went just as I had hoped."

"Oh, Chastity, you are more shatterbrained than I ever supposed," said Merrill, aghast. She shook her head slowly. "I must say, I am utterly shocked at this revelation."

Chastity laughed. "My dear, why? Simply because I neatly extricated myself from attentions that were becoming embarrassing? I had turned Jeffrey Halston down twice before I found Mirabelle and brought her to his attention. I thought it all ended very well. Except for this tragic turn, of course. I do hope that Jeffrey has been able to reconcile himself to his terrible loss."

"Well, we shall quickly see in the upcoming weeks, shan't we?" asked Merrill tartly. "I rather suspect that Jeffrey has made up his mind to wed again, and that is why he is coming down from town with Gabriel. I will lay odds that he has not forgotten you, Chastity, and that he will make a point of remembering himself to you. I leave it to you to imagine for what purpose!"

"Oh, dear!" Chastity was dismayed. "I do hope that you are wrong, Merrill."

"And I trust that I am right. It is high time that you were wed. You are not getting any younger, you know. At five-and-twenty, you must begin thinking of yourself as being on the shelf. And I simply cannot bear the thought of you reduced to wearing a cap, dear Chastity."

"Is that what happens when one attains my great age?" asked Chastity, amused. "I had wondered. Thank you, Merrill! I shall at once celebrate my new status by sending off for a drawerful of lace caps!"

"Oh, how provoking you are!" exclaimed Merrill, half laughing. She scolded some more, shaking her finger. "Yes, it is all very well to laugh, Chastity. But it really is such a pity that Henry has not made the least push on your behalf."

"Henry and I have a very comfortable arrangement. Neither of us has the least desire to marry, at least for the present," said Chastity. "We are situated pleasantly in society and do not lack for companionship. Why should we alter what suits us both so well?"

"Why—why, I cannot tell you that. Except that it is your duty," said Merrill, putting on a prim expression.

"Oh, Merrill, pray do not say so!" exclaimed Chastity, her eyes brimming with laughter. "And in just that way, too!"

"Yes, and it is Henry's duty, too!" exclaimed Merrill, determined to hammer home her point. "What is to become of the Cummings fortune if Henry does not have an heir? It will all go to Archie and Regina! *That* is food for thought, is it not? I know that it makes *me* shudder."

Chastity gave a peal of laughter. "You sound just like my aunt Mackleby!"

Merrill was instantly stricken. Her great blue eyes wide, she asked, "Do I? Oh, no! Do I truly, Chastity?"

"Just like her," said Chastity firmly, nodding.

"Now just see what you have done, Chastity! My concern for you has turned me into a ferocious old harridan before my time!" said Merrill in tragic accents, falling back against the sofa with her hand to her eyes.

"I do not think that you will ever be either ferocious or a harridan, Merrill. You haven't got the character for it," said Chastity, neatly skewering her friend's taste for the dramatic.

"Well, I like that!" Merrill exclaimed, bouncing up again, not really knowing whether she should be insulted or not.

Chastity looked at her with affection. "I meant that you are too bright and pleasant a person, Merrill!"

Merrill was pleased, but still she pouted a little. "Are you not going to say that I am ageless, too, Chastity?"

"I do try to stay within the bounds of truthfulness," said Chastity dryly.

Merrill made a face. "How perfectly horrid you are, Chastity. One should be able to tell a tale or two in order to preserve a friend's illusions!"

"Not I!" retorted Chastity. "That is a certain road to a broken friendship."

"Perhaps you are in the right of it," Merrill conceded with a quick smile. She raised her delicate brows. "Has your aunt Mackleby been after you again?"

"Oh, yes. When is she not?" said Chastity cheerfully. "Of course, we do not see her very often when we are away from London, but her unequivocal opinions follow us in the form of letters couched in the most acid language imaginable."

Chastity's maternal aunt, Lady Mackleby, still considered it a personal insult that while under her aegis, Chastity had not accepted any of the offers that had been made for her hand. She held to the opinion that it was every well-bred female's duty to marry, preferably straight out of the schoolroom.

Lady Mackleby highly disapproved of Chastity's lot in life and never let an opportunity go by when she did not express her opinion. But since Chastity saw her ladyship only in society, and then in the most genteel company, she was spared many lectures that would otherwise have fallen upon her head. Chastity had always considered it to be a blessing that she had not been obligated to make her home with Lady Mackleby, for though she had great affection for the old lady, she had no desire to live with her.

"In her last letter to me, my aunt expressed regret that I am of age and mistress of myself. Worse, I am possessed of an independence that makes it highly unlikely that I will be forced into matrimony by pecuniary circumstances," said Chastity cheerfully.

"I don't know why you even accept the post," Merrill said, shaking her head. "I know that I would not. I would either burn the letters unopened or have them sent back as undeliverable."

"But I could not be so rude, Merrill. I am fond of her. She did her best for me, after all. I simply could not meet her expectations for me."

"That much is to your discredit, certainly. However, I do think that after all of these years, Lady Mackleby must see that Henry bears some blame for your lack of situation."

Chastity's eyes gleamed with laughter. "You have underestimated her ladyship, Merrill. She naturally directs most of her displeasure at me. However, Henry does come in for his share of scolds, too. The truly boring aspect of it all is that my aunt's forcefully expressed stand merely reflects the general opinion of all my dear married sisters."

Merrill made a face. "I should not like to be so bullied and hectored as you are, Chastity."

"I admit, it can be a sad trial at times. And that is why Henry and I do not often invite our siblings and their families to an extended stay during the winter, as I am certain that they wish we might. Henry has stated flatly that he will not be scolded and reproached at his own table."

"Good for Henry," Merrill said approvingly. She reached out to lay a sympathetic hand on her friend's arm. "Oh, Chastity! If only you had wed Jeffrey Halston or one of the other of your suitors! How much more comfortable you would be!"

"Nonsense! I am very comfortable now," said Chastity with a smile.

"I meant that you would not have to bear with your relations as you do," Merrill said reasonably.

"No! Instead I would have to bear with a husband who did not suit me," said Chastity a bit tartly.

"Pooh! Even if you thoroughly disliked one another, you could go on very well. Why, no one lives in their spouse's pocket. It is so unfashionable."

"Then you have my leave to call me unfashionable," said Chastity. "For I will wed only where my heart is engaged, and his likewise!"

Merrill shook her head. "You are still such a romantic goose, Chastity. That sort of notion did very well when we were naive schoolgirls, but it won't do now. Believe me, for I know."

"Did you not love Charles when you accepted his suit?" Chastity asked, surprised. "I quite thought that you did."

Merrill flushed. "I do not recall whether I did or not. It scarcely matters, does it? Charles and I go along very comfortably. That is what you need, Chastity, more than any silly notion of undying love. You need someone who will make you comfortable and with whom you can be content."

"Like Jeffrey Halston, perhaps?"

Merrill eyed her friend. Chastity's expression had become a little remote, and there was that certain quality in her voice that was a warning to one wise enough to heed it. "I shan't deny that I see Jeffrey as a solution for you, Chastity. But far be it for me to join that same chorus that you find so trying," she said primly. "I shall only urge you to meet him with kindness."

"I am seldom so rude that I fail to acknowledge an old acquaintance," said Chastity. "And so I shall reassure you of that much, Merrill."

Merrill nodded. "Thank you, Chastity," she said, very much on her dignity.

A short silence fell. Merrill pulled one of her kid gloves through her fingers. Chastity took pity on her friend's discomfiture. "How are Sir Humbert and Lady Maria? I have not seen them since Henry and I came down from London. I trust that they are well."

Merrill brightened, obviously relieved to have gotten over uncomfortable ground. "Oh, yes! Can you doubt it? They are the same as always. Mama wrote me that they will be back in London after the Christmas holidays."

The two friends spoke easily over a broad range of topics, but neither again mentioned the advent of the Honorable Jeffrey Halston to the house party. When Merrill rose to go, they were on the best terms imaginable. Chastity accompanied her friend to the grand hall, walking arm in arm with her and taking an affectionate leave at the bottom of the wide steps.

Chastity returned to the warm drawing room. She had enjoyed Merrill's conversation overall, but it had left her feeling vaguely disturbed. When her brother had first informed her that Gabriel Salyer was coming to Chester, and that Jeffrey Halston was accompanying him, she had felt a qualm. However, she had thrown it off almost at once. It was not to be expected that there should be any discomfort associated with meeting the Honorable Jeffrey Halston again. It had been years since he had danced attendance on her, after all. And he was merely accompanying a friend to a house party in the country.

Merrill had shed quite a different light on the matter. It had never occurred to Chastity that Jeffrey Halston could have a hidden motive for accepting Henry's invitation. Now the most dominant thought in Chastity's mind was the knowledge that her old beau would shortly be descending upon Chester.

Chastity was no longer sure what to think about it. She rubbed her hands up and down her sleeved arms slowly in an unconscious gesture. She and Jeffrey Halston had once been quite an *on dit*. It had been openly rumored that they would eventually make a match of it. It had been the shocker of the Season when a betrothal between the Honorable Jeffrey Halston and Miss Mirabelle Sweeney had been announced instead.

Chastity had hoped for just such an ending, for she had begun to find Jeffrey Halston's unswerving attentions unnerving. She had twice turned down the gentleman's passionately worded offers, but she had begun to despair of convincing him that his suit was truly hopeless with her.

It was not that Chastity had disliked Jeffrey Halston or that they had been ill-suited. On the contrary, Chastity Cummings and Jeffrey Halston had become instant friends on the first time that they had met. Unfortunately, thought Chastity with vague regret, Jeffrey's feelings toward her had undergone a dramatic change while hers had not. She had continued to think of him only in a sisterly fashion, and his ardor had been both confusing and even frightening.

That had been six years ago. As Chastity stared into the fire, she wondered what feelings, if any, she might have for Jeffrey Halston when she met him again. They were both older, and their lives had taken different turns. She pulled her fringed Norwich shawl closer about her as she continued to reflect.

When she looked once again into Jeffrey Halston's eyes, would her own emotions be different? Would she see the same animated adoration in his expression as she had in the past? Or would the intervening six years and a marriage have cooled that ardor completely? Most important, which did she wish it to be?

Chastity shook her head. "How foolish I am being," she said, chastising herself a little. Seldom had she had so many conflicting thoughts. It was pointless to speculate, of course. She would simply have to wait and see what happened when she came face-to-face with her old beau.

Her woolgathering was interrupted by the chiming of the clock. Chastity glanced up at it, startled. It was an hour before dinner. She should be on her way upstairs to change, not standing about thinking about might-have-beens and improbabilities.

Banishing all thoughts of Jeffrey Halston, Chastity left the drawing room and made her way upstairs to her room.

Chapter Two

A few evenings later, Chastity presided over a larger company in the dining room. The Honorable Archibald Cummings and his wife, Regina, had arrived, as had Sir Roger Highfield. Lord Henry Cummings had greeted his brother with an affectionate clap on the shoulder, which had staggered his slighter brother, and borne him off at once to the billiards room. Chastity had been left with the task of smoothing Regina's ruffled feelings at being left practically at the front door, bereft of her husband's escort. But all had gone very well, for she had been quite won over by her sumptuous accommodations.

Merrill and Regina were acquainted, of course, and they had exchanged civil greetings, but without warmth. They had never really liked one another. However, Regina was willing to overlook Lady Peters's inclusion in the house party since she was quite certain that Lady Peters's rooms could not be anywhere near as magnificent as her own.

The conversation during dinner was graced with a flow of compliments. Regina was still so pleased with the arrangements made for her stay that she was on her prettiest behavior.

"Dear Chastity! I know that I have you to thank, for you always take such very good care of me," Regina said with a lovely smile.

She even told Lord Cummings that she was in his debt for his hospitality. "The state room is truly magnificent, Henry. I am really quite impressed," she finished. "Even Archie has expressed his satisfaction, and that must count for something."

Henry accepted his sister-in-law's kind words with an inclination of his head. He presided at the head of the table, looking every inch the gracious host in his dark evening dress. His lordship was a very tall, very large gentleman, a former member of the Horse Guards. He was wide of shoulder and his build muscular, so that there was no need of padding in his coat. He exchanged a quick glance of shared amusement with Chastity.

Brother and sister bore a striking resemblance to one another. Their features were aquiline, and both possessed remarkably fine gray eyes. However, Chastity's eyes appeared softer than did his lordship's, which habitually contained a rather hard expression.

"I am glad that our arrangements for your stay have met with your approval, Regina," said Henry.

"I should tell you that one reason that we wished you and Archie to have the state room is that there were rodents in the walls in the other wing. I knew that you would not wish to be in that locale," Chastity said.

"No, indeed," Regina agreed, quite thoroughly convinced that she had been given the better option. "I shall do famously, I assure you. And I shall not allow Archie to say one word against your arrangements, my dear, as he is sometimes wont to do. Archie is a dear, but he can be so exacting. I do not know how I abide with him, but that is what it means to be a good wife."

Archie allowed his wife's disapprobation to roll off his back. He was in a mellow mood, fathered as much by his brother's hospitality and the excellent wine as by his wife's congeniality. He caught his brother's eye and lifted his glass in a silent toast.

Unlike Henry, who was attired in impeccable elegance, Archie tended to allow his dandified preferences full rein with his evening clothes. His dark hair was carefully brushed into a semblance of disorder, and his starched shirt points and massive cravat made it difficult for him to fully turn his head. His waistcoat was striped and shot through with gold threads, and he wore several fobs and seals.

Archie sprawled carelessly in his chair, one elbow on the table. He gave every appearance of disheveled decadence, though he was not in the least drunk. His expression was considerably lighter than when he had first arrived. Remarking to no one in particular, he said, "I am always glad to come home to Chester."

"I have always adored coming to Chester. It has such a delightfully medieval touch," said Merrill with an expression of contentment on her face as she glanced around the lavishly paneled dining room, the walls of which were covered by heavy woven tapestries hung from floor to ceiling. The ornately carved dining table, flanked by thickly padded chairs covered in deep green and gold medallion-patterned upholstery, was covered with an impressive array of dishes. The glow from bunches of candles in several candelabra shed an extravagance of light that caught the wink of jewels around Regina's slender white neck.

"I doubt that our ancestors lived with quite so much show," said Chastity. "For all I have heard, those were rather grim days."

Regina threw her sister-in-law an amused glance. "Oh, Chastity! How utterly unromantic you are. You have scarcely any imagination at all, have you?"

"Well, I have always been considered rather levelheaded, if that is what you mean," said Chastity, returning her attention to the gentleman on her right.

Chastity parried yet another of the lavish compliments that had been paid her by Sir Roger Highfield all evening. The gentleman was an old family friend of their father's generation. From all accounts, Sir Roger had been a rake and an avid sportsman all of his life. Chastity could well believe it. Sir Roger's chief occupations in life seemed to be paying fulsome praise to whatever ladies came into his orbit, to eat what was set before him with all appearance of enjoyment, and to sati-

ate a keen desire for the hunt. Chastity never allowed herself
to be put out of contenance by the old gentleman's ways, but
she also drew the line if his attentions threatened to become a
bit risqué, as Sir Roger was occasionally wont to do.

Sir Roger left off flirting with Chastity to demand an ac-
counting of his host. "I say, my lord, when do we go out? The
weather has been fair this last week, so I have heard."

"I thought we would wait for the first frost," Henry said,
lifting his wineglass. "My bailiff tells me that we can expect
the weather to turn brisk by early next week. He has a fine
weather sense, as you know, Sir Roger."

Sir Roger Highfield nodded, satisfied. The candlelight
gleamed on his bald pate. He returned to forking up his portion of meat with every semblance of gusto. "We'll see some
sport then."

"Sir Roger, did you not tell me that you were not to con-
sume red meats?" asked Chastity, throwing a questioning
glance at the footman who had served at the table. "Sir Roger
should have been given a serving of the fowl and fish."

"Do not blame your staff, my girl! The man gave me what
I wanted. I told you what my physician said, but I'll warrant
that he's never seen the equal of Chester beef. This bit of meat
won't faze me, you'll see!" said Sir Roger. He reached for his
wineglass with his large hand and downed the contents with a
flourish. "You there! Fill it again, I say."

Chastity watched with amusement. It amazed her that the
elderly gentleman had such capacity. Anyone else his age
would have long ago given up such expansive gastric habits.
She suspected that Sir Roger's physician probably despaired
of ever reining in his patient.

It was a convivial dinner. When Chastity, Merrill, and
Regina rose to exit the dining room and leave the three gentlemen to their wine, their going was viewed with only luke-
warm regret. Perhaps of the three gentlemen, Archie was the
least disappointed by their exit. He was already reaching for
the bottle of port.

Noticing the relaxed atmosphere, Chastity hoped that her

brothers and Sir Roger did not intend to linger long over their wine. It naturally fell to her as hostess to entertain the ladies until the gentlemen chose to rejoin them for coffee. She had no qualms about her dear friend, Merrill, but her sister-in-law was quite another story. Glancing at Regina's beautiful, petulant face, Chastity rather thought that she was not enthused by the prospect of spending time in their company, either.

"We shall see you shortly, I trust," Chastity said, throwing a meaningful glance at her eldest brother.

Meeting the message in her eyes, Henry's own eyes gleamed with laughter. He lifted his wineglass in acknowledgment. "Of course, dear sister. You may depend on it."

"So I shall, my lord," retorted Chastity.

Regina did not particularly care for the company of her own sex and thrived best in the company of gentlemen. Her conversation always revolved around herself, with the latest fashions and newest gossip comprising the remainder of her interests. Chastity was therefore anticipating a rather tedious hour. However, she meant to make the best of it. She led her sister-in-law and Merrill out of the dining room and across the hall to the drawing room.

The autumn air was chilly, and a stiff wind had been blowing all day, making the passageways noticeably drafty. A fire roared extravagantly in every room of the old manor, and the drawing room was no exception. It was perfectly warm, especially since the shutters were closed tight at the window.

"We shall be comfortable in here," said Chastity determinedly.

"Oh, I am certain of it," Merrill said, sliding a mirthful glance at Chastity as she passed into the room. "The time shall undoubtedly fly by with a good gossip."

Regina ignored her ladyship. "I do trust that we shall find something to entertain us," she said discontentedly. She roamed about the drawing room, touching a Sevres vase here and a Dresden there. "It is such a bore to be sent away. Have you a decent seamstress in the village, Chastity? My maid discovered that my favorite gown has a bit of torn lace, and I cannot trust her to mend it. She is so very clumsy with a needle."

"I believe that there is a very good seamstress. Shall I drive you over tomorrow?" Chastity asked as she seated herself in a wing back. Merrill sat down opposite her, her expression still lively with amusement. Chastity knew that her friend was deriving huge enjoyment from watching her attempt to placate her sister-in-law.

"Oh, no. I shall give the gown to my maid and she may go in my stead. I shall rely completely upon your recommendation," Regina said. "Are you expecting a large party this Season?"

"Oh, yes, Many of our guests will be the same as we have had in the past. There will be some new faces, too. Horace and Mary Bottler will be accompanied by their houseguests, Mrs. Dabney and Miss Paige. Then there will be the gentlemen whom Henry has invited. You probably know them," said Chastity.

"Undoubtedly I shall. I am a great favorite of the gentlemen, whatever set they belong to," Regina said with a tinkle of laughter. She glanced at herself in the gilded mirror hanging above the mantel and put up her fingers to smooth a perfect curl. "I am told that Archie is quite envied."

"No doubt," said Chastity, rather dryly.

"I am surprised at you, Chastity, for letting Cordelia Dabney to set foot in Chester," Regina said in a mildly scolding tone. "Why, it was the *on dit* of the Season that the widow had set her sights on Henry."

"I know that, Regina. But Henry could scarcely have invited the Bottlers without including their houseguests," Chastity said.

"No, of course not," agreed Merrill. "It would have been thought quite odd of him."

Regina shrugged her slender shoulders. She obviously disagreed with such a nicety. "Will your aunt be coming again—the one with those horrid little animals?"

"It would not be a proper house party without our aunt Webster and her pugs," Chastity said quietly.

"You are deluded, dear Chastity. But I shall not complain, as long as those curs do not snap at my hem this time," Regina said with a smile. Her eyes, however, held a somewhat hard expression.

Chastity smiled back at her. "I am glad, Regina, for I would not like to think that you felt compelled to insult Henry's godmother."

Regina looked disconcerted. Then she gave tinkling laugh. "Oh, not for the world. Of course I would not. Henry's godmother! I had quite forgotten. How right you are to remind me, Chastity."

"I like Sir Roger. He is such a dear eccentric," Merrill remarked. "He flirted with me in the most outrageous fashion."

"You may find Sir Roger agreeable, but I do not," Regina said. She turned again to her sister-in-law. "I would certainly never criticize your friends, Chastity, but Sir Roger is rather bad *ton*."

"I think that is why Henry likes him so well," said Chastity pensively. She smiled at her sister-in-law's uncomprehending expression. Regina Cummings was considered to be quite good *ton*. It was a pity that she was so obnoxious.

"My brother, Gabriel Salyer, and the Honorable Jeffrey Halston are due to arrive quite soon," Merrill said. "I am looking forward to seeing Gabriel again and, of course, Mr. Halston."

Regina shot a surprised glance in her sister-in-law's direction. "My dearest Chastity! You did not tell me that Jeffrey Halston was coming!"

"It did not occur to me to do so, Regina," Chastity said, raising her brows the barest trifle.

Regina smiled with pity. "Poor Chastity! How awful you must feel to be obliged to entertain an old beau whose admiration you lost!"

Merrill's eyes flashed. She intervened, turning to Chastity.

"I suppose that you do have the last issue of the *Lady's Magazine*?"

"Of course." Chastity found the issue and gave it to Merrill. She was grateful for her friend's attempt to turn the conversation.

"Here we are," Merrill said as she opened to a fashion plate. "Mrs. Cummings, I do believe that this particular gown must have been made with you in mind."

Regina cried out with delight as Merrill handed her the magazine. "Only look, Chastity! How very pretty! It is a bit plain, of course, but that may be easily remedied."

Chastity was just resigning herself to a thorough discussion of the latest fashion plates when the door to the drawing room opened and a footman entered. She greeted the servant's appearance with relief. "Yes, James?"

"The Bottler party has arrived, miss, and so have Sir Edward Greaves and Lord Winthrop," said the footman.

"Winny here! And Sir Edward! Why, that's famous! Chastity, you did not tell me that they would be among the guests," Regina said, her eyes brightening.

"No, for I was not certain. Henry thought that they might be coming down for a few days only, but he did not know when. James, has his lordship been informed of their arrival?"

"Yes, miss. And he asked that you be told," said the footman.

"Pray show them in here, James, and then serve coffee immediately," Chastity said. "His lordship will undoubtedly be joining us shortly."

"How wonderful! Our numbers are already increasing," Merrill said, pleased.

Regina got up from her chair and crossed to the mirror above the mantel to check her appearance and to smooth her hair. Satisfied, she turned. "Shall we go and greet everyone?"

"Certainly, Regina."

Hurried along by her enthusiastic sister-in-law, Chastity accompanied Regina back down the private hall and through the door that opened onto the great hall. Merrill followed swiftly after them.

The gentlemen were just putting off their overcoats and gloves. The ladies were being helped with their outer pelisses by the attentive footmen. Regina glided forward with a cry of delight and outstretched hands. "Winny! And dear Sir Edward. Welcome to Chester. I am so glad that you came."

Chastity looked on with amusement as her sister-in-law fell into the role of hostess with the two fashionable gentlemen. She also greeted Lord Winthrop and Sir Edward with warmth, as they were old friends. Then she turned to the Bottlers and their companions and held out her hand. "Mr. and Mrs. Bottler, so kind of you to have come. I was delighted when my brother told me that he had issued an invitation to you."

Mr. Bottler bowed. He was a portly gentleman and wheezed a little as he straightened from such exertion. "You are generous, Miss Cummings, for well I know that his lordship included us at the last possible minute. I am sure that all of your fine arrangements were thrown sadly awry."

"Not at all, Mr. Bottler," said Chastity easily. "We always have more than enough room at Chester for our friends and acquaintances."

"Oh, such welcome condescension! It quite overwhelms me, Miss Cummings, I assure you!" exclaimed Mrs. Bottler with a nervous titter. "Friends and acquaintances, to be sure! How kind of you to include us in your circle!"

Merrill half turned her head so that she could roll her eyes expressively for Chastity's benefit.

Chastity, too, recognized at once that Mrs. Bottler was one of those who was too easily awed by those of a higher social order. Well knowing that she would be drowned in effusions if she said more to Mrs. Bottler, she merely smiled graciously at the lady before turning aside to greet the other two ladies of the party. "Mrs. Dabney, I had the pleasure of meeting you in London. I hope that you shall enjoy your stay with us."

"Indeed I shall, Miss Cummings," said Mrs. Dabney with a smile. The widow was dark of hair and eyes, but her complexion was very white. She had a lively, expressive face and a lovely, bow-shaped mouth set off with a tiny mole. She looked to be in her early thirties, and her figure was extremely good. Chastity noted that the widow dressed in an attractive fashion, making the most of her assets with an extremely well-cut pelisse. A charming bonnet framed her beautiful face.

"And this must be Miss Paige," said Chastity, turning to the last lady.

The lady blushed and acknowledged that she was indeed Miss Paige. "I, too, appreciate your kindness, Miss Cummings," she said quietly. Unlike the rest of the party, who were attired quite fashionably, Miss Paige was dressed in a slightly outmoded pelisse and an unadorned bonnet. Her gloves were plain, and her half boots were serviceable.

"My cousin is rather shy at finding herself in such exalted surroundings, Miss Cummings," said Mrs. Dabney lightly, throwing an amused glance at the younger woman. "You must not mind it if she does not put herself forward."

Miss Paige bit her lip, color rising once more into her face. It was obvious that she had taken Mrs. Dabney's words as a rebuke.

Chastity did not remark on the widow's observation. "I do not believe you have yet had the pleasure of meeting my sister-in-law, Mrs. Archibald Cummings, or my friend, Lady Peters."

Merrill greeted the Bottlers and the other two ladies with perfect civility. She stood chatting with them a few minutes, before turning to greet Lord Winthrop and Sir Edward.

Chastity recalled her sister-in-law to a sense of her social obligation. "Regina, pray come greet the Bottlers and our other guests, Mrs. Dabney and Miss Paige."

Regina reluctantly left the two gentlemen with whom she had been holding an animated conversation and came over. She inclined her head in a cool fashion to the Bottlers. "Yes, we have met before, I think. How do you do?"

"Oh, only fancy your recalling us! I am quite, quite overwhelmed," exclaimed Mrs. Bottler, pressing one hand against her amble bosom.

Mr. Bottler had bowed to Regina, and now he straightened. "Yes, indeed, that is most kind of you, ma'am. We do not always run in the same circles."

"No, indeed," Regina agreed with a final smile. She turned toward the widow and her expression visibly hardened. Her soft voice was patently insincere in tone. "Mrs. Dabney, how nice to see you again. I suppose that you were becoming bored in London?"

"The society becomes decidedly flat at this time of the year, Mrs. Cummings, as you will no doubt agree," said Mrs. Dabney, smiling.

"Oh, I can readily understand why you would prefer a house party at Chester," Regina said, showing her teeth in a large smile.

"Do you, Mrs. Cummings? How omniscient of you, my dear," said Mrs. Dabney with a shade of amusement in her voice.

Merrill listened to the sugared exchange with amusement. "I did not perfectly realize that you and Mrs. Dabney were on such good terms, Regina. What fun it will be, since we all know one another so well," she remarked. The two ladies turned as one to stare at her, but Merrill merely continued to smile in an innocent fashion.

Chastity hastily intervened, wondering what in the world had gotten into her friend. It was so unlike her to bait others. But then, thought Chastity ruefully, Merrill had never cared for Regina. "Why do we not all withdraw to the drawing room? I am certain that the other gentlemen will have already gathered there for coffee, so let us join them."

Chastity and her ill-assorted guests retired to the drawing room, where her brothers and Sir Roger Highfield were indeed awaiting them.

There was a flurry of greetings. Lord Henry was well acquainted with Sir Edward and Lord Winthrop, the latter of whom had been in the Horse Guards with Henry. He greeted them warmly, making them known to Sir Roger Highfield. Archibald Cummings knew both gentlemen. Mr. and Mrs. Bottler were formally introduced, and they in turn introduced their houseguests, Mrs. Cordelia Dabney and Miss Drusilla Paige. It was explained in a tangled way by Mrs. Bottler that Mrs. Dabney was some sort of cousin to the Bottlers, while Miss Paige was related to Mrs. Dabney.

When Sir Roger was made known to Mrs. Dabney, he took the lady's hand, but then stood staring down at her as though he had been stricken deaf and dumb.

Mrs. Dabney glanced around at the company with an inquiring expression, as though seeking advice. "My goodness, it seems that I have made a conquest all unbeknownst," she said, laughing.

Sir Roger started. He turned dull red with embarrassment and dropped her hand as though it had become too hot to the touch. "My pardon, madame," he said gruffly. He bowed and stepped back.

However, Chastity noticed that even as everyone began talking, becoming acquainted, that Sir Roger rarely removed his gaze from Mrs. Dabney. It was as though he could not help himself. His eyes constantly returned to her, like iron to a magnet. His face was nearly expressionless. The slight smile he wore was one of politeness rather than of sincerity. He appeared pale and there was a singular rigidity in his stance.

Chastity finally moved to his side. In a low voice, she inquired, "Sir, are you quite well? You appear to be operating under some distress."

Sir Roger cast a fleeting glance into Chastity's face. There was almost an expression of fear in the depths of his eyes. "You must not worry your head over me, my dear. I shall be fine, I assure you."

He moved away deliberately, turning his back, leaving Chastity to look after him with a frown. "How odd," she remarked to no one in particular.

"What is?"

Chastity turned quickly to find her brother Archibald at her elbow. He was looking at her in inquiry. He was smiling, and it struck Chastity suddenly that it really did him good to be at Chester. Since his arrival, he had seemed to have dropped some heavy burden.

"Oh, I am so glad that you are here, Archie. We miss you, Henry and I," she exclaimed impulsively.

Archie flushed, looking both astonished and gratified. "Why, it is extremely good of you to say so, Chastity."

"I mean every word of it, Archie. I only wish—" Chastity stopped, awkward over what she had begun to say.

"What? That I would come alone?" Archie asked, his gaze traveling to his wife's animated face. She was laughing at something that Lord Winthrop was whispering in her ear.

"That isn't what I was going to say," Chastity hastily said. "Regina is welcome at any time at Chester, as you know."

Archie sighed and brought his gaze back to his sister's face. "Nevertheless, it would be so much more peaceful otherwise. It is all right, Chastity. I know that you and Henry pity me, just as I know that you suffer patiently with Regina for my sake."

"She is very beautiful, Archie," said Chastity.

"So you understand?" he asked quickly.

"Oh, yes. Completely. You fell desperately in love with her."

"Yes; with her face and her pretty ways," Archie said with a trace of bitterness. "I was a bit of a fool then. I still am. No matter how badly she treats me or others, I still love her."

"Then there must be something good in her, Archie," Chastity said. She hastily changed the subject. "Did you notice Sir Roger when he was introduced to Mrs. Dabney? He looked positively shaken."

"Perhaps he was simply struck dumb by what a beauty she is," Archie said. "Mrs. Dabney is rumored to be quite skilled in collecting admiration for herself. She is also rumored to have set her cap for Henry. Does he know?"

"Yes, he does. When I asked him why he had invited her to Chester, he said that he felt obligated to when he issued an invitation to the Bottlers," Chastity said. "I hope that he does not regret it, for it could possibly become very awkward for him."

Archie nodded in agreement. "It has me in quite a puzzle, however, why Henry felt compelled to invite the Bottlers at all. They are not from his usual set, are they? I know that Regina and I are scarcely acquainted with them."

"We also are on a bare nodding acquaintance. However, Henry said something about a hunter that Mr. Bottler had expressed an interest in. I suppose that must explain it," Chastity said.

"The beauteous widow is quite thoroughly detested by my own lovely wife," Archie said. "And I do not think that Lady Peters is very high on her list of favorites, either."

"So I have already gathered," Chastity said. She shook her head. "I very much dread that this may be one of our most memorable house parties, Archie."

Archie gave a fleeting smile. "Do you dread it, Chastity? Or do you appreciate the challenge?"

Chastity eyed her brother. "Perhaps a bit of both," she admitted. "I have always disliked mere sitting about and yawning politely behind my hand. At least with Regina here and Merrill and Mrs. Dabney, I shall be kept very busy trying to keep the peace."

"And I hope you may do it, for my sake as well as Henry's," Archie said, his glance traveling once more toward his wife.

"Yes. I know that Regina's happiness means a great deal to you."

Archie looked down quickly at her. His face suddenly reddened. "Excuse me, Chastity. I do not believe that I have yet spoken to Miss Paige," he said with restraint, then walked away.

Coffee lasted for two hours. When at last the gathering broke up, it was expressed by Mrs. Bottler that she had truly enjoyed herself thus far, but that she needed her rest if she was to take as much enjoyment out of the next day.

Chastity saw to it that her guests were all comfortably situated and then retired to her own room. It had been an eventful day.

As she made ready for bed, she reflected that this year's annual house party was already becoming a most interesting one. Certainly her own talents as a hostess would be challenged, she thought, recalling the instant animosity that had sprung up between Regina and the beautiful widow, Mrs. Dabney. And Sir Roger's behavior had been so very unlike him, for that gentleman had more than his share of *savoir-faire*. Mr. and Mrs. Bottler were hardly the type to demand special attention; they would prove to be little problem. Chastity had rather liked the reserved Miss Paige. She had already made up her mind to see whether she could not draw that lady out a little, and she counted on the merry leavening that Sir Edward Greaves and Lord Winthrop represented to help her. And of course there would be the addition of two other bachelors, as well as Aunt Webster and her pets.

Chastity snuggled into her pillows. All in all, her guests offered just the sort of mix that could be counted upon to keep things from becoming very dull.

Chapter Three

The following morning Chastity was given a note at first light. Gabriel Salyer and Jeffrey Halston had spent the night at an inn not far distant. They had not wished to arrive in the small hours of the morning. Both gentlemen expressed pleasure in renewing their acquaintance with the Cummings family and planned to arrive at Chester in time for tea.

When Lord Henry Cummings was told of the expected time of their arrival, he shook his head. He adjusted the pages of his newspaper and crossed his long legs at the ankle. He was attired in the somber frock coat and tan breeches of a country gentleman and shod in top boots. "I will not be at home at teatime, unfortunately. I have already promised Lord Winthrop and Sir Edward a full day out in the field with the hounds. Archie is accompanying us, as well. I cannot renege on them now. I trust you to convey my regrets."

"Of course I shall. I know that Gabriel will be sadly disappointed to miss you, as will Jeffrey Halston, but I am certain that they will understand," said Chastity warmly, without a hint of the trepidation she felt at facing her old beau.

"It has been ages since we have seen Gabriel here at Chester," Henry remarked.

"Yes, it has. I was quite astonished when you told me that he wished to stay with us for the entire hunting season. He usually remains in London during the winter," said Chastity, folding the note.

Henry frowned thoughtfully. "I wonder whether it is low tide for Gabriel and he has decided to rusticate for a time."

"Do you mean gaming debts? I had heard rumors for months

before we left London that he had become a desperate gamester. Do you suppose the gossip is true?" asked Chastity.

"Perhaps. I hope not, however. The cards can become a capricious, cruel mistress. I would not like to see Gabriel caught fast in that trap."

Chastity heard her sister-in-law's light, laughing voice. "There are traps and then there are traps," she murmured, as Regina came into the drawing room with Sir Edward. There was a rumble of agreement from her brother's direction.

Regina stopped when she saw that the drawing room was already occupied. "Chastity! And dear Henry. Sir Edward has been telling me the most entertaining tale. So naughty of him!"

"I am a sad wag, I fear," said Sir Edward mournfully. He was a brown man, from his brown hair and dark eyes to his tanned complexion. He resembled nothing so much as a long-faced hound, being neither handsome nor of an exuberant personality. He would have been totally nondescript in any company, except for his wit. He combined this with an avid sportsman's instincts and so was a very popular addition to any gathering, being well liked by nearly everyone.

The door opened again, and Archibald Cummings and Lord Winthrop stood on the threshold. They were attired in brown frock coats and breeches. Holding the door, which partially hid Sir Edward and Regina from his sight, Archie called out cheerfully, "I say, Henry, when are we to set out?"

"Archie?" Regina, followed by Sir Edward, stepped forward round the door.

At sight of his wife's face, Archie's expression underwent a sudden transformation. All the smiling ease went out of it. "Oh, that's torn it," he muttered.

"Set out? What is this about, pray?" asked Regina with a slight pout of her lips.

Henry threw aside his newspaper and stood up. He towered well over six feet and always garnered attention with his impressive size. His sister-in-law's eyes automatically swung to him as he moved. He strode toward the door, taking hold of his brother's arm. Unceremoniously, he turned Archie around in an about-face. "We are going out with the hounds, Regina. Gentlemen, let us depart."

Without pausing or letting go of Archie, Henry exited. The other two gentlemen said hasty good-byes to the ladies and also disappeared. Shortly afterward there was heard raised male laughter and a door closing in the distance.

"Well! I have never been so ill-used in my life," Regina said, quite offended. "Archie never said a word to me about going out. And it was very rude of Henry simply to walk out like that, brushing past me as though I did not exist. Winny and Sir Edward, too! I did not think them capable of such ill-bred manners!"

Chastity knew well enough what was the crux of her sister-in-law's malcontent. "Never mind, Regina. I am sure that we shall have a perfectly wonderful time today without the gentlemen. Oh, here are Merrill and Miss Paige come to join us now!"

"Yes, Miss Paige and I met on the stairs," Merrill said gaily. "She looked quite lost and so I took her under my wing."

"You did quite right, Merrill," said Chastity, smiling. She nodded to Miss Paige. "How delightful you look, my dear. I very much like that shade of blue on you."

Miss Paige blushed at the compliment. "Thank you, Miss Cummings. It is most kind of you to say so." She was wearing a plain, high-necked day dress. The gown was devoid of decoration, except for a bit of lace at the collar and cuffs.

Miss Paige dressed much like the governess of a household might, which was a great pity, Chastity thought. "Pray call me Chastity. We are all friends here, you know," said Chastity, smiling.

"Indeed we are!" Merrill agreed. She slid an impish glance in Regina's direction. "Isn't that so?"

"I have the headache. I will be upstairs in my room should anyone care," Regina said waspishly. She swept out of the drawing room.

Miss Paige watched the lady's exit with a stricken expression. She turned at once to her hostess. "Pray forgive me. I did not mean to barge in and . . . and . . ."

"Nonsense! You are perfectly welcome to go wherever you wish at Chester," said Chastity firmly. She put out her hand and drew the other woman down beside her on the settee. "And you mustn't be anxious over my sister-in-law's crotchets, for it really has nothing to do with you."

"No doubt she is merely feeling out of sorts because the gentlemen, with the exception of Sir Roger Highfield and Mr. Bottler, who have entered into a chess game, have gone out of doors," Merrill added.

"Oh, I see," said Miss Paige quietly.

Chastity looked consideringly at her. "I do believe that you do," she said.

Miss Paige blushed and looked down at her hands. "My cousin is also very beautiful and very sociable," she said. She glanced up at Chastity and Merrill and a half smile trembled on her lips. "Cordelia does not care overmuch for Mrs. Cummings."

Chastity chuckled, understanding at once. "Yes, I know. And Regina has taken quite an unreasonable disliking to your cousin." She started laughing, and Merrill and Miss Paige joined her. Chastity said approvingly, "That is much better, Miss Paige! You should laugh more often. It becomes you."

"Pray call me Dru," said Miss Paige shyly. "It is short for Drusilla, and it is what all my friends were used to call me."

"Used to call you?" repeated Chastity. "Don't you still have friends Miss . . . Drusilla!"

Miss Paige smiled a bit unhappily. "Oh, of course I do! However, I do not see any of them nearly as often as I could wish, now that I am living with my cousin. They are all quietly situated and scarcely ever go up to London, you see. But I must not repine! My cousin has been very good to me. She takes me with her wherever she goes and has introduced me to scores of personages. So I am very fortunate to be settled with her."

"How did you come to be living with Mrs. Dabney?" Merrill asked curiously.

"My mother died just a few months ago. She was an invalid, and I took care of her. When she realized that she was dying, she wrote to Cordelia and begged her to take me in, for there was no one else with the means. My cousin was good enough to do so," said Miss Paige.

Merrill and Chastity exchanged a look.

"Forgive me, Drusilla, for I would not willingly offend you. But Mrs. Dabney doesn't appear to be quite the charitable sort," said Chastity hesitantly.

Miss Paige gave a small laugh. She had thickly lashed hazel eyes that just then were gleaming with amusement, and she looked unexpectedly pretty. "No, she doesn't, does she? And you have not offended me at all, for it is something that I have puzzled over many times. I do not understand why Cordelia offered me a place with her. I am perfectly useless to her, and she actually has very little interest in me. And we are related only through marriage."

"Is she in a position to bring you out into society?" asked Chastity.

Miss Paige smiled. "I am six-and-twenty, Chastity. What need have I of a Season? No one is likely to look at me."

Chastity was astonished. "I would not have thought it."

"No, nor I," Merrill exclaimed. "Why, you look scarcely twenty!"

Miss Paige flushed. "I know that I appear younger than my years. I always have. I suppose it is because I have very little figure to recommend me. You cannot imagine what a sad trial it is to me!"

Chastity looked closer at the other woman. She had assumed Miss Paige to be rather plain, but as she studied her, Chastity realized that her first impression was not quite correct.

Miss Paige's features, though not beautiful in the general way, were pleasing. She possessed high cheekbones, a straight nose, and a smooth jaw. Her hazel eyes were large and speaking, while her complexion was what was commonly referred to as peaches-and-cream. Her hair was a light mouse brown and was combed into a style that was unflattering to her thin face. She had a good figure that was hidden by ill-fitting, outmoded clothing. Her hands were slender and graceful even in repose.

She moved with grace, her bearing one of innate dignity rather than proud arrogance.

Miss Paige obviously knew her place, Chastity reflected, for her lineage was not exalted. However, she had been bred a lady, and her character and demeanor reflected it. She was not a great beauty and never would be, but with proper handling, Chastity rather thought that an improvement could be made in Miss Paige's appearance. The first thing that must be done was to give the woman a sense of confidence in herself.

"I envy you, Dru," said Chastity.

At Miss Paige's disbelieving look, Chastity nodded. "No, I truly do. When the rest of us have grown plump with age, you will still possess a youthfulness that has everything to do with good bones. It is a gift to be prized. And I assure you, if you were to be dressed properly in the fashions that most flatter you, you would begin to turn a few heads."

Merrill looked momentarily stunned, before hastily rearranging her expression. "Very true, Chastity."

Miss Paige looked away for a moment, blinking back tears. "Thank you, Chastity. That was very kind of you to say."

"I meant every word of it," said Chastity. She had a sudden inspiration that was borne out of her previous night's reflections. "I should like to play fairy godmother to you, Dru. Will you allow me?"

"What do you mean?" asked Miss Paige, puzzled.

"I have a few things that I would like to give to you. Oh, don't say no so quickly, Dru! I should so like to do this for you. It would give me the greatest of pleasure to take you under my wing a bit," said Chastity.

"Oh, what a simply wonderful notion," Merrill said. "It would be such fun. Do, do let us, Miss Paige!"

Miss Paige did not know what to say, though she felt that she should not take advantage of her hostess in such a fashion. "I wish you would not trouble yourself over me," she said. "I am a complete stranger to you and—"

"Nonsense! I am persuaded that we shall all become the best

of friends," said Chastity. "Come up with me to my room and
let me see what will do for you."

Although Miss Paige continued to put forward faint protests,
Chastity and Merrill persuaded her to accompany them upstairs. When Chastity informed her maid of what was wanted,
the woman embarked with efficient enthusiasm on a thorough
search through her mistress's things for items that had been discovered not to suit quite as well as had been expected or that
Chastity no longer wore very often.

Merrill went away to her own rooms and presently returned
with several offerings from her own extensive wardrobe. "Mine
ought to fit you better than Chastity's, for she is such a may-
pole," she said teasingly.

"I have been called statuesque," said Chastity with mock
dignity.

Though Chastity was a few inches taller than Miss Paige,
they were otherwise of a comparable size. Chastity privately
hoped that the few articles from her own wardrobe would fit
Miss Paige well enough to supplement the lady's own meager
closet. The gowns would have to be rehemmed, of course, but
that was a task that one of the maids could easily perform.

Miss Paige was overwhelmed with the present of two day
dresses, a modish pelisse, a Norwich shawl that Chastity declared that she could well do without, and a riding habit. Merrill contributed an elegant ball gown that she had decided was
insipid on her, some slippers, a very pretty comb, and a few
other trifles.

"It . . . it is too much," stammered Miss Paige.

"Oh, no! My maid will tell you that I squirrel away too many
items that I have not the least use for," said Chastity, with a
meaningful glance at her dresser.

The maid took the hint. "Indeed, it is quite true, miss."

"You are not half as bad as I am, Chastity. I am quite the despair of my maid," said Merrill, not to be outdone.

"We are not exactly of a size, of course. I shall have one of
the underhousemaids, who is quite a good needlewoman, to
take up the bodices and the hems a bit," said Chastity. "Do you

know, I had quite forgotten! I have several extra pairs of gloves. Pray bring a couple of them out, Martha."

"Yes, miss," said the maid.

Miss Paige was flushed with hesitant pleasure and a strong doubt that she should accept such generosity. "So kind! I do not know what to say."

"There is no need for you to say anything, Dru. I am really acting quite selfishly, for I am enjoying myself very much," said Chastity. "I will ask one of the maids to refurbish or repair any of your own gowns that require it, if you will permit."

"Of course. I . . . I can have no possible objection," stammered Miss Paige.

"That is very sweet of you, Dru," Merrill said approvingly.

In the end, Miss Paige went away to her own room quite dazed by her good fortune. Besides the gowns and the riding habit, she had become the possesser of two pairs of gloves, a silk scarf, and three precious pairs of silk stockings. The underhousemaid presented herself in short order, and there ensued a fitting session that did nothing to disrupt Miss Paige's sense that she had entered into a happy fairy tale, in which Miss Cummings and Lady Peters were firmly cast in the role of fairy godmothers.

Chapter Four

That afternoon, Chastity and the other ladies awaited the new arrivals to the party. Regina had emerged from her sulks when Chastity sent up word that two gentlemen were expected for tea. She had at once started on her toilette, and she had been perfectly satisfied with her robin's egg blue day gown with its knots of silver ribbons until she had laid eyes on Mrs. Dabney. The widow's gown was bright yellow, a most difficult color to carry off, but she appeared stunning. Regina could quite cheerfully have overturned the large vase of profuse hothouse blooms that was on the mantel over her rival's head. However, she had to content herself with several snide remarks to the effect that she had never admired warm colors because they were so commonplace.

"There is no comparison between a violet and a dandelion, for instance," she said, bestowing a smile on the assembled company.

Mrs. Dabney regarded these stabs with open amusement, which only served to infuriate Regina further. Chastity invited Mrs. Dabney to sit with her, hoping to draw her attention away from her sister-in-law. When Mrs. Dabney had joined her, that lady smiled at Chastity. "Thank you, Miss Cummings. I am certain that I shall derive more pleasure from your conversation, if not as much amusement," she said.

Chastity chuckled. "I had hoped to spare you annoyance, Mrs. Dabney. Pray do not tell me that my stratagem has been in error."

"Not at all, for I should have been bored within a very few minutes with such sport," said Mrs. Dabney. Her dark liquid eyes gleamed. "Mrs. Cummings is amusing only up to a point, as I am certain that you are very much aware."

"Regina is my sister-in-law. I am very well acquainted with her," said Chastity.

Mrs. Dabney acknowledged the slight rebuke in her statement. "Of course. Forgive me, Miss Cummings. I should not behave so ill with you, especially when you and Lady Peters have been so kind to my cousin. She told me not very many minutes past of your kindness toward her."

"Miss Paige is very likable, but I find her very reserved. I hope to draw her out while you are visiting with us. I hope that you do not mind," said Chastity.

"Not at all, Miss Cummings! Why, I am ashamed that I have not done better by my cousin, for she is usually dressed with perfect propriety but somewhat shabbily. It is scarcely to my credit, I know," said Mrs. Dabney. She was still smiling, but there was a slight hardness about her eyes and the set of her mouth.

Chastity was instantly on the alert. She did not want to set the widow's back up, for to do so would hamper her own efforts to make the house party run as smoothly as possible. "I do not know your precise circumstances, Mrs. Dabney, but I think well of you for taking Miss Paige in. It is a charge on you, of course. You are yourself far too young to sit with the matrons," said Chastity lightly.

Mrs. Dabney's expression relaxed just slightly. "Oh, yes! Was there ever such an oddity? I! A duenna! It is perfectly absurd. However, I do not complain, for Drusilla is scarcely any trouble at all. I hope to see her credibly established one day, as you may readily guess. Perhaps your influence will be a good thing, Miss Cummings, for I am sure I do not know how to encourage her to show herself to the best advantage."

"Why, certainly, I shall do whatever I can to help you, Mrs. Dabney," said Chastity. With a perfect understanding established between herself and the widow, Chastity allowed her attention to be diverted by Regina, who demanded to know when their visitors might be expected.

"It is almost half past the hour, Chastity," Regina said in gentle complaint.

"I am fully confident that Mr. Salyer and Mr. Halston will arrive in good time, Regina," said Chastity.

"Unless they have difficulty on the road, of course," Merrill said serenely.

Regina sent an irritated glance in her direction, to which Merrill paid not the least heed.

"Oh, how exciting it all is! I shall have a great deal to relate to my bosom-bows. Won't they stare when I tell them of all the personages that I have been in the way of meeting," said Mrs. Bottler with one of her tittering laughs. She nudged Miss Paige, who was sitting beside her on the settee. "And what do you think, Miss Paige? You haven't so much as squeaked since we came down. Isn't it all so very grand?"

"It is, indeed," said Miss Paige, smiling.

"For my part, I only wish they would arrive. I detest waiting about," Regina said. She moved restlessly about the front sitting room, and within a few seconds a slight smile touched her lips. "I have always liked this room."

"Indeed, it is one of my favorites. It is where we usually receive visitors who are known to us, for it is such a comfortable room," said Chastity.

The sitting room was of even proportions, its windows giving a view of the sloping lawns at Chester. A fire crackled quietly in the fireplace, and brass fire tools stood nearby for use. The cherrywood high-back chairs set about the wall were polished to a high gloss and covered with stitched tapestry cushions. Two settees were arranged at angles in front of the fireplace, with wing chairs placed nearby.

Regina ran her fingers caressingly across the gleaming top of the occasional table that stood to one side. "I do so like the feel of smooth cherrywood," she remarked to no one in particular.

"Indeed, it is a very pretty wood," said Mrs. Bottler, fanning herself. Her plump face was red even though she sat as far from the fire as she could. She was attired in a mustard day dress that clashed with her high complexion.

Regina shot a contemptuous glance at the woman. She had little tolerance for those whom she deemed to be of a lower social order than herself, especially for anyone who showed so little fashion sense.

"I must compliment you, Miss Cummings. Everything that I have seen at Chester is quite, quite perfect," said Mrs. Dabney.

"Thank you, Mrs. Dabney. I can scarcely take all credit, however. We have an exceptional household staff."

Mrs. Dabney shook her head. "Oh, no! I will not allow it, Miss Cummings. Such modesty certainly becomes you, but I suspect that it is your firm hand that guides the efficient workings at Chester."

"Indeed! Miss Cummings is what I call an excellent mistress," said Mrs. Bottler in a tone of congratulation.

Chastity blinked, still unused to the woman's overdone style.

"Quite," said Mrs. Dabney, throwing a conspiratorial glance at her hostess.

Chastity could not help smiling. The widow was infinitely better bred than her cousin-in-law, Mrs. Bottler. However, that did not exonerate Mrs. Dabney from an inexcusable fault. The widow had already made perfectly plain a preference for Lord Henry's company. Chastity rather thought that Mrs. Dabney had it in mind to wrest a proposal from his lordship before the house party was over.

As Henry had remarked to Chastity in private, "It appears that the lady believes herself to have driven straight into heaven, and I have taken St. Peter's place as gatekeeper!"

"She is a schemer, Henry," Chastity had said roundly.

"Quite. Not good *ton* at all," said Henry. "Though I must say that I prefer her to the Bottlers. Horace Bottler is a bit of a bore, and as for his wife—! I am excessively sorry for Miss Paige."

Chastity agreed, but her concern was elsewhere. "I pray that you are not so senseless that you saddle me with Mrs. Dabney for a sister-in-law. I could not like it, Henry!"

"Nor I, believe me. You may rest easy, Chastity. I am too wily to be snared by the likes of Mrs. Dabney," Henry said, hiding a yawn behind his hand.

"I hope so," Chastity had retorted.

Chastity was recalling this conversation as she looked at the beautifully turned out woman opposite her. She smiled at her houseguest. "I am happy that you find all to your satisfaction, Mrs. Dabney."

Mrs. Dabney gave a light laugh. "Oh, yes! I am confident of being pleased by simply everything. In fact, I am all eagerness to meet your friends this afternoon."

"I wonder where they are? I *do* detest being made to wait," Regina said.

Chastity took up a ladies' magazine and opened it at random to draw Regina's attention to a fashion plate. "Pray look at this. What do you think?"

Regina looked at the plate and then at Chastity, an expression of surprise in her eyes. "Why, it is very well, Chastity. But I scarcely think that it is quite in your style."

Merrill glanced over Regina's shoulder and went into a peal of laughter.

Chastity looked closer at the plate. She saw that it was a rather outrageous gown. "No, you are quite right," she admitted. "However, I do think that if one were to rid it of those hideous bows and fill in the neckline a trifle and cut it on more elegant lines, the gown could be quite tolerable."

"You might as well start with a different gown altogether, such as this one," Regina said, taking the magazine out of Chastity's hands.

Chastity relinquished the magazine without a murmur. She glanced up at the clock on the mantel. It was teatime and her visitors had not yet arrived. She got up, unable to remain sitting still, and went over to the bowl of cut flowers that had been brought in from the hothouse and placed beneath the gilt mirror. She began rearranging some of the blooms.

"Allow me to help you, Miss Cummings," said a low voice.

Chastity was rather annoyed, but she could not be angry with Miss Paige, who was looking a little lost. "Of course, Drusilla," she said, moving to one side.

The door opened, and the butler entered to announce the expected visitors. Chastity turned quickly, a long-stemmed lily still between her fingers.

Gabriel Salyer and Jeffrey Halston were ushered into the drawing room. "Gabriel!" Merrill rushed forward with outstretched hands and reached up to kiss her brother's cheek. "Gabriel, I am glad you have come at last!"

Mr. Salyer returned his sister's fond salute. "My dearest sister. How well you look."

Merrill turned to Chastity. "I trust that you will recall my brother, Gabriel."

"Of course I do," said Chastity, giving her hand to the gentleman and smiling at him. She was all the while conscious of the other gentleman. "I remember you very well, Mr. Salyer."

"And I you," said Mr. Salyer, making an elegant bow. There was admiration in his gaze as he straightened. He was a handsome man in a boyish way. He was in his early thirties, but was slight of stature. His hair was carefully brushed into a semblance of disorder, setting off a face whose features were almost too delicate to be manly. His shirt points were high, his cravat was a masterpiece that kept his chin rather elevated, and the shoulders of his coat were padded with buckram to give breadth. Several fobs and seals hung from ribbons attached to his striped waistcoat. Mr. Salyer obviously had tendencies toward dandyism.

"I am certain that you must recall the Honorable Jeffrey Halston, as well," interposed Merrill, drawing the gentleman forward.

Chastity turned toward her old beau. She looked up at him in some curiosity. Her first impression was that he appeared older than when she had seen him last, but that was a natural observation after so long. "Yes, of course. Good afternoon, Mr. Halston."

Mr. Halston smiled slightly and bowed, but he did not put himself forward in any way. In a single fleeting glance, Chastity took in his appearance. His dark brown hair was brushed into a Brutus crop. His coat was of fawn, and his snow-white cravat was intricately tied, a topaz pin nestled among its

exquisite folds. Superfine breeches molded tight to his long
limbs, and the Hessians he wore gleamed with a mirrorlike finish. There was nothing of the dandy about him, and it crossed
Chastity's mind to wonder what had caused a friendship to
form between him and Gabriel Salyer.

When Mr. Halston spoke, it was in a deep, measured voice.
"Miss Cummings, it is a pleasure to see you again."

Chastity was disappointed. He had not been even as enthusiastic as Gabriel Salyer upon being brought up to her. She
caught a speaking look from Merrill, which she ignored. It
could scarcely matter, after all. She and Jeffrey Halston were no
longer so well acquainted as they had once been.

Chastity made known the gentlemen to the rest of the ladies
and then set herself to be a good hostess, pouring tea and offering biscuits and plum cake. It was a lively tea, made so by Mr.
Salyer's gallantries directed toward her and the other unattached ladies. His flirtations swiftly put Miss Paige out of coun-
tenance, however, and she retreated to the fringes of the group
as soon as she could, leaving Mrs. Cummings to the sole enjoyment of Mr. Salyer's attentions. Mr. Halston sat down beside
Miss Paige and talked quietly with her for several minutes.
Mrs. Bottler firmly attached herself to Mrs. Dabney and Mr.
Salyer, and Merrill seized the opportunity to address Chastity.

"Well? What do you think of Jeffrey Halston? He is as handsome as ever, don't you agree?" Merrill asked in a low voice.

Chastity glanced over at the gentleman. "He appears older, of
course."

"Chastity Cummings! Is that all you have to say? He appears
older!"

"What do you wish me to say, Merrill?" asked Chastity,
amused. She knew quite well what her friend wished to hear.

"You're impossible!" Merrill said.

"Console yourself, Merrill. You are not the first to say so,"
said Chastity.

Mr. Salyer claimed Chastity's attention then, and the private
exchange with Merrill was at an end. Chastity was glad, for it
did not suit her to be discussing Jeffrey Halston.

Chastity conveyed her brother's regrets at not being present. "Henry told me that he was particularly looking forward to seeing you again, Gabriel, but he had already made a commitment to our other guests."

When she explained the nature of his lordship's prior engagement, Mr. Salyer laughed and shook his head. "We gentlemen do enjoy our sport. I myself am quite excited by the prospect of participating in the hunt. It has been too many seasons since I last coursed the fields."

"I trust that Mr. Halston shares your enthusiasm," said Chastity. It was a mechanical civility at best, for she had a vivid recollection of a certain cold autumn day, when Jeffrey Halston fairly flew past on his big hunter, his coattails soaring.

"Indeed! I suspect it is all that he thinks about day and night." Mr. Salyer gave a self-deprecating laugh. "I am far more comfortable on the dance floor than on the back of a horse, I fear."

"In that case, I hope that neither of you will be disappointed. We will be having our first soiree a fortnight hence," said Chastity.

"That will be delightful," exclaimed Mr. Salyer. "Here, Jeffrey! Miss Cummings tells me that she will be holding a soiree in a fortnight. What have you to say to that?"

"I shall attend, of course," said Mr. Halston gravely, bowing.

"Was there ever such a fellow? He is a man of a few words, but a good companion for all of that," said Mr. Salyer.

"Yes, of course," said Chastity, glancing in Mr. Halston's direction. He had returned to his conversation with Miss Paige. Regina had joined them and seemed to be enjoying herself tremendously. Chastity felt a twinge of pique that he appeared so indifferent about renewing his acquaintance with her. But really, she told herself, it was just as well. She could rest easy at last, for it was quite obvious that Merrill's assertion that Jeffrey Halston wished to woo her again was nothing more than a figment of that lady's lively imagination.

*   *   *

That evening at coffee, Henry drew Chastity aside for a private chat. "How are our guests settling in, Chastity? Have there been any complications?"

Chastity shook her head. "None to speak of. Lord Winthrop and Sir Edward are prepared to be pleased by everything, as usual. Mr. and Mrs. Bottler seem to be a little overawed by their surroundings, however. Mr. Bottler compensates with that expansive bonhomie that you have already commented on, while Mrs. Bottler is so effusive as to be annoying."

Henry nodded. "Yes, I know. I have never been around such people in my life."

"Of course you have, Henry. You have just never invited any of them to Chester before," said Chastity, laughing at him.

Henry grimaced. "You are right, as usual, Chastity. I notice that you have said nothing about Jeffrey Halston."

Chastity looked at him. "Why, what should I say? He seems pleasant enough and appears pleased to be here at Chester."

"He is an old beau. I did wonder perhaps—" Henry caught himself up.

"That he had come to renew his suit?" finished Chastity. She shook her head with a smile. "Merrill thought that he might, but she is now quite put out. He has not shown the least interest in me, for which I am very thankful. It would have been most embarrassing, to say the least."

Henry seemed satisfied. "What of our beauteous widow? I know what I have reaped for myself, for the lady scarcely lets me out of her sight. But how is it for you?"

"Oh, I go along famously with her. Mrs. Dabney has nothing but well-placed compliments for Chester and our staff. She possesses more dignity and is far more sophisticated than her cousins."

"Sir Roger seems to have recovered from his previous stupefaction," Henry remarked.

"He does not flirt with her as he is wont to do, however. Have you noticed?" said Chastity. "He converses with Mrs. Dabney very politely with not a single extravagant compliment leaving his mouth. I have never seen him behave in such a fashion around a woman who is considered to be as lovely as Mrs. Dabney."

"It is odd, indeed. However, I do not think that we need be anxious about Sir Roger. He is a rule to himself," Henry said. "What of Miss Paige?"

"She goes along tolerably well. I have taken her under my wing a little, for I feel a little sorry for her."

"I gather that Miss Paige is not used to having anyone cater to her wishes." Henry glanced down at his sister. "I would appreciate it if you would continue to keep an eye out for Miss Paige, Chastity, for I wish all of our guests to be made to feel at home."

"Of course. And you are quite right. Miss Paige is used to being ignored, yet she has a natural dignity that cannot be disguised," said Chastity.

Henry nodded. "I thought so, too. She is very different from the usual poor relation that one sees hovering in the background."

"I have arranged for one of the maids to help her to dress. She feels awkward about it, but she managed to thank me very prettily," said Chastity. She nodded toward their brother, who was seated with Sir Edward and seemed to be involved in an intensely riveting conversation. "Have you noticed how much Archie has relaxed since his arrival? I wish that he could be with us more often."

"But that would mean we would also see more of Regina. I for one can easily forgo that treat," said Henry. "Has our dear sister-in-law given you any trouble, Chastity? You have only to say the word and I shall drop a word in her ear."

Chastity shook her head. "There has been nothing that I haven't been able to handle, Henry. I should perhaps warn you that there is a burgeoning dislike between Regina and Mrs. Dabney. Regina regards her as a rival, while Mrs. Dabney treats her with a kind of indifferent amusement."

"Heaven help us, then," Henry said. "With two such cats under one roof, it is inevitable that the fur will fly."

"Pray do not be so dismayed, Henry. I certainly am not," said Chastity.

"And to what do you owe this remarkable serenity?" asked Henry.

"Why, I am relying upon you, of course," said Chastity. "I fully intend to remind you of your generous offer of help if I should ever find myself at a standstill!"

"I do not doubt that in the least!" Henry drawled. He sauntered back into the midst of their guests, while Chastity rejoined the ladies.

Chapter Five

In the fortnight before the soiree, there was one more arrival at Chester. Mrs. Webster stepped down out of her carriage, carrying one of her beloved pugs, while the other two cavorted about her feet. Mrs. Webster was ample of girth, and she always attired herself in the panniers of her youth, so that she appeared even wider. She was greeted kindly by Henry and with affection by Chastity. Mrs. Webster was an amiable soul and she would have found it difficult to bear anyone ill will.

A mountain of baggage was carried upstairs by the struggling footmen, under the direction of Mrs. Webster's formidable dresser, while Henry and Chastity drew Mrs. Webster into the front sitting room. The lady was plied with a fortifying glass of ratafia, and her three pugs were fed biscuits after their long journey.

Mrs. Webster expressed herself quite recovered from the rigors of the trip. "You are always so exceedingly kind to me and my dear doggies," she said, caressing one of the pugs in her lap.

Henry eyed the dogs with disfavor. The two that were still at liberty had discovered the fringe of the carpet. He unobtrusively toed them away with his boot, which only encouraged the pugs to think it was a new sort of game. They growled and made dashing passes at his toe. His lordship regarded the little dogs grimly. "I should like to see you established comfortably as soon as possible, Aunt. I know that you will wish to rest before being obliged to dress for dinner."

"Indeed, I shall! Do we sit down to company?" asked Mrs. Webster, turning her slightly myopic gaze on Chastity.

"Yes, but it is not a large party, as you will discover," said Chastity. "Archie and Regina are here, as are Sir Roger Highfield, Sir Edward Greaves and Lord Winthrop, all of whom you are acquainted with. There are also Lady Peters, her brother Mr. Gabriel Salyer, and Mr. Jeffrey Halston. We also have the Bottlers with us and their houseguests, Mrs. Dabney and Miss Paige."

"It sounds most promising, Chastity. I do thank you for inviting me this year," said Mrs. Webster. She looked around as the door opened. "Oh, here is Dixon now, come to escort me upstairs. I shall leave you for now, my dears. No, no, Chastity, you need not accompany me, for I see Wilkins has come in, too. No doubt he has a message for you. I know that you must see to your other guests."

The butler held a quiet conference with Chastity before exiting the sitting room.

Henry helped his aunt to rise from her chair and handed her into the care of her dresser. "You must tell me if there is anything that you require, Aunt Serena."

Mrs. Webster nodded affably. "Thank you, Henry. Come along, doggies. Henry is sorry to see you go, of course, but you will see him again later."

Henry's expression would not have led anyone to suppose that he was regretting the exit of the pugs, but he did not disabuse his aunt of her fond assumption. As soon as the door closed behind Mrs. Webster, he said, "Those little brutes have no conception of how close they came to a good swift kick."

Chastity chuckled and shook her head at him. "You shan't take me in, Henry, for I know that you would do nothing to distress Aunt Serena. They are the horridest nuisances, of course, but we have always contrived to survive them in the past."

"It is a pity that we do not learn from our past experiences and bar those confounded dogs from the premises," Henry said. He sighed and rose to his feet. "My conscience smotes me. I shall see Aunt Serena safely bestowed in her rooms."

"And I must go speak with Mrs. Timms. She has sent word

through Wilkins of a small domestic crisis concerning our sister-in-law," said Chastity ruefully.

"And so it goes," murmured Henry. "Regina is at least manageable. It is a pity that we cannot say the same about Aunt Serena's spoiled darlings."

Lord Henry's sentiment was shared by others. Archie regarded his aunt's dogs with resignation, while Regina expressed outright revulsion. The next few days were lively as the other members of the house party realized that the pugs had to be discouraged and diverted from wreaking destruction. Mrs. Webster apologized for her dogs' lapses in good manners, but it was not to be expected that any words of hers could conjure up another pair of gold tassels for Sir Edward's favorite pair of Hessians or replace one of Mrs. Dabney's expensive kid gloves.

In the meantime, Chastity worked diligently to make the first soiree at Chester a memorable evening. She consulted with the chef over the menu, carefully selected the music, and put in train all manner of arrangements. The entertainment had been planned for the full moon, so that all the neighboring countryside could drive over to partake of the famous Cummings' hospitality.

The night of the soiree, Chastity stood perfectly poised at the top of the stairs. She was attired in a new gown of wheat-colored silk sarcenet, with a set of glittering diamonds around her neck and in her ears. A gold-fringed Kashmere looped in graceful folds from her elbows. Her chestnut hair was cut in a smart crop so that the natural curls rioted about her head. She knew that she appeared at her best.

Chastity smiled and shook hands, saying a few gracious words to each person before they passed into the brilliantly lit ballroom. All those who had received an invitation made an appearance, and soon the ballroom was filled with a respectable crowd.

The houseguests at Chester were naturally already in attendance, and, with the exception of the Bottlers and Miss Paige, all had met one another in London or at Chester in previous years. Mrs. Dabney was not generally known, but such a beautiful woman was not long left without introduction. Music from the three-piece orchestra was a fine accompaniment to the increasing buzz of conversation and laughter.

When it seemed that all of their neighbors had arrived, Henry deemed it time to join their guests. "It is a good crowd this evening," he said appreciatively as he took his sister's elbow and escorted her into the ballroom.

"Yes, it is," agreed Chastity. She glanced up at her brother's strong profile. "You did say that you wanted everyone we knew from miles around to be invited."

"Indeed, I did. I wished to avoid as much as possible a flirtation with a certain beauteous widow," Henry said, lowering his voice and nodding his head in the direction of the lady standing opposite them.

Mrs. Dabney looked ravishing in a spangled gown over a white crepe slip, her unusual coloring and the glittering spangles making her appear like an ice queen. The impression was further enhanced by the diamond tiara set in her black hair. There was a circle of admiring gentlemen around her, with a smattering of ladies who were curious about the widow.

"Why did you invite her, Henry?" asked Chastity, also looking across at Mrs. Dabney. "I know you said that you were compelled by manners to do so, but surely there must have been a way. She has managed to thrust herself forward so often this past fortnight that even Winny has remarked upon it, and in general he does not say anything about anyone."

"I did not wish to deliberately offend Horace Bottler. They are related in some way, which is why Mrs. Dabney was staying with him," Henry said. He shook his head. "I almost wish that I had offended him now. It is becoming impossible to make a move from my rooms without the lady instantly sniffing me out. I wish you could find it in your heart to help me, Chastity."

Chastity twinkled up at him. "Is the huntress following too close, Brother? Shall you manage to throw her off the scent, do you think?"

"Actually, I am hoping to divert her to another trail altogether," murmured Henry. "That is why I have invited Winthrop and Sir Edward and a few other unattached gentlemen."

Chastity cast another amused glance up at her brother. "You are strangely optimistic, dear Henry, for the lady has had you squarely in her sights for weeks. And you are such a very large target!"

Henry's white teeth gleamed as he laughed. "Sadly true. But I am not one to be bagged so easily, as you will see."

Some neighbors came up to them at that moment, making further private conversation impossible. Chastity wondered fleetingly what her brother had in mind, but quickly forgot about it as she talked with her guests.

There had not been much time for Chastity to visit with her old beau since the afternoon he had arrived. However, Chastity had been struck at that initial meeting by his quiet demeanor. He did not dominate a party in the same way that he had formerly done. He had been content to stay in the background while his friend, Gabriel Salyer, had entered into a light flirtation with her.

Chastity did her duty as hostess by making certain that all had been introduced to one another and dance partners had been found for everyone. Then finally she was at liberty to seek out the one person in the ballroom with whom she truly wanted to talk. Her curiosity had grown so strong that she could not resist seeking him out.

Chastity made her way slowly through her guests toward the Honorable Jeffrey Halston. He was leaning nonchalantly against a marble pillar with his arms folded across his chest, watching the sets forming up on the dance floor. Mr. Halston straightened as Chastity came up to him. He made a slight bow. "Miss Cummings."

Chastity smiled at him. She gestured with her fan toward the occupied dance floor. "You do not dance, Mr. Halston?"

"Not at the moment, Miss Cummings," he said. He returned her smile, but there was a curious glint in his eyes.

"Shall I find a partner for you?" asked Chastity. She hoped that he would refuse her offer since she wanted to spend a few minutes in his company.

"I beg that you will not, Miss Cummings," said Mr. Halston with the glimmer of a smile.

"We are very formal," remarked Chastity. "Will you walk with me, Mr. Halston?"

"It will be my pleasure, Miss Cummings." He bowed and offered his arm to her. Chastity placed her fingers on his elbow. Sedately, they walked around the perimeter of the dance floor, in the aisle formed by the unoccupied gilded chairs and marble pillars on one side and the row of velvet-draped windows on the other. They did not exchange a word for several minutes.

Wall sconces blazed with candlelight, so that every trick of expression could be discerned. Chastity glanced once or twice at her companion's chiseled profile. She thought that if it was possible, he was more handsome than he had been. There was a resolution about his firmly held mouth that had not been there when she had last known him. She wondered what he was thinking. Perhaps he, too, was comparing what he remembered about her with how she seemed at present.

Chastity stopped before a well-cushioned settee. Letting go of his arm, she turned to face him. For the first time since meeting him again, Chastity looked full into Jeffrey Halston's face. There was a weariness in his eyes that she did not remember. She did not like to see it, perhaps because the naive boyishness that she had expected no longer existed. She wondered all of a sudden what he saw in her eyes.

So intent was she on her reflections, Chastity was actually startled when he broke the silence between them.

"How are you, Chastity?" he asked quietly.

There was a wealth of meaning in the inane phrase, which she instinctively understood. Chastity held out her hand to him, almost in appeal, and he gently clasped her fingers. She studied his face, noting the differences. There were lines carved from nose to mouth and between his brows. His eyes met her own steadily, without demand or appeal. He had become a virile man of character, tempered by life. Chastity could at once regret the passing away of the youth that he had been and feel interest in this near-stranger.

"I am very well, thank you, Jeffrey," she said, equally quietly. "And you?"

Mr. Halston smiled. "I also. May I sit with you?"

"Of course." Chastity gently retrieved her hand. She sank down gracefully on the settee, looking up at him.

Realizing that he had not let go of her hand until she pulled free, a flush rose up under his tanned skin. "Forgive me."

Chastity pretended not to notice his discomfiture. She gestured to the settee, inviting him to join her. "Pray be seated, Jeffrey."

Mr. Halston sat down sideways beside her. He laid one arm along the back of the settee. He did not take his eyes from her face. "You have not changed, Chastity."

Chastity was surprised. She had expected him to say something quite different since she had already seen such a change in him. Surely, she must have altered in some indefinable way, too. "You are kind, Jeffrey. I think perhaps too kind."

"Not at all. You are still as lovely as ever. It seems almost like yesterday when we last sat together like this," he said softly.

Chastity searched his face. The words themselves could be construed as flirtatious, but there was no corresponding warmth in his expression or in his voice. She felt some confusion. It was as though he had merely made a comment on a mundane topic such as the weather.

Chastity was at a loss for what to say. She did not know how to react to his matter-of-fact tone. More and more she was becoming convinced that he was nothing at all like the passionate young gentleman that she still remembered. It was a bittersweet discovery.

Chastity gave an uncomfortable laugh. "You are much too flattering, Jeffrey. Pray recall that six years have passed. Surely, we have both changed in that time."

"Have I changed all that much, Chastity?" he asked.

Chastity hesitated, not wishing to put it into words too baldly. "Yes, Jeffrey, you have. I . . . I cannot tell you how, though."

"Perhaps you are right. Perhaps it is wisest not to inquire too closely into what those changes may be," Mr. Halston said with a shrug of his broad shoulders. "The past is best left where it is."

A short silence fell, which felt uncomfortable to Chastity. She cast about in her mind for some light thing to say, but she could think of nothing that did not sound completely inane. In any event, her thoughts were wholly taken up with the gentleman who sat beside her. "I heard about Mirabelle. I am very sorry, Jeffrey," she said finally.

"Thank you. She was a good wife to me," Mr. Halston said unencouragingly.

"And . . . and your daughter? She is well?" asked Chastity.

At last animation lit his face, and there was a note of enthusiasm in his voice. "Yes. Alicia is two years old now and is bidding fair to become a handful if I am not careful," said Mr. Halston. His mouth had eased into a smile.

Chastity had not expected to be given a glimpse of such a side of him. "You are exceedingly fond of her, I see," she said.

"Alicia is everything to me. When she survived against all odds, I was never more glad of anything in my life," said Mr. Halston. He gave a laugh, shaking his head. The expression in his eyes was warmer than previously. "I spoil her abominably, as you might already have guessed."

"I do not think that a child can be made too spoiled by a loving father," said Chastity. "Did you leave Alicia with her nurse at your estate?"

"No, she is staying with my parents for a few weeks. My mother begged that they be allowed to keep Alicia, and most reluctantly I relinquished her into their care. I am an unnatural parent, I fear. I prefer to have my daughter with me," said Mr. Halston.

"That is to your credit than otherwise," said Chastity.

"I am glad to hear you say so," said Mr. Halston. "I have been scolded handsomely by some of my friends for burying myself for too long away from society. Gabriel Salyer and I stumbled across one another in London a few weeks ago. We had used to be good friends, and though I had neglected him badly over the past two years, he was very willing to reestablish our connection. I was therefore delighted to bear him company when Lord Cummings issued his invitation."

"Do you make a long stay with us?" asked Chastity.

Mr. Halston shook his head. "I am here only until the holidays begin. Then I must leave."

"I understand. You will naturally wish to be with your daughter during the holidays," said Chastity. She was conscious of disappointment. She had just met him again, and she was intrigued by him and all that had changed in his life. So much for Merrill's declaration that Jeffrey Halston had come to the neighborhood for the express purpose of finding himself a wife, she thought again.

"Just so."

"You must remember me to your parents when you see them," said Chastity formally.

"I will certainly do so. They have always recalled you with fondness," said Mr. Halston.

Chastity was left bereft of speech, for she could scarcely believe that to be quite true. She had spurned Jeffrey Halston's suit. Surely Lord and Lady Halston must harbor some resentment over that fact.

Mr. Halston rose agilely to his feet and bowed to her. "Miss Cummings, may I have the honor of this dance?"

Chastity thought at least that much had not changed. The Honorable Jeffrey Halston had always been graceful in company. She realized that he was still holding out his hand to her. Mutely, Chastity put her hand into Mr. Halston's and allowed him to draw her up.

Chastity and Mr. Halston partnered one another in the simple country dance with every appearance of mutual enjoyment. Behind her serene, smiling expression, however, Chastity's mind was very busy. She kept wondering why the gentleman that she had known had altered so greatly. Still handsome, Jeffrey Halston appeared to be not only more staid, but actually grave in character. There was nothing to hint at the transparent and lively young man he had once been. Surely, even the death of one's wife could not so radically change a man's entire personality.

Chapter Six

After the set, Mr. Halston escorted Chastity off the dance floor toward a vacant chair. They exchanged commonplace civilities, pausing now and again as acquaintances greeted them. It was excruciating to Chastity, for she had had enough of Mr. Halston's company. Her entire conversation with him had been disconcerting, to say the least. She felt that she needed time to evaluate what little she had learned about him.

As Chastity and Mr. Halston approached, Mrs. Webster greeted her niece's escort with a friendly nod. She had taken the neighboring seat and was engaged in feeding tidbits from a napkin to her three pugs. Her old-fashioned, wide panniered skirts spread out gracefully on either side of her. The small dogs pressed close to the satin folds of their mistress's skirts, bobbing up now and again to place their paws on her knees to beg for another bite.

"Good evening, Chastity," said Mrs. Webster. She glanced with bright button eyes at her niece's escort.

One of the pugs rushed out to growl at Mr. Halston's feet. Mrs. Webster called the pugnacious pug back, scolding. "Now you mustn't be so unfriendly to Mr. Halston, Artemus. He is a perfectly kind gentleman." She glanced up to nod acknowledgment. "I do trust that you will not take offense at Artemus. He is such a protective little fellow, are you not?"

Mr. Halston greeted Mrs. Webster politely and made a slight bow. "Not at all. I happen to like dogs, ma'am."

Mrs. Webster cocked her head as she looked up at him. "I knew a Mary Halston Lavender. I've wondered if you are by any chance a relation?"

"She was my father's sister," said Mr. Halston.

"Oh! How serendipitous, to be sure! Mary and I went to seminary together. We were great friends as girls. She died not so very long ago. A pity, for I always liked her," said Mrs. Webster. "I do not believe that I am acquainted with any of the rest of your family. However, I am glad to know you, sir."

Chastity had to struggle to keep a straight face. She could well imagine the gentleman's feelings, for her aunt and her dogs were rather difficult to accept with aplomb.

However, Mr. Halston seemed to have surmounted the difficulty. He acknowledged Mrs. Webster's comments with another bow. He bent down to pet one of the dogs. It wriggled with pleasure beneath his caressing fingers. "A nice-looking pug," he commented, straightening again to his full height.

Mrs. Webster beamed up at him. "Thank you, sir. You are too kind."

Mr. Halston bowed and walked away.

"What an exceedingly nice young gentleman," said Mrs. Webster approvingly. "You must cultivate him, Chastity, and bring him up to my salon for tea one day. I will be most happy to chaperone you, I assure you. His aunt was once a great friend of mine, did I tell you? I should like to know the gentleman better. And so do you, I should imagine."

"Thank you, Aunt Serena," said Chastity, ignoring her aunt's last comment. "I shall remember your kind offer."

Mrs. Webster absently offered another tidbit to one of the begging canines. "What was his given name, dear? I cannot quite recall."

"The Honorable Jeffrey Halston. He is an old acquaintance," said Chastity.

"He seemed to prefer your company," said Mrs. Webster.

Chastity gave a small laugh. "I do not know how you could have come to that conclusion, Aunt! Mr. Halston and I have merely spoken together a few minutes on two occasions and shared a country set. He is scarcely dancing attendance on me."

Mrs. Webster glanced at her. "I hope that you do not let him become too old an acquaintance, my dear. Otherwise he will begin to look elsewhere for a connection."

"Aunt! What an utterly inappropriate thing to say," Chastity said, flushing slightly. She was taken by surprise. As far as she had been aware, this particular relation had never taken the least notice of her unwed state.

Mrs. Webster ignored her niece's remonstration. She fed one of the pugs. "I do trust that he is an exceptional *parti*?"

Chastity sighed. It seemed that it was her lot to be possessed of nothing else but relations who were vitally interested in her lack of matrimonial state. "Yes, Aunt. Mr. Halston is quite unexceptional. He is a very respectable widower. He has an estate in Sussex and a house in London, all quite unencumbered."

"Has he an heir from his marriage?" asked Mrs. Webster with lively curiosity.

Chastity shook her head. "No. His wife died giving birth to a daughter. The death of his wife was a tragedy, which I suspect that he must still feel, though it has been two years now."

"Well, perhaps; but two years is a very long time to grieve. I know that within two years of Mr. Webster's death I was quite willing to resume my life. Mr. Halston appears to me to be a sensible fellow. He will not be wearing the willow still. I approve of what you have related to me about him, Chastity. What could be better than a gentleman already comfortably established in the world?" said Mrs. Webster. She regarded her niece's unresponsive expression anxiously. "You do agree, Chastity, do you not?"

"I suppose that I must, if only to satisfy you," Chastity said with a smile. "However, you mustn't think that Mr. Halston is at all interested in me or I in him. We are simply old acquaintances, as I have told you. I met Jeffrey when I came out. I have not seen much of him in the intervening years."

"What a pity. But all is not lost, my dear," said Mrs. Webster, patting Chastity's hand consolingly. "Why, Mr. Halston knows good breeding when he sees it. Only see how he treated my dear doggie. Mark my words, Chastity, he shan't overlook you, either."

"No, Aunt," Chastity agreed, knowing that there was no use in arguing the point. Mrs. Webster had a rather simple thought process, but her tenacity to her subject was admirable. Without much expectation, Chastity tried to turn her aunt's thoughts from this disturbing direction. "How are you finding your accommodations, Aunt Serena? I am sorry that I have not yet visited you. I fear that I have been too busy by half this past fortnight. I trust that you have been made perfectly comfortable?"

Mrs. Webster beamed. "Oh, quite, my dear! Nothing could exceed my gratification. Only fancy! My dear doggies have taken an unusually strong liking to our rooms. I have never seen anything to equal it. Why, it is at times almost impossible to persuade them to come out. We are so comfortable, aren't we, my precious ones?"

A horrible suspicion entered Chastity's mind. "Aunt Serena, precisely which rooms have you been given?"

"Why, the back bedroom and sitting room, of course," said Mrs. Webster, looking round at her with myopic surprise.

Her worst suspicions confirmed, Chastity managed to summon up a smile. Mentally, she was planning to exchange a few very pithy words with her brother over his notion of a practical joke. "Of course. Aunt . . . have you noticed anything odd about your rooms? An odor, perhaps?"

"Not at all, my dear. Have you put out mothballs? Pray do not be anxious, Chastity. I cannot smell a thing, I assure you. My nose no longer functions quite as well as it once did, as I think that I wrote you," said Mrs. Webster.

"And your dresser? Has . . . has she mentioned anything discomfiting to you?" asked Chastity.

Mrs. Webster smiled at her niece in a kind fashion. "How you worry so over a few mothballs Chastity! My dresser is quite content, I assure you. She remarked to me just last evening that it is very pleasant not to have any neighbors in the room next door. Poor woman! I debated whether I should bring her with me this visit, for she has been afflicted with a stuffed head for some weeks. I suspect that she is allergic to something in the air. I have told her to treat herself with a liberal rubbing of horse ointment to the chest each evening before she retires. I am fortunate not to be able to smell it, for I well remember how pungent liniment is! But it is bound to do her good, don't you think?"

"I trust that it will, indeed," said Chastity. Privately, she hoped that the dresser did not regain her sense of smell until well into the visit. Perhaps by then the awful odor of the dead rats in the walls would have dissipated to a greater degree.

Chastity still could not quite believe that her brother had been so heartless. She would certainly give him a piece of her mind. "I really must talk to Henry, Aunt Serena."

"Of course, my dear. You may safely leave me, for I am never alone as long as I have my dear doggies," said Mrs. Webster contentedly.

Chastity left her aunt and at once went over to her brother. Henry was standing with some of their guests. After a few minutes of civil conversation, Chastity was able to detach him from their guests and draw him aside for a private word.

Henry looked at his sister's expression. His heavy brows rose a fraction. "What has set you about, Chastity? Has something gone awry with dinner?"

"Of course not. I would not call you aside for something so paltry as that," said Chastity. As a couple of acquaintances passed close by, she lowered her voice. "Henry! I have just spoken to Aunt Serena. How could you?"

Henry flashed a grin. His gray eyes held amusement. "Chastity, I had very little choice. When she went upstairs, she let those damnable dogs of hers loose. They scrambled up the stairs and dashed away before I could say a word. Aunt Serena insisted that she had to go in search of them. Perhaps you may venture to guess where we found them?"

"In the spare rooms," said Chastity, dismayed.

Henry laughed. "Precisely! They were happily sniffing and pawing the walls when we discovered them. Aunt Serena naturally insisted that she be allowed to have that set of rooms. Nothing I could say would dissuade her."

"Didn't you tell her that there were dead rats in the walls?" asked Chastity.

"Of course I did, but she said that as long as her dear doggies were happy, she did not care what wildlife we chose to house," Henry said.

Chastity chuckled. "That is so very like Aunt Serena! I am sorry, Henry. I have very unjustly accused you. I should have known that you would not have played such a deliberate trick on our aunt."

"Quite. By the by, Chastity, I am informed by Miss Paige that you have been very kind to her. I appreciate that very much." His gaze had strayed to the lady in question, who was at that moment talking with Miss Radford, one of the local beauties, and Merrill. "I do not think that she has met with much kindness or consideration in her lifetime."

"Nor I. I discovered that she cared for an invalid mother alone for several years, and after her mother's death she went to live with Mrs. Dabney," said Chastity. "Dru says that she has friends in Bath, but she isn't able to visit them now that she resides with her cousin."

Henry glanced down at his sister, his heavy brows drawn into a frown. "You have learned quite a bit about Miss Paige, I apprehend. Are you saying that Mrs. Dabney mistreats her?"

"Oh, no. I think that Mrs. Dabney ignores her more than anything else. You mustn't think that Dru resents it, Henry. Quite the contrary. She is almost pathetically grateful that her cousin has offered her a home and chooses to take her wherever she goes," said Chastity. "Henry, I could scarcely believe it. Dru is six-and-twenty."

"I took her to be scarcely of age," Henry said, again glancing across the room at the lady. His gaze returned to his sister. "What do you call her?"

"Dru. It is short for Drusilla and is how her friends address her," said Chastity, smiling as she recalled Miss Paige's explanation. "She is a quaint creature. I like her very well."

"Do you indeed? I should like to become better acquainted with her while she is here. As the master of Chester, it is my duty to see that all of my guests enjoy their stay with us, but I cannot seem to come close to her without her beauteous cousin closing in on me," Henry said with disapprobation.

Chastity chuckled. "You invited the lady right into your lair and therefore have left yourself very nearly defenseless. You have nowhere to retreat."

"I strongly dislike your metaphors, Chastity," Henry said affably. "I do have one defense, however, which I hope to put into good effect."

He caught sight of a particular gentleman, and the gleam became more pronounced in his gray eyes. "Behold, Chastity, the instrument of my deliverance."

"Oscar Poplin?" Chastity was astonished. "Henry, she could not prefer him to you! He is a fop and a bit of a slow-top. Why, he hasn't even got a title!"

"Ah, but all of that is quite to his advantage," said Henry. "That, coupled with his exceedingly deep purse, of course!"

"Henry, just what are you about?" asked Chastity.

Henry did not reply, but steered her over to the gentleman. "Oscar, my dear fellow! I am so glad that you were able to attend this evening. I trust that you have fully recovered from your cold?"

"Completely, my lord. It was a trifle only," said Mr. Poplin, shaking hands with his host. He had to tilt his head back to look into his lordship's face. It was only with great difficulty that he did so because of the exceeding height of his neckcloth.

"Capital! Of course you recall my sister, Miss Chastity Cummings," Henry said.

Mr. Poplin took Chastity's hand and raised her fingers to his lips. "Of course! Who could ever forget such grace and elegance, my lord? Miss Cummings, your devoted servant." He made an elegant leg, his hand pressed ardently to his breast.

"I am happy to renew our acquaintance, sir. I trust that you will have a pleasant evening at Chester," said Chastity, amused by the gentleman's extravagant show of gallantry, such a contrast to Jeffrey Halston's recent quiet demeanor.

"I have not the least doubt of that, Miss Cummings," said Mr. Poplin with an admiring glance.

Chastity cast a swift look up into her brother's inscrutable face. Only Henry's eyes revealed his appreciation of the situation. Chastity again wondered what her brother had in mind. Surely, he was not preparing to shuffle Mr. Poplin off on her, she thought indignantly.

"Chastity, our friend here has not had the opportunity to meet all of our other guests, due to his late arrival this evening. Pray introduce him around, especially to the ladies. Oscar is most accomplished on the dance floor. I am certain that the feminine company will be glad to discover it."

"Of course, Henry," said Chastity, accepting her fate with resignation. She understood her brother's strategy well enough, she thought. She would discretely make Mrs. Dabney and Mr. Poplin known to one another and thereafter encourage their acquaintance as best she might. She did not share her brother's obvious optimism in such a tactic, but she was willing to put it into play.

"Thank you, my lord. I appreciate your thoughtfulness most highly," said Mr. Poplin, bowing again. "And my gratitude must also extend to you, Miss Cummings. This is favor, indeed!"

"Come, Mr. Poplin. I know of several ladies in particular who will be glad to know that there is at least one gentleman in attendance who is not so wound up in talking about the hunting season that he cannot spare a thought for dancing," said Chastity.

Mr. Poplin tittered appreciatively at what he took to be a witticism. "Just so, Miss Cummings!" He laughed again.

Chastity introduced Mr. Poplin first to Merrill and Miss Radford. After a few minutes chatting with them, she suggested that he might perhaps wish to make Mrs. Dabney's acquaintance, as well. "This is Mrs. Dabney's first visit to Chester, but perhaps you met her while in London?"

"I did not have that pleasure, Miss Cummings. My word, the lady is a diamond of the first water!" exclaimed Mr. Poplin. He was a connoisseur of beauty, and he was immediately struck with admiration. "A veritable Venus rising from the shell! A goddess come to vibrant life! A poem in all its grace and form!"

Chastity was astonished. She stared at Mr. Poplin, but he had no awareness of her scrutiny since his gaze was fixed reverently upon Mrs. Dabney. Chastity wondered whether her brother might have been more cunning than she had supposed. "Er . . . yes, I am certain that she is all of that. Excuse me, gentlemen. Mrs. Dabney, pray allow me to introduce to you Mr. Oscar Poplin. He is an ardent admirer."

Mrs. Dabney gave her hand to her latest conquest. She smiled kindly on him. "Mr. Poplin, I am pleased to make your acquaintance."

"No, it is I who have the pleasure," Mr. Poplin said, making an elegant leg. He turned the lady's hand and pressed a light kiss into her palm. The lady's fingers curled in surprised reaction.

"Well! You go to work quickly, Mr. Poplin," said Mrs. Dabney, somewhat taken aback.

"You will dance with me, of course," said Mr. Poplin, drawing her hand through his elbow. "It is a waltz. You are made to waltz. I shall worship you with the waltz."

Mrs. Dabney laughed, obviously much amused. "Very well, Mr. Poplin! I doubt that any woman could resist such an invitation." She went off on Mr. Poplin's arm onto the dance floor, while Chastity stood by watching in amazement.

"I have never seen such fast cross-and-jostle work in my life," said Sir Edward Greaves. There was a murmur of agreement among the other gentlemen who had been caught equally flat-footed by Mr. Poplin's audacious approach. The disappointed admirers began to disperse. Chastity ignored the small relief she felt at noticing that Mr. Halston was not among this number.

Chastity turned to Sir Edward, shaking her head. "Believe me, Sir Edward, I only meant to make them known to one another. I had no notion that—"

"That he would carry off the prize?" Sir Edward smiled, his brown eyes crinkling at the corners. "I acquit you of an ulterior motive, Miss Cummings." There must have been some slight altering of Chastity's expression, for his gaze sharpened. "Ah, perhaps I am being premature. In that case, Miss Cummings, you owe me a favor. Perhaps an introduction to that lady who is just now turning from Lady Peters?"

Chastity laughed and agreed. "That is Miss Radford. She is the eldest daughter of Reverend and Mrs. Radford, whom we number among our best of neighbors. She has only lately returned home from the seminary."

"And no doubt she is exceptionally good and has been warned against all men of fashion," murmured Sir Edward.

Chastity paid no heed to him, but steered him across to Miss Radford. "Lucy, I have been asked to perform the office of introduction. This is Sir Edward Greaves, a friend of our family. He is a decided man of fashion and has expressed a wish to make your acquaintance. Sir Edward, Miss Lucy Radford."

Miss Radford gave her hand to Sir Edward. A dimple quivered in her cheek as she smiled. "I am glad to make your acquaintance, Sir Edward."

Sir Edward held her hand clasped in his, looking down into her vibrant face. "Miss Radford, why have I not come across you before now?"

Miss Radford chuckled, not at all disconcerted by the implied compliment. "Sir Edward, I fear that you are a sad flirt."

"I am not at all a *sad* flirt, Miss Radford. I am on the whole quite happy, actually," said Sir Edward promptly.

Chastity realized that her aegis was no longer needed. Sir Edward and Miss Radford had apparently experienced an instant rapport. With a few words, she excused herself.

As she turned away, she noticed that Henry was whirling Miss Paige around the dance floor. She smiled, appreciating her brother's exquisite manners. There were several other, more fashionable, ladies in attendance, and his lordship had squired each of them at least once. Miss Paige certainly had no pretensions to her host's good offices, but he was scrupulously performing his duty, nevertheless. Chastity thought it was very good of him, especially when she saw Miss Paige's flushed face as they whirled past.

Chastity's arm was caught by a hand, and she glanced around, surprised. "Oh, it is only you, Merrill!"

"Did you think it was Jeffrey Halston?" Merrill asked with a mischievous glance.

"Of course not," said Chastity. "What a foolish thought!"

"I saw how you and Jeffrey spent several minutes in conversation before he led you out for the country dance. I am positively agog to hear what passed between you! Did he ask you all manner of questions? Do tell me, Chastity!"

"I fear that you would have been gravely disappointed in us, Merrill," said Chastity. "There was not a romantic glance exchanged, nor a significant word. We simply talked a little of the past."

"Well, that is a beginning," Merrill said encouragingly.

"Oh, and my aunt Webster took an instant liking to Jeffrey because he complimented her pugs. She has offered to chaperone me if I should like to have him up to her salon for tea," said Chastity.

Merrill went into a peal of delighted laughter. "Oh, my poor Chastity! You *are* hedged about by well-wishers, aren't you?"

Chastity smiled at her friend. "Yes, I am," she agreed with a significant glance.

Merrill at once understood and squeezed her arm. "I shan't tease you anymore, I promise you! I simply had the highest hopes of—but I shall say no more on the head! Tomorrow is opening day. Do you ride?"

"Of course."

The ladies spoke at length about the hunting that could be expected, before each was claimed for another set. Chastity was claimed by Mr. Salyer. He was an amusing partner, and Chastity greatly enjoyed herself while in his company. As they were leaving the floor, she noticed that his glance fell on and lingered on Mrs. Dabney.

"She is very beautiful," remarked Chastity.

Mr. Salyer looked down at her quickly, flushing as he met

her amused gaze. "I . . . yes, I suppose that she is. However, I am not a particular admirer of Mrs. Dabney."

Chastity raised her brows. "Are you not? Then you must be in the minority, Mr. Salyer. Even such a hardened flirt as Sir Roger Highfield was struck dumb with admiration upon first making her acquaintance!"

Mr. Salyer shrugged and laughed. He seemed to have gotten over his embarrassment. "I shall confide in you, Miss Cummings, that ladies such as our beautiful widow frighten me. I infinitely prefer the company of yourself or one such as my sister, who are also beautiful but possess sensitivity, as well."

"Do you know Mrs. Dabney, then?" asked Chastity curiously. He had spoken with such assurance that she could not but wonder whether he was better acquainted with the lady than either had said.

Mr. Salyer shook his head, again laughing. "Oh, no! That is to say, not at all well. We have met occasionally in London, of course. But I daresay anyone else here may say the same."

Chastity agreed to it. Mr. Salyer inquired if she would like an ice, and when she acquiesced, instantly declared himself capable of rendering her this service. He kissed her fingers in a light, flirtatious gesture before bearing her off to the refreshment table.

Chastity spent the remainder of the evening dancing. She saw Mr. Halston several times, but he did not approach her again to ask for her hand onto the floor. She was disappointed, but did not quite understand why. The Honorable Jeffrey Halston meant nothing to her, after all.

Chapter Seven

Opening day dawned cold and clear. It was perfect weather for a good cross-country gallop, as Sir Roger Highfield remarked happily to his fellow guests.

Chastity, Merrill, and Mrs. Dabney were the only ladies mounted. Mrs. Dabney's habit was an extremely flattering pale green, frogged and laced, and cut close to her splendid figure. Her hat was a dashing piece with a wisp of veil floating out from it. Her appearance won instant admiration from the gentlemen. Even Henry was not unaffected. "She is a beautiful sight, by Jove," he murmured.

Ruefully, Chastity felt that she had been quite put in the shade. Her own habit was expensive and fit her very well. She had often received compliments on it but she recognized that the widow's ensemble quite eclipsed her own.

Regina did not like to ride, and she and Miss Paige were to share a carriage out to the vantage point that would overlook most of the field. Regina expressed her discontent to be driving about with a nonentity such as Miss Paige, but she felt that the alternative was worse.

"I tell you, Chastity, I will not take up Mrs. Bottler with me. Your aunt Webster may share her carriage with that toad-eater," Regina said forthrightly.

"She is rather difficult to swallow at times," agreed Chastity. She hoped that her sister-in-law would not be unkind to Miss Paige, but it would be just like Regina to take her spleen out on the nearest person. However, Chastity had the happy thought of asking Sir Edward and Lord Winthrop to escort the carriage, which seemed to answer the purpose very well. Regina's spirits revived at once, and since Miss Paige could scarcely be considered a rival, the party went along very well.

Mrs. Webster had left her pugs at the manor for fear that the little dogs would feel compelled to leap into the hunt with the hounds. "But I do so worry about them, Mrs. Bottler," she confided. "They are like little children. I am all that they have."

"Oh, I do understand, Mrs. Webster. Why, I felt just the same about a parrot that I once had. He would fall into a deep decline if I was out of his sight for more than an hour or two. It was quite, quite affecting," said Mrs. Bottler with instant sympathy. The ladies having thus established a common ground, they passed the drive very comfortably.

Mrs. Dabney swiftly established her place riding beside Henry and engaged him in light conversation. Mr. Archibald Cummings was content to leave the escort of his wife to the other gentlemen and he rode with Chastity and the rest of the houseguests. A friendly debate between Mr. Salyer and Mr. Halston arose over the rival merits of the hunters that they each bestrode. Mr. Bottler tended to lag behind the other riders, every once in a while kicking his horse forward, but then falling back again.

At one point, Archie glanced back at Mr. Bottler. He murmured for his sister's benefit, "The man is a sack of flour in the saddle. What possessed him to ride?"

"He came to Chester to try the paces of the hunter," said Chastity, casting an amused glance at her brother. "He is thinking of buying the gelding from Henry."

Archie grimaced, shaking his head. "We shall have to carry him home on a door, no doubt."

Sir Roger overheard the comment and gave a rumbling laugh. He said nothing, however, but dropped back so that he could engage Mr. Bottler in polite conversation. So it was that the party from Chester arrived at the designated meeting place.

Others from the neighborhood around about had already arrived. There was a smattering of lesser gentry and some of the professional gentlemen, such as the local physician. Reverend and Mrs. Radford were also there with their daughter, Miss Radford.

The good reverend and Miss Radford were dressed for the chase, but Mrs. Radford declared herself quite content to follow the course of the hunt seated in a carriage with the other ladies who were not riding. "It will be quite a merry party, I daresay," she said.

"I have little expectation of it," Regina said discontentedly as she discovered that she was soon to lose her pleasant male companions. It was not to be expected that they would remain riding tamely with the carriages when the chase was on.

However, she was not to be bereft of all admirers. Mr. Poplin announced that he did not hunt. "You may rest easy, Lord Cummings. I shall take upon myself the task of entertaining the ladies," he said with a deep bow.

"That is good of you, Poplin," drawled Henry.

Mrs. Radford smiled and took Mr. Poplin's arm, saying, "Come inside the carriage, dear sir. You must not stay out in this brisk air, for I understand that you have but recently recovered from a terrible head cold."

"That is quite true, Mrs. Radford. It is very good of you to think of it," said Mr. Poplin, deeply moved by the lady's consideration.

"Not at all, Mr. Poplin."

While the riders all remounted, the brown-and-white hounds milled excitedly around, whining and barking. The whipper-in good-naturedly cursed the hounds, cracking his whip now and again to remind the dogs of his authority.

Chastity expected to have a groom's aid in mounting, but instead Mr. Halston appeared at her side. "Allow me, Miss Cummings." He made a step for her with his gloved hands. After the slightest hesitation, Chastity put her foot into his laced fingers. With scarcely any visible effort, he tossed her up into the saddle.

Chastity straightened, her color somewhat heightened. She gathered her reins. "Thank you, Mr. Halston."

Mr. Halston touched his fingers to his top hat, the faintest of smiles on his lean face. He was attired like the other riders, in a scarlet coat and buff breeches and top boots, which showed his muscular build to advantage. He moved with the economical grace of the athlete as he swung up onto his own horse.

Henry led the riders to the copse where his men had discovered a good den. The fox was flushed from cover and was gone in a red flash. The hounds sprang after it, baying madly, with the riders in swift, thundering pursuit. There was a rousing chase across plowed fields and grass meadows. The fox ran straight and true, not circling back as many did, and led the field a long chase. The carriages were quickly left behind and were not seen again.

Chastity was not one to hang back from obstacles such as fences and gates or ditches. Her mare took the jumps, landing easily each time on the opposite side. Once, however, she felt her mount stumble when the edge of a bank began to cave underneath. A chestnut surged past, and a masculine hand shot out to grasp her mare's bit, giving the horse that instant of stability so that it could scramble clear.

"Thank you, Jeffrey!" Chastity was grateful. She knew that he had saved her from a possibly nasty fall.

Mr. Halston's eyes were alight as he looked at her. There was a wide grin on his face. "Not at all, Chastity!" With a nod, he was gone again, pounding away on the powerful gelding.

Chastity urged her mare on, not taking her eyes from Mr. Halston's back. He rode well, she thought, but most of all she liked what she had seen in that all too brief moment when their eyes had met. She had seen a flash of the passion for life that she had always associated with Jeffrey Halston.

Chastity caught a fleeting glimpse of Mr. Salyer and Mrs. Dabney emerging together out of an autumn-colored copse. She could only shake her head. It appeared that there was no end to the beautiful widow's conquests. First Sir Roger, then Mr. Poplin, and now Gabriel Salyer. Despite Mr. Salyer's assertions to the contrary, it was apparent that he was as susceptible as any other gentleman to the lady's charms.

*   *   *

The day was long, and when the chase was finally over, the sun was tipping the treetops with brilliant gold. The chill of night was on the riders when they returned to Chester. The manor was ablaze with candlelight and appeared most inviting to the wearied riders. They were greeted with the welcome news that dinner awaited them.

Once again, Chastity found Jeffrey Halston beside her, this time to help her to dismount. As she slid from the horse into his arms, she felt her face grow hot. He did not appear to notice, but set her on her feet and offered his elbow to her. Chastity swept up the long skirt of her habit, along with her whip, in one gloved hand and laid the other on her old beau's arm. He escorted her inside, without exchanging a single word or glance with her. Chastity could only wonder what he might be thinking or, for that matter, feeling. She scarcely knew how to define her own feelings, let alone discern his.

It was a convivial evening, which ended well into the small hours. There was moonlight to guide the neighbors home once they had left Chester. Chastity thought that she had never been so tired in her life, but it was always the same on opening day. As the hunting season progressed and she became accustomed to the long rides, she would become fitter. The same sentiments were expressed by the others who had ridden that day.

Miss Paige hesitantly expressed the wish that she, too, had ridden in the chase. "It was very pleasant driving, of course. But I have never hunted before, and I think that I might enjoy it," she said.

Henry reached out to lay his hand on hers for an instant. "You should not forgo any entertainment that we offer at Chester, Miss Paige. I wish you to enjoy yourself."

Miss Paige blushed. "Thank you, my lord," she said in a suffocated voice.

Chastity took pity on the lady's obvious embarrassment at being singled out. "Yes, Dru, we wish our guests to take away a good report of Chester hospitality."

"Oh, I shall remember this time all of my life," said Miss Paige, almost under her breath.

Mrs. Dabney came up to them. "It is quite late, Drusilla. I think that it is time that we retire."

"Yes, cousin," said Miss Paige, rising at once.

Mrs. Dabney turned to Chastity and Henry, smiling. Her gaze however, scarcely touched Chastity, rather being fixed on his lordship's face. "It has been a delightful day, my lord. I cannot express how much I enjoyed myself."

Henry bowed. "I am glad to hear you say so, Mrs. Dabney."

"Pray call me Cordelia, my lord. I feel that we are becoming good friends," said Mrs. Dabney softly. Her dark eyes met his lordship's in a bold glance, before her lashes swept down demurely.

Henry smiled and bowed again, then excused himself to say good night to his other guests. Chastity said good night to Mrs. Dabney and Miss Paige. She, too, made the rounds and was preparing to go upstairs to her own rooms, when Henry stopped her and asked that she join him in his study for a few moments in the morning. Chastity nodded, only mildly surprised by his request. She supposed that he wished to convey something privately to her that could not be said in the vicinity of their several guests.

Henry had established a habit of retiring to the study a few hours each week, supposedly to attend to the workings of the estate. However, Chastity had long suspected that at times he simply wished to have a respite from the house party. Though Henry had never openly said so, Chastity was of the opinion that the personage that he wished to escape from was Mrs. Dabney.

The lady was rarely seen outside of his lordship's company. She deliberately insinuated herself into whatever gathering included Henry. Usually she had Miss Paige in tow so that that unfortunate lady could be foisted off onto whomever Henry was with. Occasionally such tactics failed, for Lord Winthrop and Sir Edward were quick to appreciate Henry's dilemma and sometimes took a hand in the matter. Thus it was that Henry and Miss Paige found themselves thrown into one another's company, while Mrs. Dabney was ruthlessly but very civilly diverted.

Regina had not been behind in noting what was happening, and she took Chastity to task for not protecting Henry from such insidious tactics. "For I do not mind telling you, dear Chastity, what a disaster it would be if Henry were to be entrapped by those honeyed ways of hers," Regina said.

"But what more do you expect me to do, Regina?" Chastity asked reasonably. "I have rearranged the seating arrangements at table, and I've encouraged Lord Winthrop and Sir Edward in their silly games. I had hoped that Mr. Poplin might answer and so he did for a short while; but that is obviously at an end."

"Poplin!" There was a world of contempt in Regina's tone. "Really, Chastity, how could plain Mr. Oscar Poplin, however wealthy he might be, compare with Lord Cummings of Chester? We must do better than that, or we shall have that woman lording it over us. Never mind! I shall take matters into my own hands."

Regina sailed away, leaving Chastity feeling slightly apprehensive. She knew her sister-in-law well enough to know that Regina Cummings would not be deterred by propriety if there was something that she wanted badly enough. However, all that had taken place was that Regina had appointed herself something of a jealous watchdog over Henry. She even neglected her own admirers in order to thrust herself forward whenever she perceived that the widow was steering Henry into a tête-à-tête. The air of amusement that Mrs. Dabney had originally adopted toward Regina was obviously beginning to wear thin, and Chastity could foresee that a spitting confrontation between those two ladies was in the making.

Chastity was reflecting upon all of this when she entered the study the following morning. After greeting his sister, Henry announced that he had to make a quick trip up to London.

Chastity regarded her brother with surprise. "Why, whatever for? We have several entertainments this week. What could be so important that it would take you off to London just now?"

"I am informed by my secretary that there is a slight problem with the arrangements that were made for the orchestra that I engaged for our dress ball," said Henry, signing his signature to a paper that was lying on his desk. He did not look up to meet his sister's eyes. "I wish to look in at the Horse Guards in any event, so I thought that I might as well take a personal hand with the orchestra, too."

"Oh, I see." Chastity smiled at her brother's bent head. She put little credence in Henry's somewhat lame excuse, but she kept her thoughts to herself. She had been aware for some time that her brother was feeling abnormally restless. She suspected that Mrs. Dabney's continued presence at Chester was making him feel distinctly hemmed in. It would probably do him good to be away for a short time. "Very well, Henry. I wish you a safe journey. When shall I expect you back?"

"I shan't be gone above a day or two. Can you single-handedly manage our guests for that long?" Henry asked, finally looking up.

"Of course." Chastity devoutly hoped so. She feared that the house party was beginning to disintegrate. At breakfast, her brother Archie had been wearing a peevish expression again, which Chastity had no hesitation in laying completely at her sister-in-law's door.

Regina had thrown several verbal darts at Mrs. Dabney, almost to the point of rudeness. Mrs. Dabney had never allowed her smile to slip, but more than once there had been a flash in her dark eyes. Archie was undoubtedly aware of his wife's acute dislike of Mrs. Dabney, and though it made him uncomfortable, there was nothing he could do to rectify the situation.

Chastity herself had been hard-pressed to keep at least a semblance of an amiable atmosphere intact. She was grateful when Mr. Halston responded to a few of her gambits; however, it was not enough to divert the two ladies. Miss Paige had listened and contributed only trifles to the conversation, her intelligent and worried gaze traveling back and forth between her cousin and Regina. Sir Roger Highfield had ignored everything except his breakfast, of course, as had the other gentlemen. Mr. and Mrs. Bottler had leaped into the lagging conversation that Chastity was trying so hard to promote, and for once she was almost glad of their presence.

Chastity had come to the study, wishing that her brother had been at breakfast. Now she was glad that he had not been. If he was in the frame of mind that she thought he was, nothing could have been more uncomfortable for him than the sniping that had taken place over the marmalade and biscuits.

"Of course, Henry," she repeated. "Everything shall be just fine."

"I knew that I could rely on you, Chastity," he said.

Chapter Eight

Almost from the hour that Henry left Chester, the weather took a turn for the worse. A continual drizzle fell, making it impossible to entertain out of doors. Mrs. Radford's invitation to an al fresco breakfast was necessarily postponed, as was Merrill's inspired notion of a picnic at the site of an old abbey ruins. Chastity's own soiree, which she had planned for that Saturday evening, was sparsely attended due to a thundering storm.

Lord Winthrop and Sir Edward did not allow the weather to completely ruin their sport. They took out guns and dogs to try their luck, but came back with only a paltry brace of rabbits to show for their day's outing. Chastity was surprised that Sir Roger did not go with the other two men, for he was an avid sportsman in his own right. But Sir Roger seemed content enough to while away his time playing chess with Mr. Bottler or billiards with Archie. He rather obviously avoided being in the vicinity of the ladies, and Chastity rather missed the old gentleman's extravagant gallantries.

However, she could not fault Sir Roger. She herself was beginning to dread being in the same room with her sister-in-law and Mrs. Dabney. The animosity between the two ladies was patent to everyone.

At one point, Mr. Halston murmured an aside to her. "I do not envy you, Chastity. You are all that is holding the skirmishers at bay."

"Yes, I am well aware of it," she had retorted, flashing a look at him.

Mr. Halston had given her a half smile before replying to a

query from Mr. Salyer. Chastity had hoped that having at least two gentlemen in attendance would lessen the tension between her sister-in-law and Mrs. Dabney, but her expectations had been dashed. Mr. Salyer seemed to have lost his buoyant spirits, retreating more and more often into fits of moody silence. His frame of mind did not lend itself well to gallantries. Only Mr. Halston seemed able to tease him out of these megrims, most often by prevailing upon Mr. Salyer to while away the hours in cards. Mr. Salyer had been nothing loathe.

There were few diversions for Regina and the widow, therefore. As a consequence, tempers became frayed, and the inevitable happened, despite Chastity's best efforts. Regina and Mrs. Dabney fell into a vicious argument, which ended only when Regina flounced out of the sitting room.

Miss Paige said something to her cousin, laying a hesitant hand on the widow's arm. Mrs. Dabney rounded on her, high flags of color in her white cheeks. "I do not recall asking you for your solicitude, Drusilla!" Without a word or look for anyone else in the sitting room, she stomped out. Miss Paige stood scarlet-faced.

"Come sit with me, my dear Miss Paige," said Mrs. Webster comfortably. "You must see that my dear doggies are pining for your soft touch."

"Thank you, ma'am," said Miss Paige in a shaking voice. She crossed over and sank down on the carpet beside the settee quite unconcerned that her day dress would become wrinkled, and gathered one of the pugs to her.

"I do trust that they do not come to actual cap pulling," exclaimed Mrs. Bottler.

"We must hope not," said Chastity wearily. "Pray excuse me. I must talk to my sister-in-law."

As she left the room, she heard Mrs. Bottler's pitying comment. "Poor dear! She is being run quite ragged by those two. I am astounded that such lovely creatures are such shrews."

Chastity heartily agreed with Mrs. Bottler. She knew that much of the trouble that had burgeoned up so quickly between Regina and Mrs. Dabney was because there was nothing to divert them. All of the ladies had felt the abandonment of the gentlemen, but none more than Regina Cummings and Mrs. Dabney. Both ladies thrived on male admiration and company. With all the gentlemen occupied elsewhere, and the curtailment of entertainments, it had been inevitable that the animosity that had been existing just below the surface of civility had erupted.

When Henry finally returned to Chester, Chastity was coming down the front stairs just as he entered the hall. She greeted his reappearance with relief. "Henry, thank God!"

Henry raised his brows as he was helped out of his damp greatcoat by a footman. "As bad as that, Chastity?"

She gave a tremulous laugh. "Oh, you must think me a ninnyhammer. And indeed I feel that I am! I should have been able to do better."

"Allow me to hazard a guess. Regina and Mrs. Dabney?" Henry asked, coming up the stairs.

"Precisely," said Chastity as she waited for him. "Lord Winthrop and Sir Edward have abandoned the drawing room in favor of the fields and rabbits."

"Oh, Lord," said Henry ruefully. "Let me get out of my dirt, Chastity, and I will come down to rescue you. I assume that tea is about to be served?"

"Thank you!" said Chastity. "Yes; and it will be the most pleasant tea since you left!"

Henry took the stairs two at a time. On the landing he paused and leaned over the banister. "By the by, Chastity, you may expect another guest. I have invited another unattached gentleman to join us."

Chastity made a face. "Did you not think that my plate was full enough as it is? Regina's temper will improve, at least." Henry laughed and continued on his way.

For the remainder of the week, the perverse weather continued. Henry's return was regarded very favorably by all, except his lordship's sister-in-law. Regina revealed her feelings to Chastity one evening. "I wish Henry had stayed away! Now that Dabney woman is able to work her witchery again against him."

"I do not believe that Henry will succumb, Regina," said Chastity.

"You are a fool to think so, Chastity. Henry is not immune to her beguilements. Why doesn't he deliver one of his famous set-downs to her?" Regina demanded. Her blue eyes flashed. "I shall tell you why! He has a liking for her company! Oh, I wish that I had been able to drive her away before he returned!"

"It is not for you to decide the composition of our house party, Regina," said Chastity coolly.

Regina smiled at her contemptuously. "You are worse than a fool, Chastity! You are blinded. I wonder, shall you express any regrets if that woman becomes Lady Cummings? I assure you, if that day dawns you will no longer be welcome at Chester!"

Despite Regina's disapprobation, the atmosphere at Chester improved perceptibly during the succeeding days. With the return of Lord Cummings, the other gentlemen again spent much of their time in the ladies' company. The weather improved dramatically, and that also raised spirits. The postponed entertainments went forward, with much interaction between the occupants of Chester and the surrounding neighborhood. Even Sir Roger was back to his old flirtatious self, if a bit more ardent than he was wont to be in the past.

Merrill pointed out to Chastity that Sir Edward Greaves and Miss Radford seemed to be spending considerable time in one another's company. "I wonder whether we may expect an announcement in that direction?"

"I do not think that there is any doubt," said Chastity. "Mrs. Radford has delicately inquired about Sir Edward's circumstances and expectations. And Henry mentioned not a day ago that he believes Sir Edward is quite serious."

"How wonderful for Miss Radford! And Sir Edward, too!" Merrill slanted a glance in Chastity's direction. "It is a pity that you and Jeffrey Halston do not seem to be making the same progress."

"Mr. Halston and I have developed a very amiable friendship since his coming to Chester. Indeed, I believe that I like him better than I did when everyone expected that we would wed. I trust that Mr. Halston would say much the same thing," said Chastity.

"Mr. Halston! Mr. Halston! You are so stuffy these days that it truly tries my patience, Chastity!"

Chastity chuckled. She had decided not to regard any remarks from anyone about herself and Mr. Halston. Her aunt had also made reference once or twice about the gentleman, and she had turned them aside with good humor. "Oh, Merrill! You are quite incorrigible. I hope that you and Charles have a set of girls that you may matchmake to your heart's content."

Merrill had blushed, and there was nothing more said then about Mr. Halston.

As for Mr. Halston, Chastity hoped that she enjoyed his company just as much she did any other gentleman's. He had promenaded with her in the drafty gallery just that afternoon. But she enjoyed similar attentions from her other guests. Whenever he was in spirits, Mr. Salyer continued to make her the object of his gallantry, and though Lord Winthrop was an old friend, he, too, was not behind in paying her pretty compliments when the occasion arose. Chastity began to be lulled into a comfortable enjoyment of the house party again.

Two days later, Chastity began to wonder whether it had been a mistake to hold a house party at all. She could not recall any other gathering to have been so difficult to manage. Everything seemed to conspire to provoke her.

It began with Merrill, whom Chastity had always assumed that she could rely upon. However, it was when Merrill brought forth her concerns that Chastity realized that she was really a ship alone in the sea.

"I do not know what to think, Chastity. I have never known Gabriel to be subject to such mercurial shifts of mood," finished Merrill.

Chastity had naturally noticed Mr. Salyer's change of temperament. He was merry and gloomy by turns. If someone seemed to catch him off-guard, when his expression was shut tight and melancholy, he instantly began talking in a manner calculated to turn all attention from himself. "Yes, I have observed it for myself. Mr. Halston seems to be the only one who can tease him out of it."

"Well, it's certain that I can't! I have tried. One moment he is plunged in deep despondency and the next he acts as though nothing is more important than the next dance or turn of the cards," said Merrill with a deeply troubled expression.

"It is almost as though he is feverish," remarked Chastity, thinking out loud.

"Yes! That is it, precisely. Oh, how I have tried to talk to him, but he only laughs at me." Merrill seized her friend's hand, saying earnestly, "Chastity, perhaps if Henry talked to him?"

"Henry does not know Gabriel that well. He is some years older, and they were never remarkably close," Chastity said dubiously. "But perhaps a word from Jeffrey Halston—"

"The very thing!" Merrill exclaimed, the shadows blowing away from her face. "Gabriel likes Jeffrey very well, I know. Thank you, Chastity! I knew that I could rely upon you to help. You will tell me what Jeffrey says, won't you?"

Chastity was utterly dismayed. "Merrill! I didn't mean that I would speak to him!"

"But you must, for I do not know him at all well. At least, not as well as you do. Please, Chastity. It is such a little thing, after all," Merrill said pleadingly.

"But I would not know what to say or—"

Merrill jumped up. "Oh, thank you, Chastity! Dearest, dearest friend, I knew that I could rely upon you!" She hurried away, leaving Chastity sitting on the settee in a state of utter dismay.

Chastity knew that it wasn't her place to speak to Mr. Halston about his friend. She scarcely knew how she had been thrust into such a horrid position. It was too bad of Merrill to have placed her in such an awkward situation, she thought indignantly. Yet no matter how much she disliked it, Chastity knew that she would have to approach Mr. Halston, if only because her best friend in the world expected it of her.

She did not know how to begin such a conversation, and each time she saw Jeffrey Halston that morning, she felt awkward and could think of nothing but the onerous task that Merrill had laid upon her shoulders. It was inevitable that she began to feel tense, and then she began to find herself avoiding Mr. Halston. That made her feel both guilty and furious with herself. She actually felt herself color up when Mr. Halston directed a quizzical glance at her when she made some inane excuse to step away from him.

It did not help matters when Mr. Halston followed her out of the drawing room, to say quietly, "Have I offended you in some way, Chastity? Is that why you are avoiding me?"

"No; yes! It is not at all what you are implying. I must speak with you, and I don't quite know how—" Chastity shook her head, a smile quivering on her lips. "But not here, not now. There are too many ears. Will you allow me to choose my time, Jeffrey?"

"Of course," said Mr. Halston, with a slight bow. His expression was unreadable.

Chastity had turned from him, only to be caught up by the butler, who conveyed a matter of utmost importance to her. After a debacle with underdone ducks and a burnt sauce, the chef was threatening to turn in his resignation.

Chastity went to the kitchens, scarcely with a compassionate turn of mind. The dratted man knew that he was priceless, especially in the middle of a house party. However, it would not have done to display her frustration, and she maintained her composure during the volatile consultation. She spent considerable time smoothing the chef's ruffled sensibilities and negotiating a new and exorbitant salary.

When she returned to the genteel regions of the house, she was immediately solicited for an interview by the housekeeper. "Why, what seems to be the problem, Mrs. Timms?"

she asked. Chastity was informed that her sister-in-law was up to her old tricks.

Mrs. Timms was trembling with indignation over Regina's most recent demands. She totted them up on her thick fingers. "Hot water at ten and again at four every day, miss. A special mustard bath prepared at five o'clock for Mr. Cummings. Her sheets changed daily and the new ones aired and ironed before they are put on. The wind howls at the window, and so we must muffle it with batting. The carpets are too thin and must be replaced. The placement of the furniture displeases her sense of proportion, whatever that may be, and is to be re-arranged."

"Oh, dear," sighed Chastity. "I quite thought that the state room would satisfy her. She seemed to like it so well."

Mrs. Timms took a deep breath. "Miss, I know the lady is family, but she is driving the household mad. I have had two girls threaten to give notice if they must wait upon her any-more. We are shorthanded as it is, as you know, miss, with Peggy being still out with her back and Agnes taking such a turn for the worse with the head cold and chills. Miss, we are in a spot of trouble!"

"Yes, Mrs. Timms. I understand perfectly. I shall do what I can," said Chastity.

There was relief on the housekeeper's face, as well as guilt. "I am sorry, miss. I am not one to complain usually, but I felt that I just had to speak to you."

"I know it very well, Mrs. Timms. And I assure you that your loyalty and your good heart are appreciated. I shall speak to Mrs. Cummings," said Chastity.

The housekeeper thanked her profusely, and by the time that Chastity had gotten her out of the room, the butler came in. Chastity saw at once from his wooden-faced manner that he, too, had a complaint. Her heart sank.

"Let me guess, Wilkins. Mrs. Cummings?" asked Chastity wearily.

The butler was freezingly polite. "No, miss. It is Mrs. Webster's pugs. The lady took them for a walk through the chapel. They have chewed through the new altar cloth."

"The one that I just finished?" exclaimed Chastity, appalled.

"The very one, miss."

Chastity shut her lips against a very pithy comment. When she had mastered the impulse, she said, "Wilkins, I have decided that the pugs are to be consigned to the kennels. Will you please see to it?"

"With pleasure, miss," said the butler with relish. "And what of Mrs. Webster?"

"I shall have Lord Cummings speak to her," said Chastity, determined that her brother take a hand in the affair at last.

"Very good, miss." The butler hesitated, then said, "There is one other problem that I should bring to your attention, miss, and that has to do with one of the underhousemaids."

"What now? More footbaths?" asked Chastity impatiently.

"Footbaths, miss?" repeated the butler, taken aback.

Chastity waved her hand. "Never mind, Wilkins. What were you about to say?"

The butler fixed his eyes to a point above her head. "One of the underhousemaids was discovered in hysterics over unsolicited advances from Sir Roger Highfield."

There was a short silence. Chastity could not believe that she had heard right. "Sir Roger?" The gentleman in question was very elderly, but also very active. As she thought about it, she began to see that it was more than possible. After all, Sir Roger had flirted rather desperately with her not two days past. Apparently, he had switched to easier game.

Chastity sighed. "I do not feel equal to it, Wilkins."

"Perhaps his lordship might drop a hint, miss?" suggested the butler.

"I certainly hope so, for I do not wish to confront Sir Roger with his peccadillos!" exclaimed Chastity.

"No, miss," agreed the butler sympathetically.

Dismissing the butler, Chastity went in search of her brother. She found Henry enjoying a rare private moment of conviviality with Archie. The gentlemen were laughing heartily over something when Chastity entered the billiards room, but they sobered somewhat when they saw her.

"I am glad to find you in such high spirits," said Chastity, smiling.

"I always enjoy Archie's company," Henry said easily. Archie reddened with pleasure and murmured something incoherent. Henry rechalked his stick. "I know that you have not sought us out because you miss our company, dear sister. What have you got on your mind, Chastity?"

"You know me so well, Henry," said Chastity. "As a matter of fact, I need you to exercise a bit of your awe-inspiring authority."

Archie set down his stick. "Perhaps I should leave."

"Nonsense," said Henry, catching hold of his brother's arm. "There is no need. We have no secrets here at Chester. Do go on, Chastity. I assume that it is not entirely a household affair?"

At that, Chastity gave a quick laugh. "Well, I suppose that in one way you might call it that exactly!"

Henry and Archie looked at her with identical expressions of curiosity. "It becomes interesting, I must say," said Henry.

"Actually, one of the complaints involves Sir Roger," said Chastity.

Henry raised his heavy brows. "I suppose the housemaids are all in hysterics?"

"Only one," said Chastity. "I do wish that you would speak to him, Henry, for I scarcely think that it is my place to do so!"

"No, indeed," agreed Henry. He bent down with his stick and made his shot. There was a satisfying crack of the balls. His lordship straightened. "As pretty as ever I have done!"

Archie looked from Chastity to Henry. "Do you mean precisely what I think you mean? That Sir Roger has . . ."

"Quite. The old goat has been teasing the housemaids again," Henry said coolly. "I shall attend to it directly, Chastity."

"Thank you, Henry."

Archie was shocked. "Improbable, I must say! Why, the old doddard is sixty at least."

"Yes, and he appears like a kindly old grandfather who had not a single devious thought in his head, doesn't he?" asked Chastity. "But Sir Roger is a desperate flirt. I have sustained a few heavy-handed compliments from the gentleman myself. He is hardly a saint, Archie, believe me."

Henry looked at his sister. His brows had drawn together, and there was a frowning expression in his eyes. "Has Sir Roger insulted you, Chastity?"

"Not to speak of, Henry. Not in the way that you are thinking. A few firm rebuffs always put him firmly in his place. You needn't speak to him on my behalf," said Chastity reassuringly.

"I marvel that you have such a degenerate personage here at Chester!" Archie exclaimed.

"Oh, Sir Roger is relatively harmless," said Chastity, giving a slight shrug. "On the whole, he can be amusing, and he is a famous shot, as you have seen. Henry would not think of turning him away."

Henry was still frowning. "No, I would not. At least . . . I shall speak to him, of course."

"Thank you, Henry," said Chastity cheerfully. "And while you are about it, pray do speak to Aunt Serena, as well."

Henry stared at her suspiciously. "What about exactly? It is not delicacy that prohibits you in that direction, I know."

"Oh, no. Just cowardice," said Chastity. "I wish you to explain to her that her pugs must be consigned for the remainder of her visit to the kennels. I was informed this morning that they chewed through the new altar cloth that I had finished. I fear that I would not prove to be as diplomatic as the task demands, given the circumstances."

Henry flashed a grin. "No, I can quite see how that might be!" He sobered suddenly, saying in quite another voice, "I am sorry, Chastity. I know how much work and time that you put into that altar cloth. It is a pity about it."

"I have not yet seen it. Perhaps there will be something salvageable. I do hope so," said Chastity. She turned to the door. "Now I will leave you gentlemen to your game. There are other matters that I must attend to, but I shall not bother you with them."

"Thank God. You have laid two heavy portions on my plate, as it is," Henry said, grimacing.

Chastity laughed. "However, I know that you are well able to handle them, Brother."

As she left and shut the door, she overheard Archie's sympathetic comment. "What bad luck, Henry! You've gotten the short end of the stick, I must say."

Chapter Nine

Chastity smiled to herself as she went upstairs. In actuality, she felt that she had reserved the most unpleasant and most arduous task for herself. She was not looking forward to her interview with her sister-in-law. She thought that it would be worse than all the rest. However, it was not a task for either of her brothers, Henry because he disliked anything smacking of familial dispute, Archie because he was simply too weak-willed to stand up to his wife.

When Chastity went up to her sister-in-law's rooms, she discovered that Regina had lain down to enjoy her usual before-nuncheon rest. The lady's maid who informed her of this fact also said that Mrs. Cummings could not possibly be disturbed.

"Who is it, Simpson?" came Regina's voice from a distance.

"It is I, Regina," said Chastity, firmly pushing the door open a few inches wider and stepping inside.

"Miss!" exclaimed the lady's maid with shocked affront.

"Oh, do let her in, Simpson! Pray do not be insufferable," said Regina.

The lady's maid lifted her nose in the air and with a gesture ushered Chastity into the bedroom. Chastity could scarcely control her twitching lips. Her sister-in-law was well served, it seemed.

Regina reclined gracefully on a daybed. She was attired in a confection of filmy lace and gold embroidered silk that was so stunning that it made Chastity blink. Regina noticed Chastity's reaction, and in satisfaction she ran one slender manicured hand down her shapely side, caressing the silk. "It is pretty, is it not? I had it made from my own design. You would not believe how many times I had to send it back because it was not just right. But decent modistes are so hard to find. Don't you find that to be true, Chastity?"

"No doubt I would if I demanded such a high degree of perfection as you do, Regina," said Chastity, sitting down in a wing chair near the daybed.

Regina nearly purred. "That is so kind of you, Chastity, for I do try to always look my very best."

"I have never seen you appear otherwise, Regina," said Chastity frankly.

"My dearest Chastity." Regina proffered a languid hand to her sister-in-law and squeezed Chastity's fingers in a show of mild affection. "What an utterly sweet surprise that you have come up to visit me. I was just remarking to Simpson how bored I am today. And here you are to relieve my tedium!"

Chastity smiled. "I am glad, Regina. You have certainly made a difference to my morning."

"Oh, have I?" There came a wariness into Regina's deep blue eyes. She waved a dismissing hand toward the hovering maid. "Go away, Simpson. I shan't need you while my dear sister-in-law is visiting with me."

The maid gave an audible sniff and exited from the room. Regina aimed a grimace at the departing maid's back. "Intolerable creature. But she dresses hair so divinely, and so I must keep her by me. Now, Chastity! It is so delightful that you have taken time out of your arduous duties to come see me. Do you wish to see my new ball dress? I have had Simpson unpack it just this morning and hang it up so that the wrinkles may fall out of it."

"I shall wait to see it when you have put it on, Regina, for I am certain that a simple viewing cannot possibly do it justice," said Chastity dryly. She knew her sister-in-law's vanity all too well.

"No, that is quite true," Regina said consideringly.

"Unfortunately it is not fashion that I have come up to discuss with you, Regina."

Regina opened her eyes very wide in a look of innocent inquiry. "Have you not? What a pity! I find that most other things can be such a bore to talk about."

Chastity smiled determinedly. "No doubt. However, I trust that boring or not, my conversation with you will be fruitful and civil. Regina, the fact of the matter is that you have been making unusually heavy demands upon the household. Just at this juncture, I fear that I haven't the staff to give the proper attention to your needs. I do hope that you will not be terribly inconvenienced or made unhappy by my decision to deny some of the more extravagant of your requests."

Regina stared at Chastity with a distinctly pouting expression. "My dear Chastity! I cannot recall a single request of mine that could possibly be construed as either unnecessary or extravagant!"

"Perhaps I should mention those that put the most burden on my staff. The twice-daily hot baths and the mustard plasters for Archie," said Chastity. "I am afraid that I must insist that these luxuries be curtailed, at least at present. We have such a large house party this year that our servants are being stretched rather thin and—"

Regina arranged the folds of laces at her shapely bosom. "Really, Chastity, I never thought that you would take to heart the disgruntled murmuring of a few lazy servants. Why, if this were my house, I would instantly dismiss those malcontents who could not accommodate a few reasonable requests."

"It is not your house, however," said Chastity quietly. "And I have made my decision, Regina. There will not be any more heating of the water twice a day, nor mustard plasters for Archie. Believe me, I am being quite forbearing in this matter."

Regina sat up, suddenly shedding her indolence. "No, it is not my house; but neither is it yours, Chastity! If you persist in taking this high tone with me, I shall instantly apply to Henry. I doubt very much that he will wish to offend me in this or any other matter! He positively dotes upon me and dear Archibald."

"I think that you will find that Henry is quite content to leave all household decisions to me," said Chastity, rising to her feet.

She smiled down at her sister-in-law. "However, pray approach him if you feel that you must, Regina."

"I certainly shall! What nonsense! I am really quite displeased with you, Chastity," said Regina. "I had thought your sense of hospitality more highly developed than this. I had no notion at all that you would stoop to such pettiness!"

"Good day, Regina." Chastity walked to the bedroom door and opened it. She exited, leaving her sister-in-law still castigating her back.

Regina did not come downstairs for luncheon. When her absence was commented upon, Archie threw a rather reproachful glance at his sister. "My wife is not feeling well at present," he said.

"What a pity," remarked Mrs. Dabney. She turned and engaged Henry in low conversation.

Chastity thought that she could guess what her brother had been told by Regina when he had gone upstairs to change. Archie would naturally have been torn between his wife and his sister. Chastity had merely come up with the short straw, and she sighed. It was so very difficult to negotiate the various personalities of this visit.

The horrid day was suitably crowned when it began to drizzle. Chastity dreaded what wet weather meant, for it was so much simpler when her guests could choose their own activities rather than have something constantly manufactured for their pleasure. Even then, it would not be an arduous thing were it not for the skirmishes that had continued between Regina and Mrs. Dabney that set them all on edge.

Chastity stood at the parlor window that overlooked the front lawns and drive, watching the misting rain with a frown. Lord Winthrop, Miss Paige, and Sir Edward had ridden over to visit the Radfords. The weather would undoubtedly force them to return earlier than anticipated. She had just seen Mr. Salyer and Mr. Halston returning from their venture out with guns, gamebags, and the spaniels, angling across the brown lawn and disappearing past the side of the manor. Chastity felt a slight twinge of envy and wished she could join them and escape the responsibility of hostessing. She knew that her aunt had walked down to the kennels to feed treats to her pugs and that Mr. and Mrs. Bottler were taking their exercise in the gallery. Henry had taken refuge in his study after luncheon, leaving Chastity to entertain Mrs. Dabney. However, that lady had just exited the parlor with the announced intention of going to the library and penning a letter.

Chastity knew that within a very little while most of the house party would be back together, and she should concoct some sort of diversion for their pleasure. But she had developed enough of a nagging headache that she felt quite unequal to the task.

Outside the wet window, a private chaise-and-four swept into sight, mud spraying from its iron ties. The carriage stopped beneath Chastity's vantage point. The driver sprang down from the box to let down the iron step. From the door emerged a gentleman, swathed in a greatcoat and with a beaver pulled well down over his brow to protect him from the rain.

The gentleman descended to the soggy ground and with a slight nod acknowledged his driver's courtesy. He walked up the steps that led to the front door of the manor, disappearing from Chastity's sight.

Chastity sighed. The house party was to her mind already quite diverse enough. She had not recognized the gentleman, so he must be the guest from London. How like her brother not to consider what his impromptu invitations might mean to the careful planning that went into the house party, thought Chastity with unusual self-pity. An unlooked-for addition meant rearranging the seating at dinner and choosing which would be the best room to give to the guest. If the gentleman was of social prominence, he would naturally take precedence over some of their other guests.

"Bother," murmured Chastity. At that moment, receiving the unknown gentleman seemed a formidable task. On the instant, she made up her mind that she would send word to Henry that she was in her rooms and not to be disturbed. After such a rigorous day, Chastity thought that it would undoubtedly do her good to retreat to the privacy of her rooms for an hour or two.

Chastity lay down on her bed, not expecting to actually sleep, but simply to rest until the headache was gone. Minutes later, she was asleep. Her maid, coming in after several minutes to tell her about the new guest, retreated quietly without disturbing her.

Chastity did not waken until just before time to dress for dinner. She scolded her maid for letting her sleep so long. "What will our guests think when I make such an entrance?"

"I didn't have the heart to wake you, miss," the maid said.

When Chastity walked into the drawing room, apologizing to her guests for keeping them waiting, she was quickly drawn into a discussion over the latest arrival. The gentleman had not yet made an appearance. It was said that he was still closeted with Lord Cummings, who had sent word that they would be joining the rest of the party in a quarter hour.

Mrs. Bottler was round-eyed with excitement. "It is too exciting for words, Mr. Bottler. I never thought that we would be so honored."

"No, indeed, Mrs. Bottler. I admit to some curiosity over young Cardiff, for if everything that is said about his lordship is true, then we shall be sitting at table with a true hero," said Mr. Bottler.

Chastity was disconcerted. She glanced around at the assembled company. "Who is it that we are waiting for?"

"Oh, have you not heard, Chastity? How odd, for I was certain that Henry kept you perfectly informed on all points," Regina said waspishly.

"I have not seen Henry this afternoon. I was recovering from the headache," said Chastity with a very direct look at her sister-in-law. Regina hunched her shoulder pettishly and looked away.

"It seems that Henry ran into Lord Cardiff while he was in town and invited him to Chester to join our charming party," Archie said, frowning at his wife's averted face.

"Why, I had no notion that Henry was acquainted with Lord Cardiff," said Chastity, surprised.

"Nor I," said Archie. "But apparently they met through some mutual connection with the Horse Guards."

"Undoubtedly that was it," said Lord Winthrop, nodding. "I understand that Cardiff is quite close to Wellington, being one of his top aides-de-camp. However, his father, the Duke of Cardiff, is generally held to have influence in Whitehall."

"I have the liveliest curiosity at being introduced to his lordship," said Mrs. Dabney with a smile. "It is not every day that one actually meets a hero. The poor gentlemen who are so called are generally dead before they earn that sobriquet."

There was a general laugh raised by the widow's witticism. Even Regina showed a slight smile.

Chastity was also curious to meet Lord Cardiff. She had heard like everyone else that he had been mentioned in the dispatches in glowing terms. It would be interesting to see what a real-life hero was like, she thought.

Henry entered the drawing room, ushering in his guest. He made a general introduction. "Ladies and gentlemen, allow me to introduce Lord David Cardiff."

Lord Cardiff bowed in acknowledgment of the overall welcome given him by the gathering. He was not an exceptionally tall man. However, his straight military bearing, with his shoulders well back and his head at a proud angle, gave him a presence that others might envy. His lordship was handsome, but very tanned, and he smiled easily. He wore his right arm in a silk sling.

Henry proceeded to make individual introductions. As he brought Lord Cardiff up to Chastity, she thought that she detected a gleam of amusement in the gentleman's eyes. Chastity instantly felt comfortable in his presence. Chastity smiled and held out her hand. "How do you do, my lord."

He took her hand a little awkwardly since he was using his left, and bowed. "Lord David Cardiff, at your service, Miss Cummings."

Chastity smiled at his lordship. "Forgive me, Lord Cardiff. I

apologize for not receiving you directly upon your arrival. I am
not usually so remiss."

"Quite all right, Miss Cummings," said Lord Cardiff. "I
imagine that it is rather a responsibility to attend to all of the de-
tails of a house party of this size."

Chastity appreciated the gentleman's insight. "Just so, my
lord."

He nodded, still smiling, and stepped past her as Henry drew
his attention to someone else.

While the introductions proceeded, Chastity took advantage
of the opportunity offered to move over beside Merrill. In a
lowered voice, she said, "What do you think of Henry's newest
find, Merrill?"

"I think him quite, quite perfect!" she said enthusiastically,
her eyes still on Lord Cardiff. She glanced at her friend. "How
wonderful it would be if Lord Cardiff would cast his eyes in
your direction, Chastity!"

Chastity smiled, but shook her head. "I have no anticipation
of that, Merrill." She looked across at the gentleman. "Though
I must admit that it would be very pleasant. He is very handsome."

"I shall do all in my power to help bring you to his lordship's
notice."

"Pray do not, Merrill," said Chastity, glancing swiftly at her
with alarm. "It would embarrass me so."

"Very well! I shall not lift a finger in your behalf," said Merrill, tossing her head.

"Thank you, Merrill."

"Well, you needn't sound so grateful!" Merrill retorted.

At dinner Chastity was seated too far from Lord Cardiff to
actually converse with him, but she could see that he was holding the attention of everyone around him. He was obviously
being plied with questions about the war and his own experiences, which he handled with apparent good humor.

Her own dinner partners had little to contribute, since they,
too, were more interested in what was going forward at the
other end of the table. When dinner was over and Chastity led

the ladies out of the dining room to leave the gentlemen to their wine, the ladies expressed the hope that the gentlemen would not be long in following them to the drawing room for coffee.

"For you must not keep Lord Cardiff all to yourselves," Regina said, bestowing a lovely smile on Lord Cardiff. "We, too, should like to become better acquainted with him."

The gentlemen were considerate enough to curtail their time and shortly rejoined the ladies.

At length, Chastity was able to sit down with Lord Cardiff and exchange pleasantries. She recalled the little that she had heard about the handsome officer and his circumstances. "You are a staff officer with His Grace, the Duke of Wellington, are you not? We have heard a number of things in the duke's favor."

"His Grace is a great man. Britain is fortunate to have him, though I believe that he does have detractors here at home," said Lord Cardiff.

"It is always so, I believe," said Chastity. "There is misunderstanding and envy for anyone who bears such responsibility and who is able to carry it. However, I think you will find that there are fewer critical voices now than before. The duke has run the French out of the Peninsula, after all. We here at Chester have only good to say about any of our brave soldiers."

"You are extravagant in your praise, Miss Cummings. Dare I trade upon it and beg the favor of your standing up with me in a country dance?" asked Lord Cardiff. "I understand that you are shortly to hold a grand ball, and I would deem it an honor if you would allow me to lead you out."

Chastity was surprised. With an involuntary glance at his slinged arm, she said, "Why, certainly, my lord."

Lord Cardiff smiled at her, completely understanding her hesitation. He lifted the hand resting outside the sling and flexed his browned fingers. "I am not nearly as incapacitated as my physicians would have everyone believe. It is my shoulder only that was injured. The sling is mere window dressing, as far as I am concerned. So you need not be concerned on my account, Miss Cummings. I shall endeavor to acquit myself credibly, I assure you!"

His expression was one of such friendliness, and not at all superior, that Chastity laughed. "Very well, my lord! I shall remember that. I accept the honor of standing up with you, my lord."

Chastity knew that Lord Cardiff would not have been sent home to recuperate unless he had sustained more injury than he was admitting. However, she respected his lordship's obvious wish to brush aside any coddling considerations.

After a few more pleasantries exchanged with Lord Cardiff, Chastity excused herself to mingle with her other guests. When it came time for her country dance with the tall, browned staff officer, Chastity decided that she would be very willing to accept his lordship's escort onto the floor. It would be nice to enjoy the company of a man with so much good nature in his expression, unlike the reserve so often to be found in Jeffrey Halston.

Chapter Ten

When the post arrived, it was always placed on a silver salver and taken upstairs to Chastity's private sitting room. As always, Chastity thanked the butler, who bowed and left. She sorted through the invitations and other correspondence for those that were addressed to herself, setting aside the rest for her brother's perusal. One thin, violet-scented envelope was forwarded in a familiar flourishing script, and she picked it up.

Chastity sat down with the letter in a straight-backed chair at her Sheraton writing desk. The skirt of her high-waisted day dress fell in graceful folds to the floor, so that only the toes of her slippers peeped from under the hem.

Chastity slit open the envelope from her aunt, Lady Mackleby, with a silver letter knife and unfolded the sheet. As she read, a faint frown gathered between her brows.

Letter in hand, Chastity rose from the desk, left the sitting room, and went downstairs. As she descended, Mr. Halston appeared in the grand hall below. She saw that he was dressed for riding and that he carried a crop in one gloved hand. He looked up upon hearing footsteps. "Good morning, Miss Cummings."

"Good morning, Mr. Halston," said Chastity, coming down the last few steps.

Mr. Halston waited for her. His eyes were warm, and he wore a smile. "I have been hoping to see you alone for several days. We left a most interesting conversation dangling the other evening."

"Yes, I do realize it." Chastity gave a little laugh. "I still have not discharged my obligation, and it weighs with me."

"Your obligation?"

"Yes, to Lady Peters. I must explain it to you," said Chastity.

"This obligation has been a source of embarrassment, I perceive. I hope that you can trust me well enough to unburden yourself," said Mr. Halston quietly.

Chastity was mildly surprised by his sensitivity. "Why, thank you, Mr. Halston. I appreciate your expression of concern. I do not regard the circumstances, however. I enjoy entertaining, and that supersedes all possible distresses."

Mr. Halston looked down at her. "*All* distresses, Miss Cummings?"

Since there had been a rather open exchange between the two resident beauties earlier at breakfast, which Chastity had done her best to mediate but with only moderate success, she laughed and shook her head. "Well, perhaps not all," she conceded. "Sometimes I feel as though I am walking a tightrope that is not at all stable."

"Miss Cummings, I was preparing to go down to the stables. Perhaps you would care to join me for a ride?" said Mr. Halston.

Chastity looked up at him consideringly. "I should like that very much, Mr. Halston. Shall we say in a half hour? I was on the point of consulting with my brother on a simple matter."

"Of course." Mr. Halston bowed, politely gesturing her past him.

With a last smile for Mr. Halston, Chastity continued on to her brother's study. She knocked, and upon being bidden to enter, she went in.

Chastity had always liked her brother's study. It reflected Henry's character with its heavy and massively proportioned furniture. The thick carpet under her feet was a dull green with a border of rust and gilt. The rust-colored drapes over the mullioned windows were made of heavy brocaded velvet. The busts of distinguished ancestors stood between the windows, and massive portraits hung above them. Several bookcases built straight into the paneled walls were filled with all sorts of tomes.

Chastity allowed her eyes to travel to the long fireplace with its massive grate and a stone-faced opening that took up most of the wall. The mantel above it was carved to fit its length. Hung above it was a portrait of the last Lord Cummings, seated in that very room with a summer view of the Chester gardens in the background.

A fire was blazing on the hearth to ward off the deepening chill that was apparent in the weeks before winter truly set in. Wall sconces with burning tapers shed welcome added light. Three well-upholstered chairs were arranged in front of the fireplace, but there was no one else in the room.

Chastity had half expected to find Archie with Henry. Indeed, it appeared as though he had just left, thought Chastity, noting that the chess set and a decanter of port were out on the low table between the wing chairs. Firelight flickered on the glass-fronted cabinet to one side of the fireplace. Chastity knew its contents well. The cabinet was filled with several valued books, china, and porcelain pieces, as well as other treasures that had come into possession of their family.

She turned her head, smiling. The most impressive piece in the study was Henry's desk, which was wide and ornately carved on three sides and down the legs. The drawers had heavy metal pulls and were kept locked with a large key that never left his lordship's possession. Only two other people had access to that key, Chastity herself and Henry's trusted secretary.

"Hallo, Henry."

Her brother was seated behind his desk. He looked up as Chastity spoke and put down the sheaf of papers that he had been reading. "Thank God! I have been hoping for an interruption for the last half hour. You should see the stuff that Twally has me going over," he said. "I had no notion what a can of worms I was opening when I decided that I wished to acquire that small acreage adjacent to the back field. It almost causes me to regret my decision."

"I do hope not, for you know how nicely that parcel will finish out your holdings," said Chastity. Across from the desk were two more wing chairs with an occasional table separating them. Chastity seated herself in one of them, feeling far more at ease than one of his lordship's employees might have in the same chair.

"Yes, and the squire is now so eager to oblige me." Henry sighed.

Chastity chuckled. "I sympathize, Henry, of course I do! I know how impatient you are with all such legal matters. But you cannot very well leave it all to Twally, can you?"

"If only I could," Henry said, grimacing. He leaned back in his chair. Behind him, the drapes on the two tall windows had been looped back to let in the weak sunlight and cast him into partial silhouette. "But what may I do for you, Chastity? I will welcome any turn of my thoughts just now! Has Regina turned the household on its ear? Must I speak to Sir Roger again?"

Chastity shook her head. "Nothing like that, Henry. It is this." She held up the letter. "Our aunt Mackleby has written me to say that she has decided to accept your invitation. Henry, whatever possessed you to invite Lady Mackleby to Chester for the holidays?"

Henry's expression altered. An alertness came into his eyes. "I told you that I visited her ladyship briefly when I went up to London a fortnight ago. I found her going along quite well."

"Yes, but you neglected to tell me that you had asked her to come stay with us," said Chastity.

"I am guilty as charged, I fear," Henry said, continuing to watch his sister.

"No doubt you thought she would never do so," said Chastity, sighing.

Henry did not reply, an omission that she scarcely noticed as her thoughts turned to the immediate problem at hand. "According to the date of her letter, Lady Mackleby will already have left town. We can probably expect her imminent arrival. I scarce know where we shall put her or how we shall entertain her. Really, Henry, you could have given me some warning."

"I am confident that you will rise to the occasion, as always," said Henry. He saw that his sister was annoyed by his easy answer. With a conciliating smile, he said, "I apologize, Chastity. It was not very well done of me. It was never my intention to make your duties onerous. Will you forgive me?"

"Readily, Henry. But what shall we do? You know how Lady Mackleby likes just her own select group of friends. Shall I send invitations posthaste to a few of them?" asked Chastity.

Henry feigned a shudder. "Spare me! It will be quite enough to have Lady Mackleby under our roof. Perhaps you might shuffle her off on Sir Roger instead."

Chastity's worried expression lightened. "The very thing, Henry! Why, they will undoubtedly go along famously. If only Sir Roger will flirt with her ladyship a bit. That will go far in assuaging her boredom."

Henry regarded his sister with a fascinated gaze. "Sir Roger? Sir Roger and Lady Mackleby? Are you quite serious, Chastity?"

She flashed a bright smile. "Oh, yes! What could be better? He will feel quite wicked, and she will derive great satisfaction in delivering heavy setdowns. We shall have them both very well occupied, which will ease my duties considerably, believe me! Now I must leave you, Henry, for I must go consult with Mrs. Timms about where we shall house Lady Mackleby. It must be far enough from Sir Roger for decorum, but not too far away that they might not encounter one another in the halls as they come downstairs of an evening!"

"I am almost revolted by the visions that my imagination present to me."

Chastity laughed. "My dear brother, a little flirtation will enliven things remarkably, I assure you."

Henry gave a half smile. His lids drooped over his eyes, which were suddenly agleam with amusement. "Perhaps you are right, Chastity. Well! We shall await events as they unfold. This house party may prove to be every bit as interesting as I had hoped."

When Chastity left Henry and went upstairs to change to her

riding habit, she recalled her parting comment to her brother. She found that she was anticipating her ride with Jeffrey Halston. A light flirtation would certainly be welcome, always supposing that Mr. Halston was willing to comply, of course. Then it would be so much simpler, she thought, to bring up Merrill's concerns for her brother.

Chastity was not disappointed. Mr. Halston set himself to be an amusing companion. It seemed to her that he was far more relaxed in her company than previously. Perhaps it was due to the activity more than anything else, since they both enjoyed riding. Once they had let the horses work off their initial restlessness, Mr. Halston and Chastity allowed their mounts to drop into an easy pace.

"Now what is it that you have found so difficult to discuss with me?" asked Mr. Halston.

"It is ridiculous, really. I find myself in the awkward position of go-between for Lady Peters. She feels some concern for Gabriel, and she hoped that you might speak to him, that your words might carry weight with him when hers have not," said Chastity. She was glad to have gotten it out. It had been most awkward, but he had given her the very opening that she had needed.

"I see. And how is it that you have been dragooned into this?" asked Mr. Halston, interested.

"She did not feel well enough acquainted with you to speak to you herself," said Chastity, throwing a glance at him.

"But her ladyship thought that *you* were," murmured Mr. Halston, an odd smile playing about his mouth.

Chastity cleared her throat. "I suppose it does sound utterly ludicrous."

"Not at all. I am honored that Lady Peters thinks so highly of me," said Mr. Halston smoothly. "I, too, have felt for some time that there is something wrong with Gabriel. I suspect that he is in trouble of some sort. I have tried once or twice to solicit his confidences, but to no avail. However, you may tell Lady Peters that I shall not give up. He is my friend, and I intend to help him, *if* I can."

"Thank you, Jeffrey," said Chastity quietly. There was the feel of snow in the air, she thought. She felt the tingle against her skin. Chastity breathed in, liking the clean crisp scent. "We shall see snow soon," she remarked.

"You have always done that," said Mr. Halston.

Startled, Chastity glanced at her companion. She met his steady regard. "What do you mean?"

"I can remember your sniffing the air like that, with just that same expectancy," said Mr. Halston quietly.

For no reason whatsoever, Chastity felt heat rise into her face. She gave a laugh. "What odd memories you have of me, Jeffrey!"

He smiled, shaking his head. "No, only remarkably detailed. What did you think of Lord Cardiff? His lordship seemed to make quite an impression overall."

Chastity was disconcerted by the personal nature of his words, and she was glad for the change in subject. "Oh, I found Lord Cardiff to be quite charming. He is not at all high in the instep as one might have supposed. I am glad to have his lordship here at Chester."

Mr. Halston threw an enigmatic glance at her. "Are you, indeed?" he murmured. He spurred his mount. "Come, it is time for another gallop! Let us blow the cobwebs out of our heads, Chastity! I extend a wager. I shall beat you back to Chester."

"I never refuse such a challenge, Jeffrey. Allow me to show you the way!" said Chastity, putting heels to her own horse.

It was a mad gallop across fallow fields and flying leaps across ditches and gates. At length the riders hurtled into the stable yards. Their horses were blowing, and steam rose from the animals' hides in the chill air.

Mr. Halston threw himself off his mount and caught Chastity's bridle. Then he reached up to take hold of her waist. Chastity was laughing as she slid off her mare into Mr. Halston's arms. Her eyes sparkled, and high color flew in her cheeks. "That was magnificent, Jeffrey!" she exclaimed.

He had been laughing, too. But as he looked down at her, his arms still around her, a sudden shuttering came down over his face. He dropped his arms and stepped back. "It was indeed a grand ride, Miss Cummings. We must do it again someday." He bowed and walked away.

Chastity stared after him, her laughter caught in her throat. She did not understand what had happened. He had changed in an instant from a lighthearted companion to a stiffly formal acquaintance.

Chastity picked up her riding skirt so that the hem would not drag across the ground and walked slowly toward the manor's side door. All of her pleasure in the outing had been quite destroyed. She rather thought that she would do better to stay far clear of Mr. Halston. He was upsetting to her equilibrium in more ways than one.

Chapter Eleven

The ballroom was filled with guests. Out-of-season flowers of all descriptions gathered from Henry's hothouses added a light touch to the elegance of the furnishings. The blazing candles and the burnished dance floor were reflected in several mirrors. The dance floor was a swirl of color as ladies and gentlemen went round and round to the strains of the full orchestra that Lord Henry had imported from London.

A veritable feast was laid out in the adjacent room on several occasional tables. Cold cuts and lobster shared the tables with quail in aspic and thinly sliced hams. Hot punch, iced champagne, and lemonade were available to quench the thirst after the hot work of dancing. Everyone was willing to be pleased and Chastity and Henry were repeatedly praised on the success of the evening.

Chastity herself was in high good looks and received several compliments. Her cream gown of Italian crepe had an overdress of Brussels lace. She wore a golden tiara of diamonds and amethysts and matching drop earrings flashed brilliant fire whenever she moved her head and they caught the candlelight.

Chastity gently waved a neat gilded fan. Her satin slippers tapped to the music when she was not dancing. It was just the kind of entertainment that she reveled in most.

"Oh, Miss Cummings! What a positively delightful grand ball! I am almost beside myself at my good fortune to have been invited to Chester," exclaimed Mrs. Bottler. The lady was clothed in puce and wore a huge headdress of nodding ostrich feathers.

Chastity eyed the extraordinary concoction and with difficulty transferred her gaze to her guest. "I am glad that you find all to your satisfaction, Mrs. Bottler," she said with a polite smile.

Mrs. Bottler pressed her plump hand to her bosom. "Such consideration! Such condescension! You are too good, Miss Cummings!"

Chastity dryly agreed to it and moved on gracefully to mingle with her guests. She spent a few moments in light banter with each, pairing couples for dinner and making certain that all had dance partners. Some of the more retiring ladies were more difficult to find partners for, particularly with modest or reluctant gentlemen, but Chastity managed all with aplomb.

At one point, Henry paused beside her. "You have outdone yourself this evening, Chastity."

"Thank you, Henry," said Chastity, smiling up at him. "I was in a quake earlier that it would not turn out half so well. Our temperamental Gaston threatened to mutiny when he discovered that we could not provide him with a white goose for paté. But I assured him that such a delicacy must only be served at Christmas dinner, when there will not be dancing to steal away the admiration of our guests from his masterpieces. I am happy to say that we have survived the latest rumblings from the chef's domains."

"You would make an admirable diplomat's wife. Perhaps I should bestir myself on your behalf and solicit an eligible *parti* from out of the Home Office," Henry said.

Chastity laughed, shaking her head. "No, pray do not! I have my hands full enough as it is with our domestic crises this year. It has all quite set me against the diplomatic arts. I believe I would prefer a nice snug cottage with a lovely walled garden. It would be too small to allow a great number of guests, so that I would be forced to entertain only those few whom I wished to see on a regular basis, such as you, dear brother."

"I am flattered," Henry said, bowing.

"So you should be!" said Chastity, laughing again. "I do not extend the invitation lightly, I assure you."

"What would you do otherwise?" Henry asked, somewhat amused by his sister's flight of fancy.

Chastity gave a slight shrug. "Oh, I would devote myself to such quiet pleasures as took my whim."

"Such a life sounds abominably dull. You would be heartily bored within a fortnight," Henry said, smiling.

"I could always take up some obsessive hobby, I suppose," said Chastity, though acknowledging to herself the truth in her brother's observation.

Her gaze fell on their aunt, Mrs. Webster, and her three pugs. Mrs. Webster had begged that her dear dogs be allowed out of the kennels for the evening. She had earnestly told her niece that her pets had learned their lesson and would be perfect angels. Chastity had relented with reservations, but thus far Mrs. Webster's assurances were proving to be accurate. The fat little dogs had not ruined one hem or attacked one swinging tassel.

Chastity turned a mischievous expression on her brother. "I could breed little dogs. Pugs, to be exact."

Henry grimaced. "I would disown you, Chastity."

"Yes, just as you have disowned Aunt Serena," retorted Chastity. She squeezed her brother's arm, looking up at him with an amused expression. "I know that you love me too well to ever send me away, whatever the provocation that I might offer to you. Unless, of course, you choose to marry. Then I expect that you would wish me to remove to my little cottage with the garden!"

Henry shook his head. "Even then, Chastity. You will always be welcome to make your home with me. In any event, you need not bother your head over it. I am in no great haste, for I am comfortable as I am, as well you know. I have you to play hostess, which is quite selfish of me. At least, I shall until you wed."

"I shan't do so for a day or two, at least," interpolated Chastity.

"And I have my friends and my duties," Henry said, ignoring her. "I do not intend to rush into wedlock. I shall take my time until I am certain that I have found what I am looking for."

"What are you looking for, Henry?" asked Chastity curiously. She had never discussed anything of the sort in such depth with her brother before.

Henry shrugged. "I am not quite certain. But I know that I will recognize it when I find it."

"In the meantime, there has been the occasional lady to divert your tedium," said Chastity.

Henry frowned down at her. "Chastity, you know better than to acknowledge such things."

"My given name is Chastity, dear Henry. It is not Ignorance," she retorted.

"No; you are not by any stretch of the imagination an ignorant goosecap," agreed Henry with a sudden smile. "Dash it, Chastity, you would make an admirable political hostess. You are quick-witted and discreet, as well as elegant and talented. I fear that I am not doing my duty by you as I should."

"Are you so eager to be rid of me?" asked Chastity, cocking her head.

"Not at all. I would regret losing you. But if your heart becomes attached, I will not stand in your way," Henry said in quite a different voice.

Chastity was startled. Their bantering discussion had taken an unexpectedly serious turn. She looked searchingly at her brother's face. "You are serious, Henry!"

"Of course I am. I do not wish you to ever feel that you are so obligated to me that you cannot command your own life," he said.

"You have been discussing me with Archie and Regina. No, it must have been with our aunts or our sisters!" exclaimed Chastity. "Really, Henry!"

"No, I have not," Henry said irritably, but with a slightly guilty expression. "They have been discussing you with me. It may interest you to know that I am a selfish beast to keep you cloistered and segregated as I do from eligible gentlemen!"

Chastity laughed. She could not help it. She nodded. "There is some truth to that, of course. I never see any gentleman unless he is over five score years in age. You also lock me in my

rooms at night for fear that I might elope with one of the dod-
dering dears."

Henry stared at her. A grin tugged at his mouth. "Very amusing, Chastity. You've always had a lamentable habit of poking
fun at the most opportune moments."

"Come, Henry!" Chastity tucked her hand inside her
brother's arm. "I am very comfortable with my life. So let's
hear no more of this nonsense. Our relations may continue to
spin their farragoes; but you and I know what will best suit us
both."

"Quite," agreed Henry. His eyelids had drooped over his
eyes so that his expression could not be easily read. "My mind
is now relieved of all anxiety. I am a charming fellow, after all,
and the best of brothers."

Chastity laughed. "Then I am the most fortunate of sisters."

Henry bowed. "A pretty compliment, Chastity. You have
quite put to shame my preening. I shall leave you to a better,
more self-effacing man. Lord Cardiff!"

Chastity felt herself blush as she turned to greet her brother's
newest acquaintance. She liked Lord Cardiff's frank, open gaze
and the twinkle lurking in the depths of his eyes. The slow
smile that played across his face when he looked at her made
her heart beat a little faster. Chastity offered her hand. "My
lord!"

"Miss Cummings." Lord Cummings bowed low over her
gloved fingers. The warmth of his hand could be felt through
the fabric of her glove.

"Cardiff, my sister told me earlier today that you have expressed a liking for grouse hunting. Perhaps while you are here
we might show you some sport. How is the shoulder?" Henry
asked.

"It is healing nicely, my lord, albeit still a bit stiff. But I think
that I could manage to brace a gun, however awkwardly," said
Lord Cardiff.

"Good. Then we shall try it one morning before you must
leave," Henry said.

"How long do you remain with us, my lord?" asked Chastity in quick curiosity.

Henry murmured something about seeing to another guest and slipped away. Chastity did not mind as much as she might otherwise have if it had been most other gentlemen. She resolutely turned her thoughts away from what other gentleman's company she might enjoy.

Lord Cardiff acknowledged his host's exit with a nod before replying to Chastity's question. "I do not precisely know, ma'am. I shall stay as long as my welcome at Chester is not worn out."

"I am certain that will be a long time in coming," said Chastity with a smile.

Lord Cardiff made a slight bow. He gestured toward a settee. "Will you join me, Miss Cummings? I have not yet mastered the art of dancing one-handed, to my sorrow! Or otherwise I would request that you stand up with me as you had promised."

"Of course, my lord." Chastity preceded him and sat down. She spread open her fan and waved it very gently at her breast.

Lord Cardiff joined her on the striped settee. He glanced around the crowded ballroom. "It is a very pleasant gathering. Your friends and relations have all been quite kind to the stranger in their midst."

"You have made yourself agreeable to all, my lord. It would be odd, indeed, if you had found any who wished you ill," said Chastity.

Lord Cardiff glanced around and caught her gaze. There was a peculiar amusement in his eyes. "You are kind, Miss Cummings."

"I have not had an opportunity before to speak with you at any length, my lord. At least, I have, but I have hesitated since you have been so mobbed by everyone else," said Chastity.

Lord Cardiff laughed. "Yes, I seem to be something of a celebrity. It astonishes me still."

"Were you back in England long before coming to Chester?" asked Chastity.

"A few weeks only. I did not wish to leave my company, but

my commanding officer insisted that I would regain my health and strength more quickly if I was to take wounded leave. Since winter was approaching, and the army was going to be bivouacked until spring, I did not object overmuch. I had been away from England for three years. I was glad to see that very little had changed in my absence," said Lord Cardiff, once more glancing about the ballroom.

Chastity understood to what he was referring. Those cherished traditions that had been observed for centuries were still in place. The entertaining of one's relations and friends was a staple of English hospitality.

The ball was now in full swing. The ladies chattered together as though they had not seen one another for years, instead of just a few hours before at luncheon, while the gentlemen's deep tones provided a fine counterpoint. All of the neighborhood had come, anticipating a delightful evening and fine food. They were not to be disappointed in any way. The sideboards groaned with the scrumptious offerings from the kitchen— roasted fowl, hams, puddings, pastries, sweetmeats, sweetbreads, and pies.

"Your family must have been happy to see you," remarked Chastity. She had been curious why he had not chosen to spend his wounded leave with his own kin rather than with strangers, however hospitable they might be.

"Oh, yes. However, I am so altered from my former self that I found it impossible to fit into my former comfortable role. My restlessness was such that I could not allow my relations to bear me off to the country to invalid, so I remained in London. I was slowly expiring from boredom, however, for the city is rather spare of entertainment at this time of year," said Lord Cardiff. "Lord Cummings's kind invitation to make one of a charming house party was never more welcome."

"But what of your relations, my lord? Surely, they must wish you to spend at least part of your time in England with them?" asked Chastity.

"On the contrary. They were happy for me to go, particularly since my restlessness was beginning to fatigue them in their efforts to accommodate my whims," said Lord Cardiff with a quiet smile.

"Lord Cardiff, are you hinting that you can be a troublesome invalid?" asked Chastity.

Lord Cardiff laughed. "I fear that I must admit my fault, Miss Cummings. It is not creature comforts that appeal to me, so much as the stimulation of lively minds and company. I am too much of a soldier, you see. My relations are elderly, and my habits of blunt conversation and physical exercise were a sad trial to them."

"Then I am glad that you came to Chester," said Chastity.

"Why, so am I, Miss Cummings," said Lord Cardiff with a warm smile.

Chastity blushed. Her pleasant interlude with Lord Cardiff was interrupted by the butler. "What is it, Wilkins?" He bent to whisper in her ear, and Chastity turned to Lord Cardiff. With a smile, she gracefully excused herself. "Pray forgive me, my lord. There is a matter of importance that I must attend to at once."

"Of course, Miss Cummings."

Preceded by the butler, Chastity left the ballroom and crossed into the anteroom. A short elderly lady attired in the height of fashion was giving her outer garments to the footmen. Chastity went forward, her hands held out. "My lady! How happy I am that you have arrived."

Lady Mackleby turned. She trained a penetrating gaze on her niece's face. "Well, my dear? How are you? I have heard that you are as willful as ever."

Chastity took hold of the hand held out to her and bent to kiss her aunt's withered cheek. When she straightened, she said, "I am very well, thank you. And you have heard quite correctly, Aunt. I am still unattached and likely to remain so."

"Aggravating child," said Lady Mackleby without heat. "Take me somewhere where I may sit down. I am fagged to death at being jolted over those abominable roads."

The butler threw open a door, and Chastity escorted her aunt into the front sitting room. There was a quiet fire on the hearth, and blazing candelabra were placed strategically about the room.

Lady Mackleby nodded approvingly. She sank down stiffly on a settee that was drawn up close to the hearth. "Sit here beside me, Chastity. I dislike tilting my head up to see you. It gives me a crick in my neck and makes me feel peevish."

"We must not have that," said Chastity, obeying her aunt's command. She folded her hands in her lap. "Now what may I do for you, Aunt?"

"All accommodation, aren't you? Aye, how well I know! Butter would not melt in your mouth, miss," said Lady Mackleby, shaking her boney forefinger at her niece. "We both know what would please me most, and that would be to hear of your nuptials."

"Nonsense, Aunt. It would greatly offend you to merely hear of it," said Chastity. "You would insist upon being invited!"

Lady Mackleby snorted. "You've got wit, Chastity. I've never denied it. It is a pity that you do not use it on your own behalf."

"Oh, but I do. My wits are what have preserved me from the well-meaning but misguided attempts of all of my several relations to settle my future for me," said Chastity, smiling.

"You are too independent, as I have often told you," said Lady Mackleby disapprovingly.

"Yes, as you have *often* told me," agreed Chastity demurely, but with a mischievous gleam in her eyes.

"I'll have none of your sass, miss," said Lady Mackleby, a smile quivering just out of sight. "There is not a penny's difference between you and that dratted brother of yours. You are both disrespectful scalawags of the worst sort."

"Why, what has Henry done?" asked Chastity, surprised. Surely, her aunt had not been long enough under their roof to have become offended already.

Lady Mackleby hit her cane on the floor and scowled. "He lured me to Chester with promises of fine entertainment and good company. I have seen nothing but a group of horsey gentlemen and their frumpish ladies. I wish I had stayed in London. The company is scarce, but at least it is select."

Lady Mackleby's voice and expression were irritable, but there was an underlying weariness that Chastity was quick to note. The journey was a long one for an elderly lady. It was really little wonder that her ladyship was expressing such broad discontent. Naturally Lady Mackleby did not feel equal to joining any sort of party just then, especially a grand ball. Her ladyship would probably feel more comfortable and better oriented if she was allowed to relax with a smaller company.

"I am sorry that our house party is not quite what you expected, Aunt. Perhaps you would prefer a glass of ratafia privately in your own sitting room with Mrs. Webster and Mrs. Radford to bear you company, rather than attend the grand ball. It is rather a loud gathering, I do admit," said Chastity.

Lady Mackleby grumbled some more, but agreed that a glass of ratafia would be welcome. "And I want none of these youngsters for company," she declared. "I do not know what Henry could have been thinking to invite me to mix with a bunch of young whipsters. My salad days are long over, and I do not hunt any longer."

"I understand perfectly, Aunt," soothed Chastity, as she wondered the same thing. If Henry had had any inkling at all that Lady Mackleby actually meant to honor them with her presence, surely he could have had the forethought to offer some sort of entertainment that would have appealed to the old lady. But then, he had neglected to mention to her that he had invited Lady Mackleby. Really, he had made quite a habit of it during this house party. Chastity only hoped that what she had conceived for her irascible aunt's amusement would not be found totally wanting.

As they left the front sitting room, Chastity paused only long enough to convey a few hurried instructions to the butler. He bowed his understanding. With a word to a footman to follow them, Chastity escorted her vulnerable aunt upstairs. She opened the door to the sitting room that she had had made ready for days past.

A roaring fire blazed in the grate and threw out a heat that Lady Mackleby apparently found welcome. Her ladyship regarded the fire with approval as she held out her hands to it.

Chastity hastily plumped a couple of sofa pillows and put them in a deep-seated chair. The footman pulled the chair closer to the fire so that the occupant would be situated well within the circle of heat.

"This is the first time since I have arrived that I've seen a decently stoked fire," said Lady Mackleby, turning toward Chastity. She saw the chair and sat down in it. A small sigh escaped her.

"Here is a footstool, Aunt, and I am sending Hector after your ratafia," said Chastity, moving the footstool within reach of her aunt, even as she sent a meaningful glance toward the footman.

The footman immediately went out the door.

Chastity had made a mental note to make certain that Lady Mackleby's room would have a fire kept built to a white-heat. She remained with her aunt for a few minutes until the other two ladies and Sir Roger were escorted into the sitting room by the butler.

Chastity welcomed them and in a low voice thanked them for eschewing their own amusement downstairs. "My aunt is rather wearied, and I had hoped that you would aid me in calming her," said Chastity with a smile.

"Pray think nothing of it, my dear," said Mrs. Radford. "I am always glad to see her ladyship and, truth to tell, I shall welcome a bit of quiet myself."

"I would not forgo this treat, Chastity. I have long been an admirer of Lady Mackleby, and it will be a pleasure to renew my acquaintance with her," said Sir Roger.

"Oh, do you know one another?" asked Chastity with surprise.

"As I said, I have long been an admirer of hers," said Sir Roger with a wicked glance as he crossed over to take Lady Mackleby's hand and raise it to his lips.

Chastity thought that she should have guessed. Sir Roger and

Lady Mackleby were of the same generation. They had probably been introduced to the *ton* in the same Season.

Lady Mackleby greeted Sir Roger with familiarity bordering on rudeness. "Well, my old friend! I had quite supposed that they had put you in the grave by now."

"Not I, my lady. I am too wily to be caught by the heels," said Sir Roger.

Lady Mackleby snorted with amusement, then her gaze fell on Mrs. Webster and that lady's invariable escort. "What! Have you still got those rotten spoiled dogs, Serena?"

"Oh, of course I do," said Mrs. Webster, not at all fazed by her ladyship's less than friendly accents. She sat down in a chair nearby, her panniers spreading over the sides.

"Lady Mackleby, how happy I am to see you again. It has been ages, has it not?" said Mrs. Radford.

Lady Mackleby nodded, her frowning expression clearing a degree. "Yes, it has. What have you and the good reverend been doing these last few years, my lady?"

The ratafia was brought in on a tray by the footman, and it was served. A suggestion by Mrs. Webster that they could visit over a card game was met with acceptance. The butler and footman moved a card table into position, together with a deck of cards, and the four gathered around it.

Chastity slipped out with the excuse that she must confer privately with the butler. Scarcely any notice was taken of her by the cardplayers, and she was satisfied that Lady Mackleby was well situated at least for that evening. Chastity gave instructions concerning the fire in Lady Mackleby's bedroom and other little things that her ladyship liked. Then she returned downstairs to the ballroom.

Chapter Twelve

Merrill had noticed Chastity's departure earlier and came up to discover its cause. "Is anything wrong, Chastity?" she inquired.

Chastity shook her head. "My aunt, Lady Mackleby, has arrived. She was feeling a bit wearied from the journey. The excitement of her arrival and the lack of what she considers to be suitable entertainment made her disinclined to join the company. And I was too wise to suggest that she retire to bed. That would have called down a thundering scold upon my head, for having the impertinence to suggest that she was too old to stand the pace! So I have settled her ladyship in the upper sitting room with Sir Roger, my aunt Webster, and Mrs. Radford, which seems to have answered quite well."

"Allow me to guess. Old cat's gossip and cards penny-a-point," Merrill said shrewdly.

Chastity laughed. "Exactly!"

"Well, for my part I am having a simply lovely time. If only Charles were here, then it would be quite, quite perfect," said Merrill, linking her arm with Chastity's and leisurely perambulating around the edge of the dance floor.

"Do you miss Charles so much?" asked Chastity sympathetically.

"Oh, terribly," said Merrill. She flashed a brilliant smile. "But not so much that I have forgotten how to enjoy myself." A gentleman approached to solicit her ladyship's hand for a dance, and Merrill went off with him, laughing and chattering gaily.

Chastity herself was not left alone for long. Jeffrey Halston

came up to her and asked if he could have the honor of part-
nering her in the next set. Chastity agreed, noticing again how
he was more distant and reserved than he had been in former
years. But that was certainly understandable. She had tried to
excuse his peculiar behavior on the occasion of their ride as
only part and parcel of the overall change in their relationship.
It had been a long time since they had been on such easy terms.

Of course, they had remained friendly toward one another.
On those rare occasions when they had both been in London at
the same time, Chastity had greeted Jeffrey Halston and his
wife with cordiality. However, more often than not, she had
seen them only from a distance and had merely exchanged
bows with them. Neither she nor Mr. Halston had sought to re-
tain the depth of relationship that they had once enjoyed. Once
he had wed, it had simply seemed to Chastity to be better that
way.

The music changed, sweeping into a slower tempo. With a
sense of shock, Chastity realized that Mr. Halston had requested her hand for the waltz. She glanced up quickly into her
partner's face. He met her glance, almost expressionless. His
hand clasped hers, his arm encircled her waist. They turned
across the dance floor much as in days of old, except that they
did not talk animatedly to one another as they had done then.

After several moments of silence, Chastity smiled up at him,
a little uncertainly. "This is much like old times," she commented, in line with the train of her thoughts.

"Yes, I suppose that it is," he agreed, returning her smile. His
eyes did not warm with the same light that Chastity recalled. "It
seems a lifetime ago, however."

"It does not seem so to me. But my relations have often accused me of possessing a certain flightiness," said Chastity
with another quick smile.

As the last strains of music died away, Mr. Halston said,
"You were never flighty, Chastity. You always had a level
head."

"Thank you, Jeffrey," said Chastity with some constraint.

He did not let go of her hand after escorting her from the

floor. "Will you allow me a few moments for private speech, Chastity?"

Oddly enough, Chastity recalled what Merrill had suggested could be the reason that Jeffrey Halston had come to the neighborhood. Chastity searched his face. She saw nothing in either his expression or his demeanor to suggest that he meant to subject her to an embarrassing scene. "Of course, Jeffrey. We can slip into the salon off the refreshment room, if you wish," she said.

He gestured with his hand, making a slight bow, for her to lead the way. They passed through the refreshment room and into the salon. Chastity preceded her companion into the small room and then turned to face him. She was curious what he might say in this impromptu tête-à-tête. The original thought that had leaped to her mind she had already dismissed as being highly improbable.

Mr. Halston closed the door quietly. He gravely looked across the room at her, meeting her questioning eyes without constraint. "Thank you for granting me this audience, Chastity. I had hoped that you would."

Chastity began to wonder whether she had not made a mistake. Her heart beating a bit nervously, she was reminded again of what Merrill had suggested regarding Jeffrey Halston. Hoping to forestall any sort of declaration, she began, "Jeffrey—"

He held up his hand. "Please, Chastity. Let me say what I feel that I must."

Chastity realized that to be fair she really had little choice but to allow him to continue, since she had already told him that he could speak with her privately. Besides, a part of her truly wanted to hear what he might say. "Very well, Jeffrey. I am willing to listen." The lest she could do was to make it as pleasant as possible.

Chastity moved to sit down on the settee. She gestured to the place beside her, but Mr. Halston shook his head. Instead, he walked over to the mantel to stand beside it. He was a well-built man grown stockier in the intervening years, but not to his detriment. Chastity thought that he looked very well, indeed.

When she had known him as a youth, he had been too thin for his large frame.

A short silence fell, with Chastity gazing inquiringly at him. Mr. Halston gave a short laugh. "How odd. I have given thought to what I wish to say, yet now, granted the opportunity, I find it difficult to begin."

"I hope that I am not such an ogre as all that," said Chastity jokingly, hoping to rally him.

"An ogre! No, not that." Mr. Halston also smiled, but rather briefly. "No, I know that you are not that, Chastity. But I find that it is awkward to lay open my thoughts to you, here and now, whereas before . . ."

When he stopped, Chastity nodded and made a somewhat helpless gesture. "It was quite different then, for us both. We were once such very good friends. But we have not remained so, and that has become the problem."

"You will say that was my fault," said Mr. Halston with a painful smile.

"No, I shall not. What happened was for the best. I think that we both know that. In any event, it is well behind us," said Chastity quietly.

Mr. Halston nodded. "Yes; you are quite right." He looked across at her with a strange twist of his lips. "Once again it is you who proves to have the more level of heads, while I am in danger of being carried away by my own thoughts and passions."

Chastity was at once made uncomfortable. His allusion to passion could only lead her to suppose that he was indeed working himself up to the point of declaring himself, and in the same intense manner that he had done in the past. Above all, she did not wish a distressing scene. If she could, she would keep this unwise interview as unemotional as possible. She clasped her hands tightly in her lap. "Jeffrey, what precisely are you trying to say to me?"

"You are right again, Chastity. I mustn't digress from my purpose. It will all be so much simpler if I come straight to the point. Very well."

Mr. Halston did not abandon the mantel, as Chastity was half afraid that he might. Instead, he reached up to take hold of the edge with one hand. It was almost as though he tried to steady himself. "Chastity, you are aware of my situation. We spoke of it when I first came to Chester to see you. I am widowed. I have a young daughter, who is in need of a mother. I am comfortably situated and able to offer all of the advantages of my position."

Abruptly, he turned away to stare down into the fire. The firelight cast his face into strong shadow so that his expression could no longer be easily discerned. "We once knew one another very well, Chastity. Perhaps better than most husbands and wives come to know one another in an entire lifetime. Chastity, I am offering for you again. I am asking you to become my wife."

Chastity's heart was thumping very fast. She didn't quite know what to say. "Jeffrey, I . . . I am very flattered," she began.

He turned quickly, throwing up his hand. "No, do not answer me yet. I have something more that I must tell you so that you may weigh it with all the rest."

Chastity hesitated, uncertain whether she should let the interview go on. However, she could not stand against the unexpectedly pleading expression in his eyes. It reminded her so much of the stripling that she had once known.

"Very well, Jeffrey," she said quietly. She could not imagine what else he could add to what he had already said.

Mr. Halston came over to sit down on the settee beside her. He did not attempt to close the distance between them or even to take her hand, as Chastity was half expecting. "This time it is different, Chastity. You must know that from the outset. You see, I do not offer to you my heart."

Chastity stared at him, quite at sea. "I do not perfectly understand."

Mr. Halston smiled. "I know that you do not. Chastity, you wrought better than you knew when you introduced Mirabelle Sweeney to me. Mirabelle loved me unconditionally in a way that is surely rare in this world. I think . . . I believe . . . that my heart was buried with Mirabelle when she died. That is why, even as I ask you to become my wife, I cannot offer my heart to you. Now, do you understand?"

"I think that I begin to," said Chastity slowly. "Jeffrey, are you proposing a marriage of convenience?"

He frowned thoughtfully. "Not precisely that, no. Perhaps at the first that is more what I envision. But I would hope that in time such a union between us would eventually evolve into something more intimate. I will need a male heir, you see."

"I see," said Chastity, somewhat faintly.

"What I offer to you, Chastity, is my respect and my friend-ship." Mr. Halston smiled suddenly. "Once, I would have sworn my undying devotion and love's passion." He looked at her, sobering again. "Now I know that you were right all along, Chastity. I did not truly love you."

Chastity bent her head to avoid meeting his eyes. Carefully, she made pleats in her skirt. She remembered saying that very thing to him, an assertion that he had vehemently denied. Now he was telling her that he really hadn't loved her. There was a dull ache in her heart as Chastity recognized that some very cherished memories had just that moment been destroyed. Those memories had actually been a fiction. She strongly wished that she was anywhere but in that room.

"It isn't that what I felt for you then was not real, for it was. But it was a pale candle flame in comparison to the brilliance of the sun."

Chastity took a deep breath. She felt close to tears, but she shook her head against succumbing to such a ridiculous reac-tion to Mr. Halston's revelation. All of a sudden she felt regret for what might have been for her, as well as an awe at what Jef-frey and his wife must have shared. "You have left me with nothing to say, Jeffrey." She was glad to note that her voice sounded perfectly normal.

"At least you have not turned down my proposal," he ob-served.

Chastity looked up quickly at that. She realized that he was right. How very odd that was, to be sure.

Before she could recover from surprise at herself, Mr. Halston reached over to squeeze her fingers lightly. "Pray do not feel that you must give me an answer now, Chastity. I deliberately chose tonight to approach you because I knew that there would not be an opportunity for a long discussion. You must return to your brother's guests."

Chastity was glad for the excuse. "Yes, yes, I must," she agreed. Her eyes flew to the clock above the mantel. They had been cloistered together for only ten minutes. It seemed singularly closer to a lifetime.

Mr. Halston sought her hand again, and raised it. Chastity felt a tingle go through her at the touch of his lips. "I rely upon your level head, Chastity," he said quietly.

He rose to his feet, retaining hold of her hand. He held out his other hand, and when she had put her own into it, he drew her to her feet. They stood there together for a moment, looking into one another's face.

Then Mr. Halston silently stepped back, relinquishing her hands, and made a slight bow. Without a word, Chastity turned away from him and left the salon.

Mr. Halston followed her back into the ballroom. Their absence had not gone unnoticed. After Mr. Halston had led Chastity back to her chair, bowed, and left her, Merrill hurried over. Her ladyship took the empty chair beside Chastity's.

"My dear! What a very odd expression you are wearing. Whatever has passed between you and Jeffrey Halston?" she asked urgently.

Chastity plied her fan slowly. "What do you mean? We simply conversed for a few minutes, that is all."

"You must think me a nitwit! Yes, and everyone else, too!" Merrill exclaimed. "Why, you have this positively stricken look in your eyes. It is very plain that you exchanged more than mere pleasantries."

"Oh, Merrill, do I really?" asked Chastity, abandoning her studied indifference. She attempted a smile. "Is this better?"

Merrill patted her arm. "Never mind. I shall tell everyone that you are warding off the headache. That may well be believed. Now tell me! What did Jeffrey Halston say to you? I have never seen you appear so upset."

"He offered for me," said Chastity baldly.

"I knew it! I *knew* that was why he came down from London," Merrill crowed. "And what did you say?" She looked closely at her friend's face. "Chastity! You did not reject him again, surely! Pray tell me that you did not!"

"No, I did not reject him," said Chastity in a low voice. She avoided looking at her friend while playing with the sticks of her fan.

"Chastity!" Merrill's tone was thrilled.

Chastity looked up quickly. "Hush! It is not what you are thinking, Merrill."

Merrill's eyes grew round as saucers. "But, Chastity, did you not accept Jeffrey's suit?"

Chastity shook her head. "No! No, I did not!"

Merrill looked at her in confusion. "I do not understand. Then . . . are you thinking it over?"

"Merrill, I don't know what to think!" exclaimed Chastity. "He has offered me a marriage of convenience, at least that is what it would be in the beginning. He told me that he was so much in love with Mirabelle that he has no heart left to offer anyone since her death. Yet he wishes me to become his wife for the sake of his daughter, and he hopes that warmer feelings will evolve from out of our original friendship. What am I to say to such an outlandish proposal?"

"It is outlandish, to say the least!" exclaimed Merrill. "Did he not declare any passion for you at all?"

"No, none," said Chastity, allowing her disappointment to show.

"When I recall how attached he was to you, it doesn't seem possible that he made not a single overture!"

Chastity shook her head. "Jeffrey said that I had been right when I refused him before. He said that what he had felt for me was but a pale comparison to what he felt for Mirabelle. In short, what he felt for me was calf-love!"

"How extremely rude of him," observed Merrill. She glanced

at her friend's expression. "And it is my guess that you are piqued by that."

Chastity glanced back at her quickly. Shockingly, she thought that that was true. "I am not certain. It would be quite petty of me to be affronted, don't you think?" She said it lightly, trying to disguise her confused feelings. She had the disturbing sense that she had made a terrible mistake concerning Jeffrey Halston those six years ago.

"Oh, yes, quite petty. And you do not like to think of yourself as being petty, do you, dearest Chastity?"

Chastity stared at her friend, who smiled at her.

"You are a fiend, Merrill," she said. "Am I such a self-righteous twit as all that?"

"Oh, yes. It is very difficult to remain your friend at times," said Merrill cheerfully.

"Well! You have certainly managed to burst my bubble," said Chastity with a small laugh.

"But seriously, my dear, it is a very natural feeling. None of us likes to discover that we are not the center of another's universe," said Merrill, with the slightest edge to her voice.

"Are you thinking of Charles?" asked Chastity softly.

"I don't know what I was thinking of," said Merrill with a toss of her head. "I do know, though, that we are discussing this surprising turn of events with Jeffrey Halston. My dear Chastity, he has thrown down the gauntlet. What do you intend to do?"

"Merrill, whatever are you talking about?" asked Chastity, slightly taken aback.

"Oh, Chastity! Pray do not pretend to be so naive!" Merrill's blue eyes gleamed. "Why, you have believed for years that Jeffrey had been madly in love with you. Now out of the blue he offers you a virtual marriage of convenience, and he says that he can't offer more because his heart died with his wife two years ago! My dear, how can you resist the challenge? What warm-blooded woman could?"

"That's preposterous!" exclaimed Chastity.

"Is it? Is it, really?" Merrill rose to her feet. She smiled down at Chastity. "Then why, dearest friend, did you not turn him down at once?"

With that telling question, Merrill glided away. Chastity was left bereft of speech. She wondered now why she had not given Jeffrey Halston an immediate answer. It was unlike her not to know her own mind. She excused herself on the grounds that it had been such a shock when Jeffrey had couched his suit in such unexpected terms. Yet that did not explain her present ambivalence of feelings. She had not been able to satisfy Merrill, nor herself, with her poor explanation.

Chastity fleetingly reviewed her friend's question more than once that evening. Finally, the grand ball was at last over. Those guests who had come in carriages had been seen off, and she was able to say good night to her houseguests.

Chastity went up to her bed, not so much wearied as eager to be alone so that she could reflect over the extraordinary proposal that she had received. She dismissed her maid as soon as she had been made ready for bed and then sat down at the vanity to brush out her hair.

Jeffrey Halston had taken her off-guard, of course. She simply had not been prepared for such a declaration. Chastity told herself that she had been ready to turn down his suit. Indeed, she would have done so if he had burst into a passionate speech and tried to make love to her in a reenactment of those three turbulent interviews six years ago.

However, Mr. Halston had done neither of these things. He had been controlled, presenting his case with logic and with scarcely a trace of emotion. He was definitely not the same man that she remembered, thought Chastity. It was positively eerie.

Upon the occasion of their acquaintance, Chastity had sensed at once that there was something different about Jeffrey Halston. The shuttered expression in his eyes when he looked at her had been peculiarly unsettling. She had puzzled over what it was. Now she knew without a trace of doubt that it had been indifference.

Jeffrey Halston had once regarded her with the warmth of passion and friendship. That he should have grown indifferent to her was totally unexpected. Apparently, to his eyes she was no longer a desirable woman. She had been relegated to the status of a fondly remembered, once-respected friend.

"I might as well have been wearing an old maid's cap," she grumbled at her reflection.

"That is the most nonsensical notion that I have ever heard," said a sharp voice.

Startled, Chastity whirled around on the seat. "Lady Mackleby! I did not hear you come in!"

"You were in such a brown study that it can scarcely be wondered at," said Lady Mackleby, leaning heavily on her cane and walking further into the room. "You are ready for bed, I see. I trust that I do not intrude?"

"Of course not. You are always welcome," said Chastity, rising at once from her bench. She hurried to plump a pillow in a wing chair in front of the fire. Then she offered her assistance, gently putting an arm about the older woman's waist. "Here you are, ma'am. Let me help you."

Lady Mackleby lowered herself slowly into the chair. Her boney fingers clutched Chastity's arm. "Thank you, my dear. I am not so prideful that I cannot accept a little charity now and then. Now, tell me what maggoty thoughts have been running through your mind? I thought you seemed a bit blue earlier this evening, and now I am certain of it! Caps, indeed!"

Chastity gave a laugh and sat down on the wide footstool at her aunt's feet. She hugged her knees to her breast. She shook her head. "I suppose that it was merely this dull, gray, heavy weather that we have had these two days past. I have not had a good gallop since—oh, I just wish it would rain or snow. The heavy air is oppressive. It gives one the megrims."

"I would accept that excuse from Regina Cummings or even from Lady Peters. But I do not when it comes from you, my dear," said Lady Mackleby. She cocked her head. "Do these megrims of yours have anything to do with the reappearance of one of your old suitors, my dear?"

Chastity denied it quickly. "Of course not. Jeffrey Halston

was once a very dear friend, despite his importunities. I trust that we shall always be able to offer friendship to one another."

"How very dull and pompous of you, my dear," said Lady Mackleby.

Chastity was unsurprised by her aunt's disdain. She had thought the same as soon as the words had left her mouth. "Perhaps, Aunt. Perhaps that is what has made me so unsettled this evening. I used to believe there was more to the history between myself and Jeffrey, but there is not. I suppose that I am beginning to realize that my youth is passing away. It is rather disillusioning."

Lady Mackleby rolled her eyes. "Pray spare me, child! I have seen more disillusion in my lifetime than you will ever experience. As for Jeffrey Halston, I trust that should the improbable happen, you will not be such a goosecap as you were before. If he should make you an offer, pray do not refuse it."

Chastity smiled at her aunt. She wasn't about to tell Lady Mackleby about the interview with Mr. Halston. Lady Mackleby would no doubt have some very pithy things to say to her about it. "I do not know what I would say, ma'am."

"Nonsense! You are virtually at your last prayers, my girl, and do not forget it. However, you are a bit young for caps yet. I would not take to them just yet" said Lady Mackleby.

"No, I shan't," said Chastity, laughing.

"That's better," approved Lady Mackleby. "I dislike seeing you thrown into the hips." She cocked her head, her sharp gaze fastened to her niece's face. "Perhaps you have been regretting your past follies. Jeffrey Halston does represent lost opportunities, does he not?"

"You go too deep for me, Aunt," said Chastity, feeling that she was lying from between her teeth even as she said it. But she could not let her aunt know how close to the bone she was cutting.

"I very much doubt it. You've wit enough, as I have often observed," said Lady Mackleby dryly. "Pray see that you use it wisely."

The door opened, and Chastity turned with a sense of relief.

It was her ladyship's dresser, come to escort Lady Mackleby back to her rooms.

Lady Mackleby grumbled at being treated like a child, but she got up willingly enough with the dresser's aid. She leaned on her cane a moment as she pointed a boney finger at her niece. "Remember the advice that I have given you, Chastity. I shall see you in the morning, no doubt."

"I have your cordial waiting, my lady," said the dresser, helping her ladyship to the door.

"Nasty, vile stuff. Ah, well. I pay my physician to physic me, so I must abide by his advice," said Lady Mackleby and exited.

Chapter Thirteen

The following day the entire household breakfasted late. The grand ball had not ended until the small hours of the morning, and most of the house party did not emerge from their bedrooms until the hour was far advanced. After breakfast, it was generally agreed that all would spend the day however they chose. Most opted for quiet pursuits, and Chastity found an unexpected space of time on her hands in which she could pen a few letters and try not to think on Jeffrey Halston's unexpected proposal.

When she had finished her correspondence, Chastity started down the hall from her sitting room, intending to give her sealed missives to the butler to frank for the post. She was surprised when she came upon Henry and Miss Paige on the upstairs landing.

About to call out a cheerful greeting, Chastity paused when she saw her brother raise the lady's hand to his lips. After the formal salute, Henry bowed to Miss Paige and walked away toward the stairs. Miss Paige stood staring after him with a very odd expression on her face. Slowly, Miss Paige raised her hands to her face.

Chastity continued on her way until she came up to Miss Paige. She saw that lady still stood with her hands pressed against blushing cheeks. "Dru! What is the matter?" she asked.

Miss Paige gave a startled jump, then a half laugh. "Oh! Chastity, it is only you. Forgive me! I am so disconcerted that I am all in whirl."

Chastity thought that she knew what had happened. Her brother had extended his usual innate courtesy toward Miss

Paige and she, because she was so unused to such treatment, had read more into Henry's attentions than was there.

Certainly Henry had shown a certain partiality for Miss Paige's company during the grand ball. He had danced with her three times and then chosen her to take in to dinner. Chastity thought that she ought to speak to her brother, for he was on the borderline of causing talk that he might be setting Miss Paige up as his flirt. Mrs. Dabney or Regina would have known precisely how to deal with such a situation, but Chastity doubted that Miss Paige had so much experience or sophistication. Henry must be aware of that, thought Chastity with annoyance. Yet he had exposed Miss Paige to possible gossip.

Chastity gently touched the other woman's arm. "Dru, you mustn't take it so much to heart. My brother is—"

Miss Paige turned shining eyes toward her. "Oh, I know it! Lord Cummings is all consideration. I have never known anyone quite like his lordship."

Chastity's heart plunged. She could see well enough that Miss Paige was fast falling in love with her brother, if she hadn't already done so. "Henry is considerate, yes, and a true gentleman. He always treats his guests very hospitably and, indeed, with every personal consideration. It has made him very well liked, as you may imagine," she said. More gently still, she repeated herself. "You mustn't take it so much to heart, you know."

Miss Paige had turned a little white, an arrested expression on her face. "I see." She took a deep breath and managed a wobbling smile. "Thank you, Chastity. You have stopped me from making something of a fool of myself."

"Dru . . ."

There was the blindness of tears in Miss Paige's eyes. "I . . . I think that I shall go along to my room, if you do not mind. There are letters that I really must write."

"Of course." Chastity let her go. She watched Miss Paige hurry away and saw when the other woman raised a hand to her face, obviously to wipe away a tear.

Chastity pitied her and hated that she had had to be the one to disillusion her. However, it was better to understand how things stood now rather than to be brought face-to-face with a worse disillusionment later. Of course her brother would not deliberately wound Miss Paige, for cruelty was not part of his character. But certainly he would have had to let her down somehow, and that could not be anything other than painful. Now at least, Miss Paige would keep a guard on her heart.

Chastity continued downstairs. She hoped that she would find her brother alone so that she could speak to him privately concerning Miss Paige, for the sooner that Henry knew of the unwitting havoc that he was wreaking in that vulnerable lady's heart the better it would be.

Chastity was not able to closet herself with her brother. She discovered that Henry had already made arrangements to go driving with those of his guests who were the most noted whips. With very mixed feelings, she saw her brother off with Lord Winthrop and Sir Edward. Lord Cardiff opted to sit up beside Henry and blow the yard of tin should the horn be required. Henry laughed. "Very well, Cardiff, if you trust me not to tumble you out on that shoulder of yours!"

"Devil a bit, my lord!" said Lord Cardiff cheerfully.

Chastity was not the only lady who regarded the gentlemen's excursion with disapprobation. Mrs. Dabney at once turned to lay a hand on Mr. Salyer's sleeve. "I trust that you at least shall not abandon me," she said, turning her liquid gaze up to him.

Mr. Salyer at once denied that he had any such desire. "It is my undying pleasure to accompany you, ma'am," he said gallantly.

Mrs. Dabney laughed lightly. "You are a liar, Mr. Salyer, but such an accomplished one! Pray, will you walk with me in the gallery?"

"I am your servant, Mrs. Dabney," said Mr. Salyer. There seemed to be an undercurrent to his civil words that Chastity caught. Mr. Salyer met her puzzled gaze. He bestowed a rueful smile on her, with the slightest shake of his handsome head, and went off with the beauteous lady on his arm.

Chastity instantly comprehended that Mr. Salyer would have

preferred other company. Certainly he had not been as assidu-
ous in his attentions to the beautiful widow as certain other gentlemen had been. However, his innate good breeding demanded
that he bow to the lady's wishes rather than break propriety and
serve his own desires.

"At least she is not with Henry," remarked Regina.

"You are unkind," Archie said quietly. "I do not understand
why you have taken such a dislike to the lady. For my part, I
find her company very pleasant and so does Henry, I should
imagine."

"My dear husband, I don't doubt that dear Henry prefers the
widow's company. How could it be otherwise? I am the last to
take anything away from her. She is quite, quite accomplished,"
Regina said with a light laugh.

Archie stared at his wife, his brows gathering in a frown.
"What precisely do you mean by that, Regina?"

"It is very plain to me, Archie. But if you cannot see it, I shall
say nothing more." She turned to her sister-in-law. "Chastity,
hasn't the post come? I was certain that we would have the
newest issue of the *Lady's Magazine* before this, you know."

"It is in the front sitting room, Regina," said Chastity. She
was unsurprised when Regina swept away without another
word to anyone.

"I do not understand why she is so antagonistic toward Mrs.
Dabney," said Archie. "It is not as though they do not have
things in common."

Lady Mackleby cackled. "You chucklehead! They have
everything in common, and that is precisely the sticking point!
I have never been so entertained in my life as I have been
watching those two circle each other like a pair of hissing cats.
I have yet to know a touted beauty who is not jealous of her perceived territory!"   .

Archie's brow cleared, and he reddened with embarrassment.
"Yes, I see. Of course that is it. Thank you for enlightening me,
my lady." He turned to the other gentlemen who had remained
behind. "Jeffrey, Mr. Bottler, Sir Roger! What do you say to a
game of billiards?"

Sir Roger had been sitting with a somewhat distant expression on his face. He appeared to be contemplating something that was not quite pleasant. At Archie's query, he seemed to shake himself. "Billiards? I . . . thank you, but no, Mr. Cummings. I believe that I shall take a walk round the grounds. I am feeling queerly closed in today."

"Certainly, Sir Roger," said Archie, mildly surprised. Since his arrival, he had learned that Sir Roger was game for any sort of competition. He opened the door for the elderly gentleman.

"I shall join you, Archibald," said Mr. Halston, with a glance toward the ladies.

Chastity met his eyes, but only briefly. She was half afraid that he might wish to request another tête-à-tête and demand an answer from her. It was an answer that she was not prepared to give. Notwithstanding Lady Mackleby's unexpected counsel of the night before, she still could not settle the confusion existing in her own mind.

"I think that I shall pass. Someone must stay to entertain her ladyship and Miss Cummings," said Mr. Bottler, beaming with the greatest good humor on the ladies.

The ladies did not appear particularly gratified by the gentleman's gallantry. Lady Mackleby looked sour. Chastity's eyes flew to her brother and Mr. Halston. They seemed both to read her mute appeal.

"Come, come, Bottler! I insist, for I want my revenge on you," said Archie, putting his hand under the gentleman's elbow.

"Indeed, it would not be a proper game without you," said Mr. Halston, catching him up on the other side.

As he was determinedly propelled from the room, Mr. Bottler looked from one side to the other at his taller companions. "Well, well! This is something unlooked for, indeed. I never thought to be so sought after in my life. It is quite a compliment, gentlemen, quite a compliment!"

Chastity and Lady Mackleby were left to themselves. Chastity met her aunt's eyes, and she chuckled. "Yes, ma'am, we have thankfully been abandoned!"

"It is fortunate, for I was about to deliver a set-down that would have turned that man's head around on his neck," said Lady Mackleby.

"I could see that you were, Aunt," said Chastity.

"Well, how do you intend to amuse me, Chastity? I warn you, I shan't be fobbed off on that Bottler woman nor Serena. I cannot stand the one, and the other drags along those dratted pugs of hers wherever she goes," said Lady Mackleby.

"You need not concern yourself, dear ma'am. Aunt Serena and Mrs. Bottler appear to have discovered a liking for one another. They have taken the pugs on a short drive so that they might get some air," said Chastity.

Lady Mackleby stared suspiciously at her. Then she snorted. "I never thought that Serena had more than the wit of a squirrel. I see that I was right! Preferring that Bottler woman over my company, indeed!"

The door opened, and Regina swished into the room. She glanced around swiftly and the slightest pout touched her lips. "Chastity and dear Lady Mackleby! How cozy you look without the gentlemen. You must let me join you," she said.

"Of course, Regina," said Chastity cordially, rather amused. Apparently her sister-in-law had found nothing of true interest in the *Lady's Magazine*.

Her assumption was proven correct. Regina cast herself down in a chair. "I am so utterly bored. You can have no notion what a sad trial it is to go without the comforts to which one is accustomed."

"I am sorry, Regina. I did not know that you were feeling so despondent," said Chastity.

"Oh, you mustn't think that I am complaining," Regina said, shaking her head and smiling.

"Mustn't we?" asked Lady Mackleby, raising her brows.

Regina bestowed a lovely smile on the elder lady. "But you will understand perfectly, my lady, for you, too, are far out of your venue. It is such a provincial setting, is it not? Not at all like what we are used to in London."

"I have been made most comfortable at Chester," said Lady Mackleby in an unencouraging voice.

Regina was not abashed. "I am certain that Chastity has done her best, of course!" With a commiserating expression, she reached over to pat her sister-in-law's hand.

Lady Mackleby regarded Regina with dislike. "My niece has always had a particular knack for entertaining."

"Thank you, Aunt," said Chastity, stifling a chuckle. It had not been even five minutes that Lady Mackleby had been demanding to know what entertainments were to be offered to her.

"Indeed! I certainly take nothing from you, Chastity. You have made our visit somewhat memorable, at least," Regina said. She turned her bright, wide-eyed gaze on Lady Mackleby. "Imagine my surprise and delight when I discovered that dearest Archie and I were to have the state room. It was opened expressly for us. Isn't that so, Chastity?"

"Yes, it was, Regina," said Chastity, hiding her growing amusement. It was obvious to her that her sister-in-law, who disliked Lady Mackleby equally as much as that lady disliked her, was hoping to rouse envy in her ladyship's bosom. Chastity threw a glance at her aunt, and judged from Lady Mackleby's expression that the bland provocation had definitely generated annoyance. Obviously, Lady Mackleby did not appreciate the assumption that she must have been put out that such an honor had not been bestowed upon her.

"I trust that you have slept comfortably enough in the state bedroom," said Lady Mackleby affably.

"Oh, it could not be otherwise, my lady," assured Regina with another lovely smile. She was obviously preening over what she considered to be a coup.

"I am so glad to hear that, Regina. Your lack of sensibility stands you in good stead," said Lady Mackleby. She added with relish, "The last person to sleep in that bed was foully murdered. He had his throat cut from ear to ear, and it was days before the bloodied posts and hangings could be scrubbed clean. Some said that the murderer gained access to the bedroom through a secret passageway. I don't put much stock in it, however, for to the best of my recollection the last of the priest's-holes and passageways were said to have been bricked up some time before that."

Regina was looking a bit white, and she stared at Lady Mackleby round-eyed, her mouth half open. Chastity hurried to repair the damage. "That was more than fifty years ago, Aunt! And we are not at all certain that the tale was true."

"Oh, indeed! Every old pile has its own legends and tales attached to it," said Lady Mackleby off-handedly.

Regina suddenly flushed. She rose hastily to her feet. "I have seldom been more entertained, my lady! Such romantic stuff, I swear! You will excuse me if I leave you. I have just recalled something that I wish to discuss with my maid." She whisked herself out of the room, skirts rustling with her indignation. The door closed behind her with a sharp bang.

Lady Mackleby gave a cracked laugh. Chastity looked over at her disapprovingly. "That was very ill done, Aunt."

"Nonsense! It will serve the silly, vain creature right if she is given the shivers tonight when she retires," said Lady Mackleby. "I have no patience for such posturing, especially from such as Regina Cummings. Your brother was a fool to have married her."

"Archie was carried away by her beauty and her breeding. Whatever else she may be, Regina at least has those qualities to recommend her," said Chastity.

"There is more to good breeding than one's lineage, and as for beauty, age has a way of leveling us all to common ground," said Lady Mackleby forthrightly. "Pray do not tell me that you like her, Chastity, for I shall not believe you."

"No, I do not like Regina. But I understand her to a degree, and so I pity her, too," said Chastity. "Unless she changes, I fear that Regina will become more and more an exceedingly lonely, discontented woman. She drives away those whom she should be closest to, not realizing or caring that she does so."

"You have a good heart, Chastity," said Lady Mackleby, patting her niece on the hand. "I am glad of it, for I doubt that you would put up with my crotchets as you do otherwise!"

Chastity laughed at her aunt and said teasingly, "Quite true, ma'am! I am a paragon of the first degree."

"Now that I shall not allow, for you have one great fault," said Lady Mackleby.

Chastity threw up her hand. "I know, Aunt, I know! I have not wed!"

Chapter Fourteen

Chastity's afternoon was whiled away very pleasantly with a short drive in her gig with Miss Paige on a shopping expedition to the village. She had been feeling guilty over how she had hurt Miss Paige by what she had told her. Miss Paige had always been reserved in her manners, so that scarcely anyone but Chastity realized that she had become more subdued than before.

Henry had mentioned the matter to Chastity, however. "Chastity, I have noticed that Miss Paige seems to be a bit blue-deviled. I trust that she is not sickening for something? Or that she has not been offended by anyone?"

Chastity shook her head. "No, I do not believe that she is sickening for anything, Henry, though I do not know that I could give the same assurance about Sir Roger. His appetite has not been as healthy as it usually is. As for Dru, I think that *you* better than anyone else knows the answer to her malady."

Henry stared at her from under his heavy brows. "I? What do you mean? Are you saying that I have offended Miss Paige?"

"Not offended, but perhaps you have inadvertently misled her a little," said Chastity gently. "I had wanted to discuss the matter with you earlier, but I have not had the opportunity to do so."

"Chastity, do not toy with me. What have I done?" Henry asked.

"Dear Henry! I know that you did not intend to do any harm. You are always the consummate host and a gentleman to your fingertips. But you see, Dru has taken your civilities for something more. I think that Dru has fallen a little in love with you," said Chastity.

Henry's attention was riveted on her, a sharp intensity in his gaze. "What precisely has led you to this conclusion?"

"Just a few small things. You spent considerable time with Dru at the grand ball. She did look quite lovely, I shall admit. And her shyness of manner is very taking. She did not lack for partners all evening, did you notice? You yourself danced with her three times and then took her in to dinner," said Chastity.

Henry expelled his breath heavily. "I see. You think that I have exposed her to gossip, is that it?"

"It is not only that, Henry." Chastity hesitated. "Henry, I saw you taking leave of Dru on the upstairs landing. When you left, she had stars in her eyes. And what she said! Henry, I fear that Dru has truly mistaken your intentions toward her."

"So you took it upon yourself to drop a hint in her ear." Henry's mouth was tight, and there was a hardened edge to his voice. "I appreciate your thoughtfulness, Chastity. It was good of you to warn Miss Paige against my insufferable attentions!"

Chastity was dismayed and confused by her brother's reaction. "Well, not quite that, Henry! Your attentions could never be insufferable to any lady!"

"Thank you, dear sister! My God, when I reflect on what Miss Paige must be thinking of me!" Henry exclaimed.

"Oh, Henry, I am sorry. It never occurred to me that she might be thinking ill of you," said Chastity, rather dismayed. "I just thought it would be kinder to let her down gently than to allow her to become firmly attached to you and to suffer certain disillusionment. Then there is her cousin to think of, also. I did not wish Mrs. Dabney to take it into her head that Dru was a rival for your attentions. She could make Dru very uncomfortable if she chose to do so."

Henry drew himself up. His expression was austere. "Yes. Yes, quite right. Thank you, Chastity. I shall endeavor to do better where Miss Paige is concerned. I do not wish her to suffer in any degree, from my hands or anyone else's."

"I knew that you would understand, Henry," said Chastity, smiling up at him.

"I only hope that I may amend matters," Henry said.

"I doubt that you can do anything at this juncture, Henry. However, perhaps I might help. I shall take Dru with me to the village shopping. It will do her good to get away from Chester for a few hours and give her thoughts a different turn, don't you think?" said Chastity. It would also serve Chastity well to be away from the possibility of running into Mr. Halston, in whose presence she could not help but be awkward.

Lord Cummings gave a slight smile. "Are you prescribing a visit to the shops as an antidote for the blue-deviled?"

"Why not? It seems to work in any number of situations," said Chastity cheerfully. "It has never failed to bring Regina out of the mopes, at least."

Henry laughed and shook his head. "I trust that you are right, Chastity. However, I think that you will find that Miss Paige is a far cry from our sister-in-law in character. You made reference to Sir Roger. I, too, have noticed that he is not his usual self. He appears to be dropping weight. Have you any insight about what ails our friend?"

Chastity shook her head. "No, I don't. I have been wondering whether we should have a physician in to him. However, Sir Roger has not complained of any ailment and so I have been reluctant to go to that extreme."

"Sir Roger is not the complaining sort, Chastity. I have seen him finish a twenty-eight mile course after taking a rattling fall that broke his arm. He uttered not a syllable, and the pain must have been excruciating," Henry said with a frown. "But like you, I hesitate to step in where we may not be wanted. Perhaps we should await events a little longer. If it becomes apparent that he is ill, then we shall call in a physician."

"Very well, Henry." Chastity reached up to kiss his lean cheek. "Now I must leave you. I shall go see whether I can persuade Miss Paige to go shopping with me."

*   *   *

The shopping expedition did indeed prove to be worthwhile. Miss Paige's spirits revived markedly, and Chastity was congratulating herself on a successful mission on their return, when her horse stepped into a hole and went lame.

The hour was already advancing, and there were dark clouds scudding across the horizon. A brisk breeze had begun to blow, carrying with it the unmistakable chill of winter.

Chastity cast a glance up at the sky. "Oh, dear. I am afraid that we are in for it, Dru. I do not think that we can walk back to Chester before the rain catches us."

Miss Paige also studied the sky. "Well, we have very little choice in the matter. But what shall we do with all of these packages, Chastity? We cannot very well leave them here, especially the butcher's meat."

"No," agreed Chastity. She snubbed the reins of the gig and caught her skirts up in one hand as she climbed down. "Perhaps we can tie them all together with their strings onto the horse's back and thus lead him home."

Miss Paige agreed to it and she, too, got down out of the gig. The brim of her bonnet blew back with a gust of wind, and she shivered. "I am glad that I wore my half boots," she remarked.

The two ladies worked together in tying the bundles and packages together with their strings and then laid the awkward pack over the lame animal's back. Chastity had already unhitched the horse from the gig, and she took the bridle reins in her hand. "Well, here we go. It is not above two miles, Dru. Do you think that you are up to it?"

"Of course. I often walked when I lived with my mother in Bath, and the streets are very steep. I am quite used to it," said Miss Paige cheerfully.

Chastity was glad, since the little adventure had to happen, that she was with Miss Paige. She could have been with her sister-in-law, for instance. Chastity did not believe that Regina would have been so prosaic about the circumstances as was Miss Paige.

The wind was blowing hard and whipped their skirts and pelisses about their bodies. Chastity and Miss Paige leaned into the cold gusts. The horse favored its lame leg, and progress was excruciatingly slow. Miss Paige kept one gloved hand on the jumble of packages to steady them. She stumbled once, then righted herself.

They had walked three-quarters of the distance when the rain sheeted across the fields toward them. It came pouring down in huge, cold drops. Within seconds the two women were soaked to the skin. Their bonnets hung sodden over their cold cheeks. Chastity's hands were numb. She could scarcely feel the tug of the reins in her tight fingers, and she glanced back to reassure herself that she still had hold of the horse.

Miss Paige trudged beside the horse, her head down. She was trying to hold up the hem of her skirt so that it did not drag in the mud, but her efforts were useless.

"Are you quite all right, Dru?" called Chastity.

Miss Paige looked up. There was misery in her pinched white face, but determination, too. She nodded. "How much farther?" she shouted.

"Not far!" Chastity had already spotted the gates to Chester. She thought she had never seen anything better in her life. However, her joy was nothing compared to that which she felt when she saw the curricle that swept through the gates onto the road.

The carriage pulled up abruptly beside the ladies. Mr. Halston jumped down. There was concern in his eyes and Chastity felt a jolt at his expression. He caught her shoulders between his hands. "Chastity!"

"Oh, I *am* glad to see you!" exclaimed Chastity. "The horse went lame, Jeffrey!"

Lord Winthrop had snubbed the reins and also jumped down out of the curricle. He hurried over to Miss Paige and led her back toward the curricle. "We must get them indoors, Halston! They are soaked through!"

"Yes, I shall let loose the horse. It knows it is home and will find its own way to the stables," said Mr. Halston, prying the reins out of Chastity's frozen fingers. "Go to the curricle, Chastity! I will join you in a moment."

Chastity obeyed stiffly. She was shivering and could not recall ever being so cold in her life. She reached out to take hold
of the side of the curricle and fumbled with her skirt.

Hands caught her around the waist and lifted her straight up
into the curricle. Chastity fell onto the seat, her head bumping
Miss Paige's shoulder. She straightened herself and moved over
to press close to Miss Paige. She could feel the shudders that
were going through the other woman, and she looked at her in
swift concern. "Dru! You are blue with cold!"

"So are you, Chastity," stammered Miss Paige through chattering teeth.

Lord Winthrop wasted not a moment in turning the curricle
around in the narrow road, expertly backing the horses and then
sending them through the gates.

"Here, let me cover you," said Mr. Halston. He had stripped
off his greatcoat and now he spread it over both of the ladies,
tucking it around them with impersonal hands.

"You'll get wet, Jeffrey," said Chastity inanely.

"Do you think that I care for that?" he asked shortly.

The drive up to the front door of the manor was accomplished in short order. Mr. Halston leaped down almost before
the curricle had time to come to a stop. He ran up the steps and
banged the knocker. Then he turned and came bounding back
down the steps to the curricle. "Here, put your hands on my
shoulders, Chastity. I will lift you down."

Chastity did as she was told. She felt his warm hands on her
waist, his thumbs firm against her midsection. Then she was
whirled down to the ground. She did not have time to think before she was picked up and gathered tight against Mr. Halston's
chest. It felt too comforting in his embrace. "Jeffrey!"

"Hush, Chastity!"

The front door had been flung open by the porter. Several individuals stood by anxiously. Mr. Halston carried Chastity up
the steps and into the manor. "Hot water for baths! They are
chilled through!"

"Yes, sir!" The butler snapped his fingers at the footmen, and
they ran to carry the order to the kitchens.

Lord Winthrop had followed Mr. Halston's example. Miss Paige's arms were about his neck, crushing his white cravat. "We must get the ladies upstairs, Halston, so that their maids can minister to them."

Mr. Halston nodded and started up the carpeted stairs two at a time. Chastity was seriously concerned that he would drop her in his haste. "Jeffrey, you needn't hurry so. I don't wish to take a fall."

He glanced down at her face and the tight corners of his mouth lifted. "Don't you trust me, Chastity?"

"I suppose that I have lit . . . little choice," stuttered Chastity, her teeth suddenly clattering together. He laughed at that. They traversed the long hall in very short order.

When Mr. Halston reached Chastity's door, he unceremoniously kicked it open. The maid whirled, her hand flying to her throat. "Sir!"

Mr. Halston took no notice of the servant woman's fright. "Your mistress is soaked from the rain. See to her!" The maid gasped and at once hurried forward.

Sparing the rest of the bedroom hardly a glance, Mr. Halston carried Chastity around the corner of the huge four-poster canopied bed to the fireplace. With his foot, he pushed a wide upholstered footstool closer to the fire. Carefully he lowered her onto it. Now that she was out of his arms she was cold again; and surprisingly bereft. "You see, I did not drop you after all," he said quietly.

"No, you didn't," agreed Chastity, pushing up the sodden brim of her ruined bonnet so that she could smile at him.

Down on one knee Mr. Halston helped to take off her muddied boots. He peeled off her sodden stockings and then proceeded to rub Chastity's cold feet.

"Mr. Halston, sir! It isn't decent!" exclaimed the maid.

"Never mind that. Just cut the ribbons of that bonnet and get it off her head," said Mr. Halston impatiently.

The bedroom door opened, and Regina swept in. "Well, Chastity! I am certainly glad that you did not ask me to go with you this afternoon! Mr. Halston, I think that we shall do better without you now."

"Regina, what . . . whatever are you doing here?" asked Chastity, huddled on the ottoman in front of the fire. Her maid had with difficulty peeled off her gloves. She had immediately held her hands out to the warmth of the fire, but her fingers were still frigid and clumsy. She was making poor work of undoing the buttons of her pelisse.

"I have come to help you, my dear. I have brought Martha with me, as you see. Now, Mr. Halston, why do we not go down to the drawing room?" said Regina. The gentleman had risen at her entrance, and she now slipped her hand about his arm to gently persuade him toward the open door. Regina's maid held the door open for them.

Mr. Halston was obviously reluctant to comply with the lady's wishes. He glanced down at Chastity.

"It really isn't quite the thing for you to be in Chastity's bedroom," Regina said in a lightly scolding tone.

Mr. Halston flushed suddenly. "No, perhaps not. You will be all right, Chastity?"

Chastity nodded. She tilted her head to look up at him. "Thank you, Jeffrey."

"Come along, Mr. Halston. You may tell me all about it," said Regina, smiling up at him.

"Regina, what of Miss Paige? Is someone with her?" asked Chastity quickly.

"Oh, yes. You have never heard such cluckings and exclamations. Our dear Mrs. Bottler has taken Miss Paige firmly in hand, I assure you. Mrs. Dabney, of course, is quite useless in this sort of crisis," Regina said, closing the door behind herself and Mr. Halston.

Chastity bent closer to the grate to spread her fingers to the welcome heat. She had not really realized how chilled she had become. Behind her, Regina's maid bustled around the four-poster bed. Chastity turned her head to see that the canopied bed was turned down to expose inviting linen sheets. A cambric nightshift lay neatly folded across the foot of the bed. The maid was briskly sliding a warming pan under the coverlet.

Her own maid noticed the direction of her gaze. "We'll soon have you properly settled, miss. Now let me help you with the rest of those clothes."

Chastity was stripped of her wet garments and sat wrapped in a blanket in front of the fire until her bath was brought in. When she was first helped into the warm water, her skin felt to be on fire. However, as she began to thaw out, she started to feel alive again. Afterward, she was dressed in a warm night-gown and robe.

Her duty discharged, Regina's maid excused herself and quietly left the bedroom.

As the woman did so, a footman came to the door, and Chastity's maid took from him a small tray with a glass on it. They exchanged a few words, the maid nodded, then closed the door again. She placed the tray on the bedside table and turned to her mistress. "Now, miss, you are to go straight to bed."

"Nonsense, I—"

"I have his lordship's orders, miss," said the maid. "Now here's a spot of hot tea and honey. You are to drink it up."

"His lordship's orders?" asked Chastity dryly, going over to sit on the bed and obediently accepting the cup. Her fingers curled around the warm cup, and she could smell the fragrance of the tea.

"Precisely, miss."

Chastity felt ridiculous about being coddled, but at the same time the thought of slipping into bed was extremely tempting. She allowed herself to be put into bed. The sheets were toasty from the warming pan and felt wonderful. Chastity gave a tiny sigh and closed her eyes.

It was a few hours later when Chastity wakened. Her maid had pulled a chair up beside the bed to watch over her. Chastity was touched by the serving woman's loyalty. She announced her intention to get up and get dressed, quite expecting some protest from the maid.

However, the maid nodded and immediately went over to the wardrobe. "I thought you might, miss, so I have already laid out a gown for dinner."

"Is it that late?" asked Chastity, startled.

The maid acknowledged that it was, and Chastity threw back the covers.

When she had dressed, Chastity made her way at once to Miss Paige's bedroom. She was told that Miss Paige had already gone downstairs, so she hurried down herself.

Chastity and Miss Paige were the focus of attention at dinner. Even Jeffrey, although reverting to his previous polite distance from her, looked at her quietly with a concerned expression. Chastity handled the ado with aplomb, but Miss Paige blushed and cast down her eyes. Her cousin rallied her teasingly.

"Come, Drusilla, there is little reason for you to color up so," said Mrs. Dabney. "It is not as though you have tied your garter in public."

"As though I would!" exclaimed Miss Paige involuntarily. There was a bit of laughter over her remark, which rendered her completely tongue-tied.

Chastity kept wondering why her aunt, Lady Mackleby, had not joined them downstairs in the dining room. It was unlike her ladyship to isolate herself, and she said so.

"Oh, hasn't anyone told you, Chastity? Lady Mackleby is not feeling well this evening," Archie said.

"Not feeling well! Why, she is never ill!" exclaimed Chastity, at once concerned.

"I have myself spoken with her ladyship's maid, Chastity. The woman assures me that there is nothing wrong with our aunt that a little rest will not cure," Henry said reassuringly.

Chastity subsided, but she could not quite let go of her anxiety for her aunt. As soon as the after-dinner coffee was served, she quietly excused herself and went upstairs.

She knocked on her aunt's door, and her ladyship's dresser let her into the bedroom. Standing just inside the door, Chastity asked in a low voice, "What is toward with her ladyship?"

The dresser shook her head, pursing her lips. "Her ladyship

has knocked herself into flinders, miss, keeping such late hours as she has lately. She'll not admit that she cannot burn the candle at both ends anymore, and this is the result of it."

"May I see her?" asked Chastity.

"Of course, miss. It will do her ladyship good."

Chastity advanced into the bedroom. Lady Mackleby was propped up on several pillows in her bed. The huge four-poster dwarfed the elderly woman. When she saw Chastity, she put on a slight smile and raised her hand.

Chastity went forward quickly to the bedside and caught her aunt's frail hand. "Dear ma'am, what is this? You are never taken ill," she said lightly, though she was shaken at how frail her aunt appeared.

"Of course I am not ill," said Lady Mackleby, her voice a bare thread compared to its usual vigor. "But I feel devilish unwell, and I was bored with my own company. So I am very glad that you came up to see me."

Chastity smiled. The dresser had moved a chair next to the bed, and Chastity quietly thanked the servant woman as she sat down in it. "I hope that you do not find my company worse than your own, my lady. I am feeling very sorry for myself this evening, I warn you."

Lady Mackleby looked at her niece from beneath half-lidded eyes. There was a spark of interest in their depths. "Are you? Isn't your house party going along to your liking?"

"It has been a disaster today," said Chastity. She proceeded to tell her aunt of her shopping expedition with Miss Paige, drawing out the tale for its full effect. She made light of the horrid cold discomfort when she and Miss Paige had been caught in the rain. She described how the packages had slipped and threatened to fall off the horse and how certain she had been that Mr. Halston would trip with her on the stairs. Lady Mackleby cackled.

"So you see, Aunt, it is no hardship to me to visit you. In a manner of speaking, I have sought sanctuary from the world here with you," ended Chastity.

"You are being nonsensical, Chastity," said Lady Mackleby with a smile.

A short silence fell. Chastity was beginning to think that Lady Mackleby had drifted off, and she looked around for the maid. The woman nodded and came forward. Chastity started to rise from the chair, carefully placing Lady Mackleby's hand on the coverlet.

A log fell in the grate with a shower of sparks. The sound jarred her ladyship awake. "You should have married him, Chastity."

Chastity was startled. "Who, Aunt?"

"Why, Jeffrey Halston, of course. I visited with him for several minutes this afternoon. I knew his family very well. It was a disappointment to us all that you would not have Jeffrey. But you were such a foolish girl," murmured Lady Mackleby.

Chastity gave a wry laugh. "Aunt, I have been a sad disappointment to a great many personages. My married sisters all scold me for my follies. They say that I should have made my home with one of them since I am grown into a spinster. But I prefer Henry's roof."

"And with good reason," said Lady Mackleby with a bit of her old energy. "Such a bunch of ninnyhammers! Why, you are worth more than all the rest put together!"

"Thank you, ma'am. I believe that is the finest compliment that you have ever paid me," said Chastity.

"Oh, aye! How often have I said that butter wouldn't melt in your mouth?" said Lady Mackleby, sinking back again onto her pillows as she smiled up at her niece.

"Many times," said Chastity, bending over to adjust and plump one of the pillows. "Can I get you anything, dear ma'am?"

"I should like a neat glass of wine, but my watch guard will not hear of it," said Lady Mackleby wrathfully, rolling her eyes in a baleful glare at her maid.

"Your ladyship will recall what the physician told me," said the dresser in a slightly scolding tone.

Lady Mackleby lifted her hand to wave dismissal. "Yes, yes,

I remember," she said irritably. "But I am not ready for my cordial. I am talking to my niece. Go away."

"Very good, my lady," said the maid, dropping a curtsey and withdrawing from the room. The servant woman did not close the door entirely, however, so that it was evident that she was just outside within hearing distance.

"The woman is a dratted nuisance, but I could not do without her," said Lady Mackleby.

"I am glad that you have someone so devoted to you," said Chastity.

"I wish that I could say the same for you, Chastity," said Lady Mackleby.

"Oh, Aunt! You mustn't be anxious over me," said Chastity. "I do very well, I assure you."

Lady Mackleby did not appear to hear her. "Do you know, I was surprised when Jeffrey Halston wed the Sweeney chit. Mirabelle Sweeney was a sweet thing, perfectly respectable, of course, but scarcely the sort that one would think would attract someone like young Jeffrey Halston. He had such dash, such fire! Mirabelle Sweeney was so docile and passive. I saw them afterward on several occasions, and I did not think it a happy union."

Chastity was astonished. "Not happy? But I had heard quite otherwise."

Lady Mackleby looked at her. "Who told you that? Whoever did so knew nothing about it, I assure you. I was good friends with Olivia Sweeney, Mirabelle's grandmother. I miss Olivia. She died a year or so ago, you know. She confided to me her concern over Mirabelle's marriage, which I never breathed a word about to anyone else. It was not my place to do so. Nor am I an inveterate gossip."

"But what did Mrs. Sweeney tell you?" asked Chastity.

"Only that it was not an ecstatic union," said Lady Mackleby. "Halston and his bride were not precisely unhappy, but they were not happy, either."

Chastity's mind was buzzing with questions and conjecture. Mr. Halston had told her quite emphatically that he had been devoted to his wife. However, it seemed that others had perceived something slightly different.

"As I said earlier, it is a pity that you rejected Halston's suit. He would have made you a good husband," said Lady Mackleby. She gave a yawn. "I have grown tired, my dear. Call my woman to me. She'll want to give me that hideous cordial before I go to sleep."

"Very well, ma'am." Chastity bent over to kiss her aunt's withered cheek. "I shall visit you again in the morning."

"Not too early," said Lady Mackleby. "I am irritable if I am made to hold a decent conversation before eleven o'clock."

"I shall remember that." Chastity called for the maid, who came back into the room instantly, giving credence to Chastity's assumption that the servant woman had been waiting for just such a summons right outside the bedroom door.

Chastity said good night to her aunt and left the bedroom. As she went on her way, she puzzled over the strange conversation that she had had with her aunt. Lady Mackleby did not often make mistakes in what she heard or saw. Therefore, there was a grain of truth in what her ladyship had just told Chastity concerning Jeffrey Halston's marriage to Mirabelle Sweeney. If that was true, then why had Jeffrey told her such a blatant falsehood? It didn't make a bit of sense to her.

Chapter Fifteen

The next morning dawned cold but clear. The Radfords had invited everyone at Chester to come to the sprawling parish for an informal breakfast party. It was a very pleasant gathering, though two faces were missed. Mrs. Dabney had failed to accompany them, her maid bringing word downstairs that the lady had awakened with a heavy head. Sir Roger, also, was absent. He had apparently gone out before daybreak to the stables and had not returned from his solitary ride before the party set out for the parish.

One of the most notable aspects of the breakfast party was the announcement made by Reverend Radford. Miss Radford and Sir Edward Greaves had become betrothed.

"How perfectly marvelous!" Merrill exclaimed. "It isn't as though it comes as any great surprise, of course. Sir Edward was clearly besotted."

Regina turned her head, her blue eyes rounded. "For my part, I am quite astonished."

Chastity only smiled, for she understood her sister-in-law's amazement all too well. Sir Edward Greaves had participated in a light flirtation with Regina, and that lady simply could not comprehend how the gentleman could have become enamoured of another woman when she had chosen to honor him with her favor.

"Oh, they do make such a lovely pair," said Mrs. Bottler, wiping a tear from her eye with a lace handkerchief.

"Indeed, they do, Mrs. Bottler," said Mr. Bottler.

Lord Winthrop slapped Lord Cummings on the shoulder.

"Well, Henry? Will it be you or I that parson's trap will close on next?"

"I beg to be excused from the question," Henry said with a flash of a smile.

Lord Winthrop laughed. "I wager that neither of us will follow Edward's example very quickly! Come, let us go wish him well. He has won a rare prize, I think."

The betrothed couple were congratulated from all sides. The atmosphere was festive, and the guests remained longer than intended. When the Chester party left the parish, they did so with openly expressed reluctance.

Sir Edward declined to return to Chester with the others, saying that he wished to spend a few hours with his betrothed and her parents. Sometime during the flurry of good-byes, Mr. Salyer rode off by himself.

"Well, we have lost another of our gallant escorts," Regina said with a light laugh.

"I believe that Salyer mentioned that he wished to stop by the village before returning to Chester. I imagine that there was some matter that he wished to attend to," said Lord Winthrop.

"No doubt. He shall catch up with us later, I suppose," Henry said.

As the carriages and their mounted escorts made their way back to Chester, an animated discussion arose on how best to spend the remainder of the day.

"It seems such a pity to remain indoors when the weather is so lovely," remarked Miss Paige.

"Quite right, Miss Paige. There will be fewer and fewer clear days as winter closes in," Henry said, casting a glance at the sky. "Perhaps you might enjoy a leisurely ride to view one of our local historical points. We are quite proud of the ancient abbey."

"It sounds just the thing," said Lord Winthrop, glancing at Miss Paige's interested face.

"Oh, yes! It is a long ride, but I think it well worthwhile. The countryside is lovely," Merrill said.

"Of course, there is nothing there but a tumble of old ruins,"

Regina said. "But I daresay the ride will be enjoyable, if I may be certain of your company, Lord Winthrop?"

Lord Winthrop bowed from the saddle. "I would count it an honor to accompany you on this or any other outing, Mrs. Cummings."

Regina bestowed a complacent smile on his lordship. Watching his wife preen, Archie sighed. "I must admit that I shan't mind seeing the ruins of the old abbey again. It has been years since I have ridden that way." He turned to his sister. "Chastity, surely you were with me then?"

"Yes, I remember. However, I am afraid that I shan't go with you today."

"But you must go, Chastity! Our pleasure must be quite spoiled if you do not," said Miss Paige in dismay.

Chastity shook her head. "I am very sorry, Dru, but I mustn't. I really feel that I should stay at Chester so that I may check on my aunt through the day. Lady Mackleby's unusual bout of sickness concerns me, for her ladyship is never ill. I already feel quite guilty in going to the breakfast party."

"We understand perfectly, Miss Cummings," said Lord Winthrop, riding alongside the carriage. "Naturally you will be missed."

Also mounted, Mr. Halston turned his head and looked directly at Chastity. "Yes, his lordship speaks for all of us in that."

Chastity felt heat rising in her face at the flare of expression in Mr. Halston's eyes.

"You have such a good heart, Miss Cummings! Her ladyship is quite fortunate to have you," said Mrs. Bottler.

"Thank you, ma'am," said Chastity quietly.

"Mrs. Bottler and I shall also beg off from the party," said Mr. Bottler. "We haven't the energy of the younger set. And I daresay that you, dear Mrs. Webster, will say the same?"

"Oh, dear me, yes. My dear doggies are waiting for me, you know," said Mrs. Webster.

"Then I rely upon you, Lord Winthrop, and Mr. Halston to escort the ladies. I, too will be absent from the party," said Henry.

There was a strong outcry against his lordship's bowing out of the expedition, since he had been the one to originally propose the outing. However, Henry explained that he had set an appointment with his lawyer, who was traveling down from London to meet with him, and he would not put off duty for pleasure.

"As for my proposing the ride, I did so from a strong desire to accommodate the least whims of my guests," he said with a smile.

No one was really astonished that Lord Cardiff, also, decided to remain behind. It was quite understood that it would not be easy for a man convalescing from a serious wound to ride for several hours.

Within an hour of arriving back at Chester, the two gentlemen and three ladies had changed for riding and left again on the best mounts in Henry's stable. They promised to be back in time for a late tea.

Chastity whiled away the hours with reading a new novel and by penning a few letters. After looking in on Lady Mackleby for the third time, and being assured by her ladyship's maid yet again that her ladyship was still sleeping peacefully due to the cordial she had been given, Chastity wandered down the stairs.

The manor felt oddly empty. Mrs. Dabney was still closeted in her rooms. Sir Roger had returned, but that gentleman had apparently been wearied by his solitary ride. He had settled in the parlor with the newspapers and subsequently fallen asleep in his chair. Chastity was informed of it by Mr. Bottler, who had gone down to the parlor in search of the newspapers, and was returning upstairs when she met him.

"I discovered the poor gentleman quite worn to the bone, Miss Cummings. He had spread the newspaper over his face and was snoring. I suppose that the noise he was making was enough to cover my own entrance into the room, for he did not stir," said Mr. Bottler with a deep chuckle. "Naturally I exited at once, not wishing to disturb Sir Roger's nap."

"I am sorry, Mr. Bottler. Shall I retrieve some of the newspapers for you?" asked Chastity.

Mr. Bottler waved his pudgy hand. "Pray do not bother, Miss Cummings! I shall read them later. I think that I shall go up and see whether I might not interest Mrs. Bottler in a game of backgammon. We play it quite often."

Chastity parted from Mr. Bottler with a smile, but she was feeling a little out of sorts. She would have enjoyed very much an outing with her friends. Until their return, with only the mystery of Jeffrey Halston to occupy her thoughts, the time would undoubtedly continue to weigh somewhat heavily on her hands.

When Chastity had descended the stairs, she saw that the door to her brother's study was standing partially ajar. She crossed the hall, expecting to find Henry inside. Perhaps she could while away a few minutes in talking to her brother.

As Chastity pushed open the door, a shocked gasp escaped her. She stood transfixed at the sight of the ravaged room.

Henry and Lord Cardiff stood in front of his lordship's desk, speaking in low tones. They heard her and turned quickly. "Chastity!" Henry exclaimed.

"Henry, what—"

Lord Cardiff moved swiftly. In two strides, he reached Chastity and took hold of her arm, pulling her fully into the room. He did not glance at her, but looked out at the empty hall. "Forgive me, Miss Cummings! It is not my intention to take liberties with you."

"No, of course not," said Chastity mechanically.

"I will check the outside grounds, my lord," said Lord Cardiff. He stepped out of the study and closed the door.

Chastity scarcely noticed Lord Cardiff's exit. She was appalled as she viewed the destruction. "Dear God!"

Henry's study had been his sanctuary, and now it had been violated.

Chastity stepped gingerly from point to point. Glass crunched underfoot. She grasped her skirt high as she stepped over yet another shattered or displaced object as she approached her silent brother.

Nothing had been left untouched. The Sevres vase that had had a place of prominence on the mantel had been smashed to pieces against the flagstones. Books had been swept off the bookshelves and pages ripped out of some of them. Chess pieces were scattered wildly over the Aubusson carpet, and the lighter chairs had been overturned. The poker lay on the carpet, where it had been tossed after being used to break the glass-fronted cabinet. The contents of the cabinet had been virtually destroyed. Two portraits were slashed; a third had been snatched from the wall and driven down over a stone bust. A velvet drape was rent almost from top to bottom.

Chastity turned a stricken face toward her brother. "Oh, Henry!"

His lordship stood quite still, stone-faced. Only the glitter of his eyes and the whitened brackets about his mouth betrayed the control that he was exerting over his emotions. "A pretty turn-out, is it not? Even my desk is not untouched. But whoever tried to force it open was unsuccessful. Lord, I should like to put my hands on the fellows responsible for this!"

"It . . . it is horrible," said Chastity, tears pricking her eyes. The safety and sanctity of their home had been breached. The vandalism had been committed with audacity and obvious contempt. There was demonstrably no safety even behind bolted doors and locked windows.

Henry looked at her quickly. He reached out to press his sister's shoulder. "Chin up, there's a good girl. We'll catch the rogues responsible, I daresay."

Chastity gave a watery sniff and dabbed at her eyes with her handkerchief. "Yes, I am sure of it. After all, you are the magistrate."

It was especially horrid that such a thing had happened when they had a house full of guests. She could well imagine the impact that it could have on their house party. A reaction of panic could set in with some of their guests, most notably with her sister-in-law. Regina had been known to succumb to hysterics on a small number of occasions. Chastity thought that something of this sort could well trigger one of her fits.

An even more horrendous thought occurred to her. Chastity glanced up quickly at her brother. "Henry, do you suppose that one of our guests—" She could not bring herself to even finish the sentence, for such a suggestion was unthinkable.

Henry looked thoughtfully at her. "I would not like to think so," he said quietly.

Chastity noticed at once that he did not immediately refute her suggestion. She shivered as further conjecture went through her mind. If the perpetrator of this outrage was a guest in their home, who could it be and why had that person done such a thing?

Inevitably, she thought of Sir Roger, who had gone off alone and come back to the manor sometime during their absence. Sir Roger, who was so weary that he had fallen asleep while reading the newspapers. But he was an old and valued family friend!

Mrs. Dabney had been at Chester all day. She had sent a message by her maid that she was ill; but no one knew for certain that that was the truth. The widow had absolutely no motive, unless she was less well situated than was assumed and supplemented her income with theft!

Their aunt, Mrs. Webster—Chastity had a sudden vision of the dotty old lady and her dear doggies wreaking havoc. It was preposterous, of course!

She had just met Mr. Bottler on the stairs. He had told her a tale of looking in on Sir Roger, but what if he had been here, in the study, instead? And exactly how did Mrs. Bottler fit in with it all?

Chastity did not like the train of her thoughts. The ugly suspicions had risen instantly, but she was reluctant to allow them to fall on any one of their guests. However, she reflected without wishing to, it was perfectly true that they had opened their doors to several individuals who were not at all well known to them.

"Henry, surely this could not have been done while we have been at home," said Chastity. "Otherwise, someone must have heard the breakage and come in to investigate. Any of our guests or a servant could have surprised the culprit."

"Yes; that is precisely why I am inclined to believe that it must have happened while we and our guests were at the Radfords'," said Henry, frowning. "Which means, of course, that whoever did this knew precisely the time that the house would be empty except for the servants. They, of course, would have been busy with their usual morning tasks, well away from this end of the house."

Before Chastity could comment on her brother's staggering observation, Lord Cardiff came back into the room. He carefully closed the door behind him.

Chapter Sixteen

"I saw nothing out in the garden, my lord. The ground is so hard that it is impossible to see any prints or scuff marks below the window," said Lord Cardiff, looking grave.

Henry nodded. For a moment he was silent, then suddenly exclaimed, "It is damnable, Cardiff. If I only knew who or what to look for!"

"Indeed, my lord. We are working totally in the blind at present," said Lord Cardiff. "However, perhaps it would profit us more to speculate on what the intruder hoped to achieve or to find in your study."

Henry's gaze sharpened as he met Lord Cardiff's steady eyes. "Yes, you may have something there, Cardiff."

"But what could they have been looking for?" asked Chastity. She gestured at the scene of destruction. "The disorder looks so random. There is no rhyme or reason to it. If it was a particular object or money that they were looking for, would they not have concentrated their efforts on just those things? Why would there be such wholesale destruction at this?"

"I cannot answer you adequately, ma'am. However, it does occur to me that there is no better way to disguise the object of a search than to erase its traces by drowning it in a sea of destruction," said Lord Cardiff.

Henry nodded. His eyes glittered, his expression was quite hard. "I have a feeling that you are correct, my lord." He glanced around them. "It is a rather clumsy attempt, now that I look at it in that light. It appears as though the intruders went through everything in haste, taking those things that they wanted and tossing aside the things that they had no use for."

"Precisely, my lord. What we must do is to make a thorough search through all of this to find a common thread. Perhaps we shall discover in truth just what is missing and what was of such interest to our housebreaker," said Lord Cardiff.

"Oh, Henry, do you think that it was a housebreaker, after all?" asked Chastity quickly, hopefully.

Lord Cardiff glanced at her, his expression startled. Then his face smoothed to inscrutability. He glanced toward Henry, and they shared a mute communication. Henry nodded and turned toward his sister.

"I think it very likely, Chastity," he said. "I do not like to think that any of our guests have so abused our hospitality."

"No, nor I," agreed Chastity. "I must admit that, as terrible as it all is, I am more comfortable with the notion that this was done by someone unknown to us."

"Quite," Henry said. He placed a large comforting hand on his sister's shoulder and gave a slight squeeze. "Courage, my dear. We shall no doubt have our answers before long. However, we will not advertise this, Chastity. Our guests must not be made alarmed."

"No, indeed," said Chastity, automatically responding to her brother's calm. "That would not do at all. You will want someone to clean up this room, of course. I shall send Wilkins to you. He will be able to suggest one or two discreet servants who can be trusted not to gossip."

"Thank you, Chastity. I knew that I could rely upon your innate good sense," Henry said. He dropped his hand from his sister's shoulder and half turned toward Lord Cardiff. "Lord Cardiff, I would appreciate your discretion, as well."

"Of course, my lord. You may rely upon me completely," said Lord Cardiff quietly. Chastity appreciated Lord Cardiff's extraordinary understanding. It was obvious that was why her brother felt able to trust him.

"Damn! I had forgotten Tisdale. He is supposed to arrive within the hour," Henry said, scowling. "I shall have to send

word to him at the posting house that I will not be able to meet
with him after all. He will have made the journey for nothing,
poor man!"

"Why don't you invite him to come to you later this afternoon? You may meet with him in the library, and he may have
dinner with us, spending the night here at Chester and leaving
in the morning," suggested Chastity.

"A very good notion, Chastity," Henry said. "I'll be able to
finish the business without any further delay."

"I shall inform the staff of your plans," said Chastity.

Henry nodded acknowledgment, then looked around the
room. "I scarcely know where to begin. I suppose that some of
the debris can be safely removed at once, such as those broken
shards. A pity, for I rather liked that vase. Then I can begin to
look about for whatever may be missing."

"I shall send Wilkins in to help you, Henry," said Chastity.

Lord Cardiff had been standing silently by, listening. Now he
said, "If you do not object, my lord, I will leave you for now."

At his host's level stare, Lord Cardiff smiled. "It is not my
intent to abandon you, my lord. It is nearly time for tea. I
thought that I may better assist you at the moment by going out
to meet the riding party, with the object of delaying their immediate return by a quarter hour, at the least."

"An excellent notion," Henry said with a nod. "I am obliged
to you. Keep them away as long as you can. I will be able to
have some of this mess straightened up, then, without exciting
undue curiosity. After I am finished, I shall lock the door
against your return, Cardiff, so that you and I may go through
the rest at our leisure."

"I trust that your confidence in me is not misplaced, my
lord," said Lord Cardiff with a bow. "However, I believe that
with Miss Cummings's help I shall be able to accomplish my
objective."

"Good. Chastity, pray see to whatever requests Lord Cardiff
might have," Henry said.

"Of course," said Chastity. She was glad to have something

constructive to do, for when she looked around at the study, all she felt was fear and helplessness.

Lord Cardiff opened the door and politely waited for Chastity to precede him out of the study. He was smiling in a friendly fashion, and as Chastity went past him, she returned his smile. She was unaccountably regaining her buoyancy of spirits. She supposed the initial shock was wearing off. It helped, too, that both her brother and Lord Cardiff were treating the situation with such remarkable calm.

When she and Lord Cardiff had exited the study, Chastity told the footman in the hall that Lord Cummings had requested the butler to wait upon him. Just as Chastity had finished relaying this message, the study door opened and Henry put his head out.

"Send my secretary to me, as well," he commanded, before retreating back into the room and closing the door.

The footman bowed his understanding and hurried away.

Chastity invited Lord Cardiff into the drawing room. "We may be private in here, my lord," she said. Once in the room, she turned and looked into his face. "Now, my lord, what may I do for you? How do you propose to delay the return of the riding party?"

Chastity was disconcerted when Lord Cardiff caught up one of her hands in his and lifted it to his lips. "My lord!"

With a warm expression, Lord Cardiff said, "You are marvelous, Miss Cummings. I do not believe there are many ladies who could have reacted with such calm upon discovering such a terrible scene in their homes."

Chastity felt a blush rise in her face. "Thank you, my lord. However, I must confess that it is shock that paralyzed my inclination to hysteria, rather than any quality of character."

"That I take leave not to believe," said Lord Cardiff, giving her fingers a squeeze before releasing her hand. "Now, may I prevail on you to order a cold collation and wine to be packed into picnic baskets to be ready in half an hour? It is my intention to meet the riding party with an impromptu al fresco luncheon."

"What an ingenious notion, my lord," said Chastity. She walked over to the bellpull and tugged on it. "I shall drive out with you."

"I would not wish to put you to that inconvenience," said Lord Cardiff.

"Nonsense. I shall enjoy such an outing immensely. I have been indoors too long today." Chastity saw by his expression that he had not told her the real reason for his polite objection. She was suddenly amused. "I assure you, my lord, I will not keep you waiting any longer than the packing of the picnic baskets! I will scramble with unseeming haste into my driving attire."

"You leave me with nothing else to say, Miss Cummings, except to express my pleasure at your unexpected company," said Lord Cardiff smoothly, bowing.

The butler came in answer to the bell, and Chastity relayed her orders concerning the picnic baskets. She requested also that her gig be readied and brought around to the front door in fifteen minutes. Then she held out her hand to Lord Cardiff. "I shall meet you in the great hall in a quarter hour, my lord."

As he took her hand, Lord Cardiff uttered another objection. "It was not necessary to order out your own equipage, Miss Cummings. I could easily have driven another one."

"But you see, my lord, I intend to drive and I prefer my own gig," said Chastity. She nodded toward his incapacitated arm. "I think it will be easier that way, don't you? You would find it rather difficult to drive one-handed."

"Oh, yes; quite," said Lord Cardiff. He had looked momentarily surprised, but his expression had turned to rueful amusement. "I was forgetting. My shoulder is healing so well that I scarcely notice it any longer."

"Well, I do not wish you to suffer a relapse through any remiss of mine," said Chastity, turning toward the door.

Lord Cardiff reached the door before she did. He opened it with a smile and another bow. The look in his eyes was warm. "I shall see you in a quarter hour, then?"

Chastity inclined her head. She swept down the hall to the

stairs, where she caught hold of her skirt and lifted it out of the way as she hurried up to her apartment.

Chastity's bedroom was furnished elegantly. Tapestries accented the handsome paneled walls. Two wing chairs were set against the wall on the other side of her bed. A small sitting area, with a settee and twin wing chairs arranged around an oval table, had been created in front of the windows. The draperies at the windows were slate blue, and the carpet underfoot was also blue with a deep gold border.

When Chastity told her maid about the proposed outing, the woman enthusiastically opened the wardrobe and swiftly helped her mistress change. Within moments, Chastity stood freshly attired in a smartly cut driving pelisse with half boots on her feet. A bonnet with a curled feather graced her head, and she clutched a whip in her kid-gloved hand.

Chastity left her bedroom and traversed the landing toward the stairs. She was well within the allotted time. Glancing down over the oak balustrade, she saw Lord Cardiff standing in the great hall below. He had put off his frock coat and was now attired in driving coat and beaver. He was holding a gold watchpiece in his gloved palm and was frowning over its open face.

Chastity ran down the stairs. She rallied him on his obvious lack of faith in her promise as she joined him. "I am a woman of my word, my lord, as you see."

Lord Cardiff laughed. "Indeed you are, Miss Cummings!" He snapped the watch shut and slipped it into his waistcoat pocket. "I am fairly caught in unbelief. I hope that you can forgive me?"

"Of course, my lord," said Chastity graciously. Lord Cardiff offered his elbow to her. Chastity accepted his escort and they walked out the front door.

The picnic baskets were already loaded into the gig. Chastity gathered her skirt and let a footman help her up into the carriage. She settled on the seat, whip in hand, and gathered the reins. She noticed that Lord Cardiff had managed to climb up into the gig without assistance. Apparently he had spoken entirely truthfully when he had said that his shoulder was mending well.

Chastity thought that she could guess how the riding party would be returning to Chester, and she turned the gig in that direction. It was only a few minutes' drive before she and Lord Cardiff intercepted the riders. From the distance Mr. Halston smiled gently at Chastity, only to have his greeting fade as he noticed the gentleman seated next to her. When the five equestrians drew up beside the gig to greet them, Chastity announced that she and Lord Cardiff had brought an al fresco luncheon out to them, deliberately avoiding looking at Jeffrey.

"What an utterly delightful notion," Merrill said, her eyes very bright in a face whipped rosy by the wind.

"Yes, isn't it!" exclaimed Miss Paige.

"I, too, think it a splendid idea," said Lord Winthrop approvingly. "Fresh air and exercise always gives one a healthy appetite. Where shall we set down, Miss Cummings?"

"I think there, close by that grove. The trees will offer us some protection from the wind," said Chastity, pointing with her whip.

"It is ideal," said Lord Winthrop. "Come, Halston! Let us make haste to help Miss Cummings and Lord Cardiff unload those tantalizing baskets."

"With pleasure, my lord," said Mr. Halston.

The gentlemen trotted over to the trees. They dismounted and tied their horses. Rugs had also been packed in the gig, and the gentlemen began to unload these and the baskets. The ladies walked their horses over to the copse of trees. Mr. Halston went over to help each of them to dismount. The party began to converge on the spread rugs and baskets, chattering merrily.

Chastity climbed down from the gig. Merrill was waiting for her. Her ladyship slipped a hand into Chastity's elbow and arm in arm, the two friends walked over to join the rest of the party.

"I had quite pitied you this morning for having to stay behind to support your aunt. But you've come about very nicely," Merrill said in a soft voice, nodding in Lord Cardiff's direction.

"You are incorrigible, Merrill. I thought it was Jeffrey Halston that you had in mind for me," said Chastity lightly.

"Oh, Jeffrey is very eligible. But he is not in Lord Cardiff's league. I must say, Chastity, I am most agreeably surprised at your resourcefulness," murmured Merrill.

Chastity felt heat rise in her face, feeling a bit defensive on Jeffrey's behalf. "His lordship and I shared the gig for barely ten minutes, Merrill."

"I do hope that you put the time to good use."

Chastity was unable to make the retort that she wished because they had come up to the rest of the party. She settled for giving her friend a slight pinch, and Merrill laughed.

She then slipped free from Chastity and held out her hand to Lord Cardiff. "My lord, I am glad that you are able to join us. I can't think why none of us had this delightful thought earlier, for it has brought you into our midst."

"You are most kind, Lady Peters," said Lord Cardiff, taking her hand and bowing.

The impromptu picnic was an unqualified success. Very nearly an hour was whiled away. Once, Chastity saw Lord Cardiff take his watch out of his pocket. As he replaced the timepiece, he chanced to meet her gaze. He gave her a reassuring smile.

Chastity exerted herself to be pleasant and sociable, but all the while her thoughts remained fixed on the destroyed study. It still bothered her that such a terrible thing had actually happened in her home.

Mr. Halston leaned close to Chastity, ostensibly to pour another glass of wine for her. He said quietly, "Is Lady Mackleby recovering all right from her illness, Chastity?"

Chastity's startled gaze flew to his face. For an instant she did not know what he was talking about. "Oh! Oh, yes, she is; thank you!"

Mr. Halston looked at her more closely. "Chastity, what is troubling you? You have several times fallen silent. I thought that perhaps you were still concerned for Lady Mackleby. But that is obviously not the case."

"Have I seemed inordinately distant? I do apologize! Pray do not regard it. It is all the fault of the chef. He is very temperamental these days, but I daresay I shall iron out our little differences," said Chastity quickly.

Mr. Halston regarded her steadily. His expression became distant. "As you say, Miss Cummings."

Chastity instantly regretted the coolness that had sprung up, but with Jeffrey's unanswered proposal still hanging between them, she thought it best not to make an overture. She did not want to lead Jeffrey to believe that she would accept his suit.

Shortly thereafter, the party started the return to Chester. In the lane they came across Mr. Salyer, who was just then returning from the village and had turned aside to meet them when he had glimpsed their coming.

When Chastity entered the manor, she looked quickly around. All was peaceful. Nothing seemed out of the ordinary. Henry emerged from the billiards room when he heard the noise of his guests' return. He greeted them all affably and inquired how the expedition had gone. During the explanations, his lordship met his sister's anxious gaze. He shook his head slightly and smiled. Chastity interpreted that to mean that the study had been put back to rights as nearly as possible and that nothing was to be said to their guests.

It was close to being time to dress for dinner, and all separated to go upstairs. Mrs. Dabney was apparently feeling much better, for she joined the company for dinner. Lady Mackleby, however, took dinner in her rooms.

After such a traumatic afternoon, Chastity found the evening rather flat. There was the usual conversation and cardplaying. After coffee she was glad enough to say good night to everyone and go up to bed.

Chapter Seventeen

Though Chastity did go to bed, she did not fall asleep immediately. She stared up into the canopy above her head. The brocaded bed curtains could be drawn at night to protect the sleeper from drafts, but Chastity usually left one curtain slightly open so that she could see the fire if it was still burning. Shadows from the firelight played over the rosettes and vines carved into the headboard.

A small table beside the bed held Chastity's candle and flint. Her books were tumbled across the tabletop. She had read for a short time before snuffing the candle and sliding under the covers.

Chastity was just drifting off to sleep when in the distance a dog began to bark. Another chimed in, howling, then the third. Chastity pulled a pillow over her head, but it only muffled the noise.

"I would like to strangle those little brutes," she muttered, thumping her pillow and trying to get comfortable again. Since the grand ball when Mrs. Webster had demonstrated that her pugs could be trusted, Chastity had rescinded her ban against having the dogs in the house. Now she heartily wished that she had insisted that they be sent back to the kennels.

The howling lessened, almost dying away, then crescendoed again.

Chastity gave up. It was easier simply to get up than to lie tossing and turning and becoming angrier and angrier. She reached out for the flint and lit her candle. The bedroom lightened, long shadows flickering across the walls. She had finished the last book that she had on her bedside table. Chastity decided to go down to the library to find a new selection.

Chastity threw back the bedclothes and reached for her wrapper. She belted the robe tightly around her small waist. Shielding her candle flame with her palm, Chastity cautiously eased open the door, hardly daring to breathe when it softly creaked. The hall remained quiet. She sped swiftly down the hall, her bare feet soundless on the carpet.

On the stairs, she moved more cautiously with one hand on the smooth balustrade as she felt her way down. Suddenly, a stair creaked loud underfoot. She froze instinctively, her heart pounding. Straining her ears, she could detect nothing out of the ordinary disturbing the silent dark.

It struck her as amusing that she was reacting much as a housebreaker must, and on a breathless laugh she continued her descent. At the bottom of the stairs she turned right, the candlelight glinting dully on the metal of the suit of armor as she passed it. She traversed the deserted great hall, her figure reflecting eerily in the huge mirror, and went through the door to the private hall. She walked quickly to the double doors of the library and soundlessly turned the knob. She went into the darkened room, holding her candle high.

Moonlight filtered through a part in the drawn draperies so that even without her candle Chastity would have had no difficulty in making out the placement of the furniture. A massive oak library table dominated the center of the room. Chairs of a bygone age, with wooden arms and carved backs and red velvet cushions, were placed around the table. Without needing to look, Chastity knew that the walls were graced with floor-to-ceiling bookshelves and between them hung several gilt-framed portraits of ancestors and bucolic scenes. The bust of a grim-faced predecessor stood in the darkened corner.

Chastity set her flickering candle on the library table. The shadows danced and something seemed to move across the bust. Chastity looked quickly, her heart thumping a little, but she saw nothing untoward.

Then as her gaze became more focused, she perceived the

figure of a man in shirt and breeches watching her from the shadows of the room. He was near the door that gave directly onto Henry's study. Chastity gave a frightened gasp and started to turn, to run.

The man moved swiftly. With two bounds he was beside her. A hard palm clamped over her mouth, stifling the scream that rose in her throat. He yanked her back against him, pinning her against him with his arms. Chastity twisted frantically in his tight hold. His hand shifted slightly, and she sank her teeth into this thumb, drawing the salt of blood.

With a smothered oath, his grasp slackened. Chastity yanked herself loose and fled. Before she had reached the door, she heard the man coming up swiftly behind her. A hard blunt object crashed down on the back of her head. Chastity sprawled forward, falling against the wall beside the open doorway.

Dazed, she struggled to sit up. She put her hand up to her head, where she could already feel the beginnings of a swelling egg. She dimly realized that she was no longer alone with her attacker, that there were two men fighting with one another almost within arm's distance.

Suddenly, one threw the other against the wall. The thrown man cried aloud in pain. His assailant spun around, leaped through the open door, and fled through the hall.

The other man got up and stumbled toward the doorway. One hand was clamped against his shoulder.

Looking up just as he crossed in front of a shaft of moonlight, Chastity recognized him. "L . . . lord Cardiff!" she said hoarsely.

Lord Cardiff stopped short, as though in surprise. He swayed slightly, then dropped to one knee. With his good arm, he supported Chastity's shoulders. "Miss Cummings! Are you quite all right?"

"Yes; at least . . ." Chastity ran her tongue over her dry lips. "My head hurts abominably."

"I am sorry. I was not close enough to prevent him from hitting you," said Lord Cardiff. He sounded tense, frustrated, as he glanced again into the deeply shadowed deserted hall. "Damn! I almost had him!"

Suddenly, another figure loomed in the doorway. "Lord Cardiff! And Chastity!"

"Oh, Jeffrey," said Chastity, on something that sounded like a sob.

Lord Cardiff rose swiftly to his feet. "Mr. Halston, you are in good time! Pray see to Miss Cummings!" He left swiftly, running down the hall in the direction that the unknown man had taken.

Mr. Halston helped Chastity to her feet. With his arm around her waist to support her, he led her to a settee. "I suppose that I may well imagine what has gone on before my arrival," he said stiffly. "I am disappointed in you, Chastity."

"Pray do not be an idiot, Jeffrey!" begged Chastity. She held her pounding head in her hands.

"Are you denying that I have discovered you tête-à-tête with Lord Cardiff?" asked Mr. Halston angrily.

"It was no such thing!" exclaimed Chastity crossly. "Which you would realize if you would but use your head!"

"Why are you holding your head like that? Here, let me see." Mr. Halston moved the candle closer and explored her head with gentle fingers. He withdrew his hand. In a very different voice, he said, "You are bleeding! What happened, Chastity? Did Lord Cardiff hurt you?"

"Of course not! It was that other man—the one that surprised me," said Chastity. "The one that Lord Cardiff was fighting with."

"I do not perfectly understand. Perhaps you should start at the beginning," said Mr. Halston.

Chastity told him a somewhat garbled story about picking up a book from the bookshelf, of being attacked and hit on the head, of Lord Cardiff appearing like magic, the scuffle between the two men, of the other's escape and Jeffrey's own appearance.

While she was talking, Mr. Halston had gotten out his handkerchief and soaked it in wine from a decanter. He pressed it against her wounded head, which made her wince. He also got her a glass of wine and made her drink it.

"It is Madeira! I don't like Madeira," said Chastity fretfully.

"Drink it anyway. You will feel better after sustaining such a shock," said Mr. Halston, putting the glass to her lips and supporting her head with his other hand.

Chastity obediently swallowed. She choked and gasped, tears springing to her eyes. She clutched Mr. Halston's lapel. "I feel so vile, Jeffrey."

"I am not at all surprised. We must get you up to your bed, so that your maid can minister to you," said Mr. Halston, setting aside the empty wineglass. He helped her to her feet, keeping his arms about her for support. "Can you stand, Chastity?"

"Of course I can," said Chastity, even though her head was spinning.

"You are brave, sweetheart, but I think a bit less than truthful," said Mr. Halston. There was a thread of laughter in his voice.

Suddenly, a candle appeared in the doorway, held up over the head of a newcomer. Mrs. Webster peered at Chastity and her companion, a slightly shocked expression on her face. "My dear Chastity! And Mr. Halston!"

"It is not at all as it appears, madame," said Mr. Halston quickly. His arms were still around Chastity, and he was aware that his assurance was less than convincing.

"How very shocking, to be sure!" exclaimed Mrs. Webster, completely unheeding. Her expression was distressed as she drew her wrapper more firmly about her throat.

"Aunt Serena, what are you doing here?" asked Chastity.

"My pugs began barking, and I came down to see what was disturbing my dear doggies," said Mrs. Webster. "Oh, Chastity, this is so indiscreet of you. Anyone at all might come upon your little clandestine rendezvous."

"We are not meeting clandestinely, ma'am, I assure you!" exclaimed Mr. Halston.

Mrs. Webster waved her hand at him. "Yes, yes! I quite understand! You are *not* having a clandestine tryst with my niece.

Very good of you, sir." Lowering her voice and putting her hand up to shield her mouth, she said in a loud whisper, "But truly, dear Chastity, it would have been far better to have asked me for the use of my salon, where you could have been quite, quite private!"

"Mrs. Webster, this is not a clandestine tryst or rendezvous or tête-à-tête!" exclaimed Mr. Halston forcibly. He had had no difficulty at all in overhearing the lady's words.

"No, of course it isn't. Who said that it was? How unfortunate that I came by just at this fragile moment. I do apologize," said Mrs. Webster.

Chastity was embarrassed. She could feel the tension radiating from Jeffrey Halston, and she felt that she really could not bear to meet his gaze just then. "I am going up to bed," she announced. She did not know whether she felt more like crying or laughing. It was such a ridiculous, awkward situation.

"I shall help you up the stairs," said Mr. Halston, taking her elbow.

"No, Jeffrey, I rather think not," said Chastity, pulling away. She swayed slightly without his support, and he caught her arm, steadying her.

"I do not think that you can mange on your own," he said.

"Really, sir! Would you set all of the tongues wagging? Most certainly you will not escort my niece to her room!" said Mrs. Webster, her eyes widening with outrage.

"You will go with us to light the way, Mrs. Webster. It will all be perfectly decorous then," said Mr. Halston reasonably.

Mrs. Webster was uncertain. "Oh. Well, perhaps that will be all right."

"It will be of immense help, ma'am," said Mr. Halston. "I do not wish Chastity to stumble on the stairs in the dark."

"No, we mustn't have that," declared Mrs. Webster, at once convinced. "Very well, then. Come along, my dears. And the next time that you wish to indulge in a romantic tryst, you really must use my salon." Holding her candle up high she led the way up the stairs.

"You mustn't pay attention to what my aunt says," said Chastity, flustered. "She is quite shatterbrained."

"Actually, once I had gotten over my initial embarrassment, I rather enjoyed her assumption," said Mr. Halston.

Chastity's eyes flew to his face. In the shadows, it was difficult to make out his expression, but she thought that he was smiling. "You are laughing," she accused.

"Am I? I was not aware of it," said Mr. Halston gravely.

They arrived outside Chastity's bedroom door. He raised her hand to his lips. "You are a sweetheart, Chastity," he murmured.

Color flew into Chastity's face. She backed away and fumbled for the door handle. Mr. Halston reached around her and opened the door. "Thank you," said Chastity and entered her bedroom. She closed the door with a snap.

Mrs. Webster had watched the byplay with approval. "That is just the way to handle her, sir. You will not find another like my niece. She is very well bred, you know."

"Yes, I am quite aware of it, ma'am," said Mr. Halston, humor lacing his voice.

Chapter Eighteen

The breakfast room was empty, with the exception of the butler, when Chastity entered. She was rather glad to be the first downstairs. She had wakened early with a sense of wellbeing that seemed odd after the shocking event of the night before. Chastity really had no idea why she felt so well, except that she had slept dreamlessly after returning to her bedroom. She was loath to have her peace spoiled by the inevitable tensions among her houseguests.

Tall, narrow windows shed pale sunlight across the mahogany breakfast table laden with covered dishes. It appeared quite warm out, she thought. However, the sunshine was deceptive. The chill of morning penetrated her long-sleeved muslin gown, and she drew up over her slim shoulders a Kashmir shawl bordered in red and gold.

"Shall I serve you, miss?" asked the butler.

"That won't be necessary, Wilkins. I shall do very well for myself," said Chastity.

"Very good, miss." The butler exited the breakfast room.

Chastity seated herself in a high-backed chair and lifted the silver covers from the dishes. Small clouds of steam rose, enticing her with fragrant aromas. There were kippers and eggs, veal and fish, and an assortment of breads, cheeses, and marmalades.

The door opened, and Chastity looked up as she was transferring some of the veal to her plate.

Lord Cardiff entered. He glanced around the empty room,

then smiled at Chastity. There was warmth in his eyes. "May I join you?"

"Of course, my lord," said Chastity graciously.

Chastity and Lord Cardiff spoke commonplace pleasantries for several minutes while they breakfasted. Then Lord Cardiff brought the conversation around to the incident in the library.

"Miss Cummings, I have been feeling very guilty. I want to apologize to you for leaving you the way that I did," he said.

"I completely understand, my lord. Did you catch up to the housebreaker?" asked Chastity.

"I did not, unfortunately," said Lord Cardiff, a crease appearing between his well-shaped brows. His mouth tightened. "The man knew exactly where he was going."

"I haven't yet seen my brother to tell him about it," said Chastity. "He will naturally be greatly disturbed over this further incident."

"I have already seen Lord Cummings. He agrees with me that we must have help in bringing these ruffians to account, especially in view of what happened to you, Miss Cummings," said Lord Cardiff. He gently laid his hand over hers. "Indeed, that was my primary concern."

Chastity blushed. "That is very good of you, my lord," she said quietly.

Lord Cardiff smiled. He lifted her hand and carried it to his lips.

The door opened, and Mr. Halston entered. He stopped stock-still at the picture presented to him, astonishment on his face. Blushing even more vividly, Chastity snatched her hand away from Lord Cardiff.

Lord Cardiff glanced toward Mr. Halston. His expression became rueful. He rose from the table. "Pray excuse me, Miss Cummings, Mr. Halston. I think that I shall step upstairs."

Mr. Halston held the door for his lordship. Then he closed it with a snap.

Chastity had risen, ready to quit the breakfast room, as well. She had regained her composure. "Good morning, Mr. Halston. I trust that you rested well?"

"Very well, thank you," said Mr. Halston with an edge to his voice. He advanced toward the table.

Chastity gestured toward the table. "We are serving ourselves this morning, as you see. If there is anything that you would like but it has not been brought to the table, pray let Wilkins know."

"What I should like to know is why Lord Cardiff is allowed to be on such intimate terms with you," said Mr. Halston shortly.

"I beg your pardon?" asked Chastity, looking at him with mingled surprise and affront.

"Pray do not look so innocent, Chastity! I saw how you were looking at each other. I saw how he was making love to you over the covers!" exclaimed Mr. Halston heatedly.

"Lord Cardiff was not making love to me! He was merely expressing his devotion and concern for me," said Chastity. "Now, Mr. Halston, you will excuse me!" She swept past him, her head held high.

Mr. Halston caught her arm. "Perhaps you were not quite forthcoming with me last night, after all. Perhaps there was more to your being down in the library alone with his lordship than I was told. Tell me, Chastity, have you set your cap for Cardiff? Are you keeping me hanging for an answer while you see if you can snare a better catch?"

Color flew into Chastity's face. She shook herself free. "How dare you!"

"Tell me the truth, Chastity," demanded Mr. Halston.

"Even if I did have feelings for Lord Cardiff, Mr. Halston, what business would it be of yours? You have no claim on me whatsoever, nor any right to question me on this or any other topic!" exclaimed Chastity.

The door opened again. Henry came in accompanied by Sir Roger. His lordship greeted them cheerfully. "Oh, good morning, Chastity! How are you, Halston?"

Mr. Halston nodded. His expression was closed. "My lord, Sir Roger. Pray excuse me."

"You are not going, surely! Why, the kippers haven't even been touched," Henry said.

"You must hold me excused, my lord. I find that I do not have the appetite for kippers this morning," said Mr. Halston. He strode out of the breakfast room.

"A testy young fellow," remarked Sir Roger, going to the table and taking a chair. "I shall take a few of those kippers, my lord. And some of the eggs, as well, I think. Ah, there is ale, too!"

Henry looked at his sister. Her color was high, and her eyes held a flash of anger. He made a fairly accurate deduction, but he chose not to ask the obvious question. He picked up the teapot and poured a cup. "Here you are, Chastity. I trust that you shall stay and sip your tea with us."

Chastity hesitated. Then she nodded and sat back down. She glanced significantly at her brother. "Of course I shall. Henry, I was talking to Lord Cardiff a few moments ago. He mentioned that he had seen you already this morning."

"Yes, he did. We had quite a chat. I trust that all is well with you this morning?" Henry asked.

"I am perfectly well, thank you," said Chastity.

"If you two are going to talk in riddles, I wish that you would drop a few hints for me," complained Sir Roger.

"I apologize, sir. It is very bad of us," said Chastity.

Sir Roger inclined his head. His gaze transferred to Henry. "I have something for you to think on, my lord, but it is scarcely a riddle. I have a few reservations concerning your young friend Salyer."

Henry raised his brows. "I am surprised, Sir Roger! I would not have thought that Gabriel Salyer would be so gauche as to offend you."

Sir Roger waved his hand. "No, no! It is nothing like that. Merely that I would like to pass on a bit of advice to him out of my own large experience, but I do not know him well enough to broach the subject."

"Ah, so you wish me to become your go-between," Henry said, somewhat amused.

"Precisely, my lord. Yesterday when I returned from my ride, I came into the house through the side door. I was walking down the hall toward the front stairs when I saw Mrs. Dabney and young Salyer emerge from your study," said Sir Roger.

Henry straightened in his chair. "You begin to interest me profoundly, Sir Roger."

Sir Roger turned to Chastity. "Forgive me, my dear. It is very bad *ton* for me to speak so openly in front of you. However, I feel that you should know as well, since you must deal with all the idiocyncrasies of your houseguests."

"Pray do not hesitate on my account, Sir Roger," said Chastity quickly. "I promise you that my calm shall remain unshaken."

"No, you are not the hysterical sort," agreed Sir Roger. He turned back to Henry. "It appeared to me that young Salyer and Mrs. Dabney were engaged in a heated argument. I could not hear what was being said, for they were speaking too low. But I could not mistake the signs, my lord. It appeared to be a lovers' quarrel."

"Gabriel and Mrs. Dabney!" exclaimed Chastity, astonished. "Why, they scarcely notice one another!"

"Perhaps they have become better acquainted," Henry said.

Sir Roger gave a short bark of laughter. "That is very good, my lord!"

Henry regarded the old gentleman with some impatience. "What is it that you would have me tell Gabriel Salyer, sir?"

"Only this, my lord. I speak from a vast experience. A woman such as Mrs. Dabney—beautiful, widowed, but only comfortably situated—is often on the lookout for a suitable *parti*. Young Salyer may be getting in deeper than he realizes or wants," said Sir Roger.

Henry was frowning into space. "Yes, he very well could be." His attention returned to the elderly gentleman. "Thank you, Sir Roger. I shall certainly give this matter some consideration."

Sir Roger nodded. He placed his napkin on the table beside

his plate. "I shall leave you now, my lord. Miss Cummings, your most obedient."

Chastity murmured something polite, a smile fixed on her lips as Sir Roger left the room. She turned immediately to her brother. "Henry, did you hear?"

He nodded, his lids halfway down over his eyes. "Indeed I did. They were seen emerging from my study on the day that it was destroyed. It makes one wonder precisely what Mrs. Dabney and Gabriel Salyer were doing, does it not? I am not at all convinced that Sir Roger interpreted that little scene correctly."

"Henry, Gabriel returned to Chester at the same time that Lord Cardiff and I and the excursion to the abbey did," said Chastity. "Isn't it a bit odd that he was seen here before we ever arrived? And if you will recall, Mrs. Dabney remained behind that morning because she woke with a sick headache."

"It is all very interesting," Henry said.

"What are you going to do?" asked Chastity.

Henry looked over at her. "Do? Why, nothing. At least, not for the moment. I haven't seen my way clear yet."

The door opened, and several of their other houseguests began to come into the breakfast room. Chastity looked at her brother, knowing that their confidences were at an end. Certainly the time would hang rather heavy on her hands until the next opportunity that she could seize to speak privately to her brother. Chastity was not at all satisfied with the way things had been left.

Her gaze fell on Sir Roger's plate as Mr. Bottler pushed it aside and sat down. "Do you know, Henry, Sir Roger did not eat at all well this morning," she commented.

"I wouldn't fret over Sir Roger, Miss Cummings," said Mr. Bottler with a hearty chuckle. He started in on the mountain of food that was piled high on his own plate. "That gentleman strikes me as being as tough as old shoe leather. He'll outlast us all, no doubt."

"Quite," said Chastity.

Despite her best efforts, Chastity was not able to speak privately to Henry again. When the evening came, she was feeling frustrated and annoyed. Every little thing seemed designed to irritate her. There was nothing remarkable about the day itself. It could have been pleasant enough if her mind had not been preoccupied with thoughts about Mrs. Dabney and Gabriel Salyer. Chastity watched them closely, but she could not detect any sort of warmth or animation between them.

Of course, there was also Mr. Halston. That gentleman had avoided her all morning and most of the afternoon. Chastity was perfectly content with the gentleman's obvious snub. Of course she was. She had been very much angered and affronted by his extraordinary liberty in speaking to her in the way that he had. For her part, she had behaved with perfect dignity all day, addressing him civilly only when she was pressed to do so by circumstance. Otherwise, Chastity was quite content to let Mr. Halston indulge in his sulks.

That evening, another large soiree had been arranged. All the neighborhood had attended, as usual. Chastity never failed for partners for the dance floor, nor for escort to and from the refreshment room. Chastity took note that not once had Mr. Halston begged for her hand in a set although she wished that he would dare. It would give her a sense of satisfaction to deny him, she thought.

However, when the opportunity seemed about to arise, Chastity realized that she really did not wish to speak to Mr. Halston at all. She was with Mr. Poplin when she saw Mr. Halston begin to make his way toward her across the crowded room. Chastity turned to her companion and requested that he escort her to Lady Mackleby's side, pleading the beginnings of a ruinous headache.

Mr. Poplin at once expressed himself most willing to be of service. "I am all sympathy, dear Miss Cummings. I cannot bear the thought of you suffering. I do hope that you will soon recover. It is undoubtedly the fault of the heat, for I feel it, too. I do not know why it is that we insist on roaring fires and bunches of blazing candles at such a frightful squeeze. The air becomes too close to breathe."

"Yes, yes! Pray, may we find my aunt, sir?" said Chastity, scarcely curbing her impatience.

"I know precisely where to find Lady Mackleby," said Mr. Halston smoothly. He took Chastity's hand and slipped it into the crook of his elbow, holding her fingers trapped in his when she would have pulled free. "I shall take good care of Miss Cummings, Mr. Poplin."

"Oh, in that case!" Mr. Poplin bowed to Chastity, his hand to his breast. "I am your most obedient servant, Miss Cummings. You may call upon me at any time."

Chastity was annoyed with the gentleman. "Thank you, Mr. Poplin! I shall certainly remember that!"

Mr. Halston and Chastity walked away. He glanced down at her. "Poplin is a very good sort of fellow."

"He is a twit," said Chastity roundly.

"Yes, I can understand why you must think so," said Mr. Halston, laughter lacing his voice, though his expression was grave.

"And you are an unprincipled opportunist," said Chastity swiftly. "You just walked up and commandeered me as though I were a frigate!"

"I perceive that you are still angered," observed Mr. Halston.

Chastity threw an expressive glance up at him. "Indeed! And what has caused you to draw that conclusion?" She suddenly realized that he was guiding her out of the ballroom. "You said that you knew where my aunt is, Mr. Halston!"

"So I do, Miss Cummings. However, I did not say that I was taking you to her," said Mr. Halston. "In fact, I am escorting you to the salon, where we may be private. And you will not create a scene, for you would spurn to behave anything like a spoiled beauty such as your sister-in-law, Mrs. Cummings."

"You are shameless, Mr. Halston!" exclaimed Chastity, very much annoyed that he knew her so well.

When they entered the salon and Mr. Halston closed the door, Chastity looked at him with a great deal of annoyance. She had taken control of her initial anger. She was determined that she would not betray herself again into unseeming conduct or speech. The quicker that the interview was over, the better she would like it. Very coolly, she said, "Well, Mr. Halston?"

Mr. Halston looked at her with a steady expression. "Chastity, I love you," he said.

Chastity stared at him. She felt as though the breath had been knocked out of her. She had been set for a siege, and he had come at her from a completely unexpected direction. She tried to speak and had to clear her throat more than once. "What . . . what did you say?"

"I said that I love you," said Mr. Halston somberly. He watched the expressions flit across her face.

Chastity shook her head quickly. All of her former outrage had dissipated like so much smoke. The emotions she felt now were almost suffocating. She half turned from him so that he could no longer see her face. In a strangled voice that did not sound like her own, she said, "Oh, do not say so! It is Mirabelle that you love."

Mr. Halston took hold of her elbow, turning her around and forcing her to face him. "No, Chastity. I love you more than life itself. I always have."

Chastity stared at him. Her eyes roved over his expression, trying to discern the truth. She was totally confused. She shook her head again, as though to clear her tumbling thoughts. "I don't understand you, Jeffrey! You told me that you loved Mirabelle and that a part of you died with her. You said that you could not offer your heart to me because of what you had felt for Mirabelle."

"I did love Mirabelle, Chastity. But not with the same passion that I feel for you," said Mr. Halston.

"I have thought that you cared nothing for me," said Chastity. When he shook his head, she made a helpless gesture. "What else could I believe? Ever since you arrived, you have been so cold and indifferent."

"No! The truth is that when I saw you again, I was almost overcome by the power of my emotions. In those scarce moments before you turned to greet me, I struggled to regain my composure so that I would not make a fool of myself," said Mr.

Halston. "I dared not trust my feelings. I thought that they must be only an echo of the past."

Chastity searched his face again. She had to ask, if only for the satisfaction of quieting the questions in her own heart. "And later? When you made that outrageous proposal to me and implied that I had been your calf-love?"

Mr. Halston sighed. "Forgive me, my darling. But in many ways what I felt for you as a feckless young man was calf-love compared to my feelings for you now. I have pretended a coolness toward you that was never real. I see now that I have made a grave mistake."

He released her and took a quick turn about the room. "Then when I thought that you and Cardiff . . ."

Chastity watched him in an agony of suspense. At length Mr. Halston stopped and took hold of a chair back with tightened fingers. She recognized at once the tension in his stance and the intensity of his gaze. This was the face of the man that she had seen six years before, the man who had pledged his eternal love to her and whom she had spurned. Her heart began thumping painfully.

"Chastity, six years ago, when I realized that you would have none of me, I was devastated. I turned to someone who did love me. That was Mirabelle Sweeney." Mr. Halston shrugged with an air of regret. "In the despair of the moment, I offered for her and she accepted. I told you a portion of the truth, at least. A part of me did die with her. Mirabelle loved me unstintingly, without regret and without demands. I could scarcely do less than to grow to love and admire and respect her. Can you understand that?"

"Yes," whispered Chastity. She was uncertain where all of this was leading, but she found that she could not have stopped him whatever her feelings. She had to hear, to know, what had gone before.

"My wife was a rare woman. I regret that I could never be the husband that she truly deserved," said Mr. Halston heavily.

Chastity felt tears come to her eyes. "Oh, Jeffrey."

Shockingly, he laughed. It was a harsh sound. "Pray spare

me, Chastity. I haven't asked for your pity, but only for your understanding. If you must pity anyone, pity Mirabelle, for I was a bad husband to her."

"I am sure that you were not, Jeffrey," said Chastity quickly.

He smiled, rather wearily. "Chastity, you do not understand. I was faithful to her in all ways but in my heart. My heart—my greatest love—was reserved for you. And Mirabelle knew that, though I tried to hide it from her."

Chastity turned away from him, pressing her hands close against her cheeks. She found his confession very hard to bear, for every word he spoke was like a knife twisting in her heart. She blamed herself. She had sent Jeffrey away. She had introduced Mirabelle Sweeney to him. It was she who had been instrumental in creating such a terribly unhappy outcome.

How odd, though! Jeffrey spoke quite matter-of-factly about circumstances that to her seemed tragic. His life had been blighted, while Mirabelle's had been stunted and foreshortened. It did not bear close scrutiny, Chastity thought somberly.

"I am so very, very sorry, Jeffrey. I would change it all if I only could," said Chastity, forcing herself to turn around and face him.

Mr. Halston shrugged. "Why? We each have a destiny in this life, Chastity. We cannot escape it or change it. Are you thinking of Mirabelle? She of all people would tell you that such sentiments are foolish. She did not think of herself with self-pity. No, she accepted all that she was offered and made the best that she could out of it. As I said, she was a remarkable woman."

"Why did you propose a marriage of convenience to me, Jeffrey? Was it for revenge?" asked Chastity.

"No, of course not! How could you even think such a thing?" exclaimed Mr. Halston.

"You are so different, so changed," said Chastity slowly. "And now that I know about Mirabelle, I thought perhaps that—"

"That I blamed you?" asked Mr. Halston. He suddenly smiled. "You did not force me to offer for Mirabelle, nor influence her to accept my suit. We made our own choices, Chastity, just as you did six years ago."

Chastity flushed. "I am sorry, Jeffrey. I could not have married you then. I hoped that you would come to understand why one day. I thought that you did when you wed. Now I understand how wrong I was to think so."

Mr. Halston nodded. "Yes, for I turned to Mirabelle for solace. I was foolish to pretend that I no longer wanted you."

"Then why, Jeffrey? If that is true, why did you couch your proposal in such a way?" asked Chastity.

"Because it had been my ardency that caused you to refuse me six years ago. You were not used to a man's passion, and my attentions frightened you," said Mr. Halston.

"That is true enough, I suppose," said Chastity slowly, not liking to admit it, but honest enough to look back at herself as she had been. She had been a naive girl, straight out of the country, gauche and shy in company. Her aunt, Lady Mackleby, had whipped her into shape, and she had debuted with some success. But inside, she had remained that unsophisticated maid.

That memorable spring, Jeffrey Halston had been the first and most trusted friend that she had made in London. It had been shocking to her when he had begun to court her with such intensity. Her trust in him had necessarily suffered, for it could not stand when he tried to make love to her. She had rejected him without even having the opportunity of exploring what feelings might have been developing toward him. She had rejected him out of self-preservation.

Chastity looked questioningly at him. "And so your proposal was deliberately couched in almost businesslike terms, because you thought that I might otherwise reject you just as I did before?"

"I thought such an approach might meet with more favor than if I was to show you just how strongly I still adore you," said Mr. Halston. "As I told you, I was relying on your level-headedness that you would make the decision that I was hoping you would."

"Am I such a cold fish?" wondered Chastity aloud.

"I don't know. Are you?"

Suddenly, he was right beside her, his breath warm on her startled, upturned face. He bent his head and kissed her, taking his time. Chastity stood quite still, as much from delight as from shock. Then of their own volition, her hands slid up around his neck.

When Mr. Halston raised his head, he smiled down at her tenderly. "I don't think you are precisely a cold fish," he said.

Chastity colored up to her hairline. She whisked herself out of reach, putting a chair between them. "You took advantage of me, sir."

Mr. Halston laughed. "I shan't comment on that!"

"So I should hope," said Chastity primly.

Chapter Nineteen

M r. Halston sobered suddenly. "Chastity, I do not know what is going on in this house. Whatever it is, I know that Cardiff and Lord Cummings are involved, and that there is some danger attached to it. I wish that I had the right to protect you, for I have seen for myself that you are at risk."

"I was foolish, Jeffrey. I should have realized, after what happened to Henry's study, that it was not a particularly clever notion to traipse about the house at night," said Chastity. "I will not put myself into such a position again, believe me."

"What happened to his lordship's study?" asked Mr. Halston quickly.

"Oh, I forgot that you did not know! Henry's study was destroyed the day that we all went to the Radfords' breakfast party," said Chastity. "Jeffrey, it was appalling! Everything that Henry held most dear was shattered or torn apart. Someone had tried to pry open his desk, too."

"Can you tell me what is afoot? I may perhaps be of some small help," said Mr. Halston.

Chastity shook her head. "I am sorry, I cannot. It is not that I do not trust you, Jeffrey. You mustn't think that! I simply do not understand what is happening. Henry and Lord Cardiff seem agreed that ordinary housebreakers destroyed the study. But I am not so certain of that."

"No, I should say not!" said Mr. Halston, frowning. "A housebreaker would not return to the same house twice, for fear of the occupants having been put on their guard."

"Yes, so I think, too," said Chastity. "Yet it certainly seems

that Lord Cardiff was lying in wait for just such a return
visit."

"All of which gives me a fair notion that there is something
very ugly and very unusual taking place during your fine
house party, Chastity," said Mr. Halston, his frown deepening.

"Quite," said Chastity. "I admit that I am not at all comfortable with the notion. It is the not knowing that is the
worst."

"I shall keep a close eye on you," said Mr. Halston. "And I
will also begin to take a closer interest in what each of your
guests is about."

"Thank you, Jeffrey. I admit that I shall feel more at ease
knowing that," said Chastity with a wavering smile.

"It will be my pleasure to serve you, ma'am," said Mr. Halston, making a short bow. He smiled when he saw her expression lift. He reached out to cup her chin in his fingers. He bent
forward and kissed her again. Very softly, he said, "I believe
that my previous proposal must necessarily undergo a few re-
visions. I will leave you to imagine what they might be."

Chastity colored up, and he laughed again.

Soon after, Chastity and Mr. Halston returned circum-
spectly to the ballroom, strolling decorously into the company
and exchanging quiet pleasantries. But for the remainder of
the night, Chastity felt as though she were walking on air. Her
heart was singing, and all was suddenly right in her world.

The soiree ended in the early morning hours. Chastity tumbled into bed and into a dreamless sleep. She felt that nothing
whatsoever could disturb her equilibrium again.

The next day, she discovered how wrong she was.

The morning progressed as had many others. At breakfast
Lord Winthrop and Sir Edward Greaves agreed that they
would go out shooting. None of the other gentlemen cared to
join them, so that it was just the two who left for the day's
hunting. Mrs. Webster announced that one of her dear doggies
had the colic and that she meant to spend the remainder of the
morning physicing her pet. This program scarcely appealed to

anyone else, and the elderly lady was allowed to exit without a single offer to keep her company.

Mr. Halston and Chastity spent the morning together, conversing about everything that came into their heads. Chastity had no idea where the rest of her houseguests were, nor did she greatly care.

It was just before luncheon when the sounds of a terrible argument drew everyone within hearing to the drawing room. A woman's shrill voice rose in vicious denouncement.

"What in the world!" exclaimed Lady Mackleby.

Chastity pushed open the door and went in, followed by most of her houseguests.

Henry and Lord Cardiff were already in the drawing room. Mrs. Dabney faced them. It was she who was screaming invectives, which were directed at Mr. Salyer. The gentleman stood, a shocked expression on his face, cornered against the occasional table. The butler and two footmen had hold of the widow's arms.

As the others entered, Henry drew himself up to his full height, roaring, "Enough, woman! I shall not tolerate any more of this. Wilkins, if she utters one more sound, stuff your handkerchief in her mouth!"

"With pleasure, my lord!"

The widow's bosom heaved, and the dagger glance that she threw at Henry spoke volumes. But she apparently believed that his lordship's threat was perfectly serious, for she clamped her lips tightly together.

"Pray take her away. Lock her securely in her room, along with her maid," said Lord Cardiff quietly. "I have already sent for the authorities to come take her to jail."

Those standing in front of the door parted on either side as Mrs. Dabney was led forth by the servants. The beauteous widow's color was high. She did not look left or right, but passed through the stupefied crowd as though she did not see them.

"Well, Salyer?"

Henry's voice was like a whip crack. Nearly everyone

jumped, none more visibly than the gentleman he had addressed. For a second, Mr. Salyer met his lordship's fierce gaze before his own eyes dropped away.

Mr. Salyer sighed. He sagged against the table, the very picture of a man defeated. "It is true. I have been in the employ of the French."

"Gabriel! No!" Merrill exclaimed, her face whitening.

Her brother did not appear to hear her. Very tiredly, he said, "I was being blackmailed by Mrs. Dabney. She threatened to expose me to my creditors. She had somehow gotten hold of all of my notes, you see."

Mr. Salyer looked up suddenly, glancing round the circle of shocked faces. It was as though for the first time he became aware that he had an audience. He flushed deep red. "I had no choice, I tell you! I can offer no more apology than that!"

Mr. Salyer was suddenly thrust backward onto the table. With startled eyes, he stared up, aghast, into Henry's furious face. An ungentle hand gripped his throat. He tried to pry aside his lordship's fingers, without success.

Lord Cummings spoke through bared teeth. "You dared! You dared to play your rotten games in my house!" Fury glittered in his eyes, and his hands tightened. Mr. Salyer began making strangled sounds and flopped helplessly.

Merrill flew to her brother's defense. She tugged unavailingly at the lethal fingers wrapped tight about Gabriel Salyer's throat. "My lord! Pray do not! I beg you not to kill him!"

"Lord Cummings! You must not!" Miss Paige gently exclaimed.

Henry looked up at once. He met her appalled gaze. He let go of Mr. Salyer and straightened. "My apologies. For a moment I was beside myself. When I recall that it was he who hurt Chastity and—but I will say no more!"

Mr. Salyer rolled to the edge of the table and levered himself up until he could support himself on one hand. The other hand massaged his reddened throat, where the cravat had been torn away. Merrill put her arms around him, quietly crying.

"You are a disgrace, Salyer. I pity your parents," Henry said harshly.

"I could do nothing else, I tell you," protested Mr. Salyer in a rasping voice.

Henry's eyes blazed. "I am a magistrate as well as your friend. You could have come to me. I might have helped you."

Mr. Salyer looked up at that, his eyes holding a question. "Would you have helped me, Henry? Would you have believed me?" He made a despairing gesture and shook his head.

"What do you want done with him, my lord?" Henry asked, swinging around toward Lord Cardiff.

"The information I have gathered suggests that Mr. Salyer was drawn into this net late in the game. It is my belief that he has not actually committed treason," said Lord Cardiff. A flicker of a smile touched his lips, though it did not enter his eyes. "There is every reason to believe that he would have done so if he had not been uncovered, however."

"I do not believe it!" cried Merrill passionately.

Mr. Salyer freed himself from his sister's clinging embrace. "Enough, Merrill." He rose to his feet and straightened his shoulders. He appeared strangely dignified in the face of the appalling circumstances. "I place myself in your hands, my lords."

Lord Cardiff glanced at Henry. "You are the magistrate here, my lord. It will be as you decide."

Henry nodded. "Very well. Lord Cardiff has pointed out the only saving grace in this matter, Salyer. For the sake of your family and their honor, I shall release you."

Merrill gave a glad cry. Mr. Salyer looked utterly stunned. Without a word, he turned and walked out of the room much as a man asleep. His sister hurried after him.

"I don't understand anything!" Regina exclaimed.

"Apparently we have been entertaining French spies, my dear," Archie said as he turned an inquiring look on his brother.

Henry nodded, somewhat tiredly. He walked over to Miss Paige and gently urged her to seat herself in a chair. "You have sustained a grave shock, Miss Paige. Forgive me! I allowed my passions to carry me beyond the boundaries of what is acceptable."

Miss Paige shook her head mutely. She cast a single glance up at his lordship, which seemed to satisfy him.

"This is preposterous! Mrs. Dabney and young Salyer! French spies! Why, I cannot believe it!" exclaimed Mr. Bottler.

"Oh, no! No, indeed!" said Mrs. Bottler.

"I can believe anything of that woman. I disliked her from the instant I first set eyes on her," Regina said.

"But, Henry, how has this all come about? How did you discover them?" asked Chastity.

"It was not I, but Cardiff. He was sent here to Chester because Mrs. Dabney had fallen under suspicion some months ago," Henry said. "But no one knew who her contacts might be, nor how she was able to influence certain young men—oh, yes! there are others besides Salyer!—to join her in conspiracy."

"Once I was situated here, it was put about in certain circles that I was a secret courier for Wellington," said Lord Cardiff. "I was supposed to be carrying the plans for the next British campaign to a contact here in England, who unfortunately had fallen ill. Thus my stay at Chester, with a trusted member of the Horse Guards who, incidentally, was said to have one of the most impregnable houses in England."

"Then it was Gabriel Salyer who made such a shambles of your study, Henry?" asked Chastity, looking questioningly at her brother.

"No, that was Mrs. Dabney." It was Lord Cardiff who answered her. "She stayed behind that day, as you will recall, Miss Cummings. Salyer arrived here only after she had finished. Then he rode back out to wait for the return of the riding party."

"I saw young Salyer and Mrs. Dabney come out of Henry's study," said Sir Roger. "I thought that they were having a lovers' quarrel."

Lord Cardiff nodded. "So his lordship informed me, sir. We were able to set a trap for them, then. Lord Cummings let drop, quite inadvertently it seemed, a small tidbit of information to Mrs. Dabney."

Henry flashed a smile. "I remarked that I was the proud owner of two safes at Chester. One was in my study, and the other was in the library."

"Then that was why—" Chastity stopped. She felt a hand fall on her shoulder and looked round quickly, meeting Mr. Halston's somber gaze.

"Did Gabriel and Mrs. Dabney find the bait, my lord?" asked Mr. Halston quietly.

"Yes, they did. There were some very authentic-looking documents in his lordship's safe," said Lord Cardiff. "I watched Salyer take them. I tried to apprehend him, as you know, Mr. Halston; but I failed. However, that was all to the good. Mrs. Dabney did not trust him with the prize, and she hid them away in her trunk. Lord Cummings authorized a search of Mrs. Dabney's rooms this morning and the damning evidence was found."

"No wonder the woman was screeching," remarked Lady Mackleby. Her eyes were bright with interest. "This is better than a play. I am very glad that you invited me to Chester after all, Henry."

Henry bowed. "I am glad that you have found your visit to be entertaining, my lady."

"What I wish to know is how that woman ever managed to worm her way into polite society at all?" asked Regina. "Who is she, really? I cannot believe that we have all the truth. Oh, I know that you have said that she is your cousin, Mr. Bottler, but . . ."

Mr. Bottler looked singularly distressed. "As to that, Mrs. Cummings, I would not say that she is a cousin, precisely. The family connection is a bit removed."

"Oh, yes! Indeed it is!" said Mrs. Bottler, nodding vigorously.

Archie uttered a bark of laughter, but he did not voice his opinion.

"I believe that better than anyone else, I can shed some light on who Mrs. Dabney really is," said Sir Roger. He appeared a little gray.

Henry raised his brows. "Indeed, sir? And who is she?"

Looking very old and very tired, Sir Roger said flatly, "She is my daughter."

Chapter Twenty

"How is this?" asked Henry sharply.

Sir Roger glanced at him. "She is the exact image of her mother. When I first saw her, I thought that I was seeing an apparition. It seemed as though the years had rolled back and I was looking at Marguerite Fontaine again."

"Who was Marguerite Fontaine?" asked Chastity.

"I can answer that," said Lady Mackleby. She glanced at Sir Roger. "There was something that I could not quite recall, until you mentioned that woman's name. Marguerite Fontaine! There was a scandal over her."

Sir Roger nodded. "Yes. She was my mistress. I was married then. I should have known better than to become involved with her. She was an emigré from France—beautiful, vulnerable, helpless. At least, so I thought. When she told me of the babe, she threatened to reveal all to my wife." His lips twisted with a caricature of a smile. "My dear wife, whom I thought would not be able to stand the humiliation. I paid Marguerite Fontaine for her silence."

"She was a schemer and avaricious," said Lady Mackleby. "I never liked her. I always wondered what became of her. No doubt it was a poor ending."

Sir Roger seemed to be locked in the mists of the past. "I had thought myself to be well out of it when Marguerite returned to France." He snapped back to the present and looked around at his fascinated audience. "The woman bled me dry for support of my daughter, until the scandal broke. Then I became free of her blackmail. Marguerite married afterward."

Lady Mackleby expressed surprise. "I have never heard that before."

"It was not generally known, my lady. I knew because I tried to keep contact for the sake of my daughter, but eventually I lost track of them. I didn't know what had happened to her, until I saw her here at Chester," said Sir Roger. His face twisted. "And she is a Bonapartist spy! My God, my sin has reaped an ugly harvest! It killed my wife's trust and has endangered my country."

Henry gently put his hand on the elderly gentleman's shoulder. "Sir Roger, you could not have foreseen what would happen. You are not responsible for Mrs. Dabney's choices, man."

Sir Roger looked up at him. There was a blinded look in his eyes. "I did not know whether to reveal myself to her or not. She is my daughter. I knew it at once. I was tormented by indecision. I did not know what I should do. In the end, I did nothing, coward that I am!"

"It is too late, sir. No possible good could have come out of such a confrontation," Henry said quietly.

"No, indeed. You are too old to survive another terrible scandal, Sir Roger," said Lady Mackleby decisively. "I would not be a bit surprised if the daughter had not turned about to do the same as her mother, given the woman's obvious lack of character. She would have blackmailed you, sir, for her silence. You could not have stood for that."

"No, no, I could not. You are quite right, my lady. I would have blown my brains out, rather," said Sir Roger with conviction.

His suppressed passion was shocking, and the listeners stirred, not knowing where to look anymore. Sir Roger looked around at his audience, and he appeared to shrivel before their eyes. He looked at that moment as though he wished the ground would open up and swallow him.

Mr. Halston cleared his throat. "Sir Roger, if you should like it, I shall be more than happy to bear you company upstairs. You have had a very trying afternoon. Perhaps a brandy in the privacy of your room?"

Chastity cast him a grateful glance. She hadn't known what to say or do.

Sir Roger avoided meeting anyone's eyes. "Yes, yes, thank you, Mr. Halston. I am feeling very tired this afternoon. I should like to lie down." He took Mr. Halston's arm and, leaning heavily upon it, walked slowly out of the room.

When the door had closed behind them, Chastity exclaimed, "Poor Sir Roger! What a nightmare he has endured. It is no wonder that he seemed to be wasting away before our eyes. He was being torn apart by guilt and fear."

"Indeed. And that woman, Mrs. Dabney, was hardly worth such extremes of agony," said Lady Mackleby.

"I wonder how someone like Mrs. Dabney became so well received in society?" said Chastity.

"That is easily enough explained. Her mother was probably shrewd enough to marry respectably, giving a legitimate name to her daughter. The daughter furthered her place in the world when she snared Eric Dabney, who was a well-bred fribble of impeccable lineage," said Lady Mackleby in a tone of deep disapproval. "Eric Dabney and his family would have opened doors to her that would otherwise have been closed. Naturally, no one knew her true background, or otherwise no amount of connections would have done her much good. She would have been barred from the innermost circles if it had ever become known that she was a bastard."

"And she used her connections most adeptly, gaining entrance to influential personages and betraying their confidences," said Lord Cardiff quietly.

Through all of the revelations, Miss Paige had sat petrified. Now she gave a little sob and covered her face with her hands. "I did not know. I knew nothing. How could I have been so ignorant, so blind?"

"Oh, my dear! How could you have known? You had never met her, living in such seclusion as you did," said Chastity, going at once to her knees beside the distraught woman and taking her hands away from her tear-streaked face. "Listen to me, Dru. You are not to blame for any part of this. You were used just like everyone else that she came into contact with. Don't you understand?"

"That is quite true, Miss Paige," said Lord Cardiff, nodding. "You were part of Mrs. Dabney's camouflage. She could excuse much of her busy social activity to others on the grounds that she had an obligation to see to it that her husband's poor, neglected relation was presented to a better society. It worked very well, after a fashion."

"Despicable," uttered Henry. He offered his handkerchief to Miss Paige, which she accepted and began to dry her eyes.

"There is no one here who will condemn you, Miss Paige," said Archie.

"Thank you!" exclaimed Miss Paige gratefully.

"I believe this to be as appropriate a moment as any to make a certain announcement," Henry said. He glanced down at Miss Paige. "If you do not mind it, Miss Paige?"

She looked up at him and gave a wavering smile. "I do not mind, my lord."

Henry held out his hand to her. When she had placed her hand into his, he drew her to her feet to stand beside him. He turned to face the gathering. "As you may have just guessed, I have the honor of announcing that Miss Paige and I are to be wed."

There were exclamations of surprise and even of dismay, but these were tactfully ignored by most. Chastity was astonished at her brother's unexpected announcement. She had been so caught up in her own concerns and what was going forward in the house that she had not paid much attention to her brother's actions. She saw now that she had been blinded also by her assumption that her brother was still satisfied with his bachelor state. However, as she thought back, certain incidents and utterances by her brother or Miss Paige took on a new context.

"Why, Henry, what a deep game you have been playing!" she exclaimed under her breath.

She felt at once foolish and amused that a romance had been carefully launched under her very nose and she had not stumbled onto it. Of course, Henry had moved toward his object in a guarded fashion. She realized that her lack of perception had served him well because her manner had not given anyone reason to suppose that anything of the sort was afoot.

The remaining guests gathered about the newly affianced couple to wish them well. Chastity was one of the first to offer her congratulations to her brother and her prospective sister-in-law. She kissed Miss Paige on the cheek and watched her color up.

"You are most sincerely welcome to the family, Dru," she said, smiling.

"Thank you, Chastity. You are so kind," said Miss Paige quietly. Her gaze slid to a point behind Chastity.

Chastity half turned and saw that Regina was beginning to indulge in a mild fit of hysterics. Archie was standing beside her, red-faced with embarrassment as he attempted to hush his unheeding wife.

"I cannot believe it! Chester is lost to us, Archie, lost! Chastity must have known and not a word did she breathe to me. What shall we do, Archie? What shall we do now?" Regina's loud utterances were beginning to gather strength and attention.

"Excuse me, Dru. I think that I must address this minor contretemps," said Chastity. She moved gracefully away, picking up a large flower-filled vase on her way. Very coolly and deliberately, she turned the vase upside down over her sister-in-law's head.

Water and flowers splashed down over Regina, dousing her head and shoulders. The lady spluttered in shock. A flurry of gasps and quickly stifled laughs passed over the few who witnessed what had happened.

Chastity motioned to the butler and a footman, who had returned some minutes before. "Pray help Mrs. Cummings to her room. She has sustained an unfortunate accident," she said.

"Yes, miss," said the butler impassively. He gestured to the stalwart footman and each of them took an arm, quietly removing the weeping woman from the room.

"I apologize, Miss Paige. I do not know what came over

Regina. She has never put on such a display before. And I had no idea she seriously believed I would inherit the title. Not for the world would I have wished such a scene to have happened during such a happy announcement," said Archie, red-faced with shame.

Henry put his arm around his prospective wife's waist. "I will be in your debt, Archie, were you to remove Regina from Chester," he said.

Archie became even redder. He started to make a stiff bow. "Certainly, Henry, if that is what you wish."

Miss Paige put up her hand, looking up at Lord Cummings. "Pray, my lord, do not send your brother and Mrs. Cummings away on my account! I am to be part of their family now. I do not wish to begin with such ill feelings."

Henry met her pleading eyes. "Very well, my love. It will be just as you wish."

Miss Paige turned to Archie and held out her hand to him. "Say that you will stay, Mr. Cummings! I could not bear it if I was to come between you and my lord."

Archie slowly took her hand and clasped it. "Thank you, Miss Paige. I am grateful. I apologize for my wife once more. She will be better presently."

"I am certain of it, Mr. Cummings!" said Miss Paige with a warm smile.

Mr. Bottler came forward and bowed. "Congratulations are in order, my lord! You have made a very pretty choice for your bride. Miss Paige, I am happy for your good fortune. You have been a sly one, though!"

"Oh, yes! Who could possibly have guessed that you would capture a lord, Miss Paige!" exclaimed Mrs. Bottler, tittering.

"And who could have guessed that your cousin would be unmasked as a Bonapartist spy?" Henry said, showing his teeth. "It quite brings into question your own loyalties, does it not, sir?"

Mr. Bottler took out a handkerchief and wiped his ample forehead. "As to that, my lord, I had not a single clue. I assure you of that! My only motive for accepting your kind invitation to Chester was to inspect that hunter that you had once mentioned you were wishing to sell."

"And now that you have bought it, Mr. Bottler, perhaps we should consider our business to be at an end," Henry said suggestively.

Mr. Bottler gave an uncomfortable laugh. "I take your meaning, Lord Cummings. My only regret is that we must leave you so soon. Come, Mrs. Bottler, say your good-byes. We must take our leave at once. We do not wish to outstay our welcome, as it were."

"Of course, Mr. Bottler. It is quite understood." Mrs. Bottler hung back for a moment longer, anxious to exonerate herself and her husband. "We do not know Mrs. Dabney at all well, you understand, my lord. She was related to a distant branch of the family. Why, it was during a chance meeting in Bath that we made her acquaintance at all. I never liked her, never."

"Quite true, Mrs. Bottler. I recall that you said so on more than one occasion," said Mr. Bottler.

"Of course, dear Miss Paige was quite a different story. I do trust that you will recall us fondly, Miss Paige," said Mrs. Bottler, bowing in her turn.

"Yes, yes! You must let us know when the wedding is to be so that we may send a proper gift," said Mr. Bottler expansively.

Miss Paige murmured something conciliating. Lord Cardiff clapped Mr. Bottler on the shoulder. "Allow me to escort you upstairs, sir. I shall set things in motion for your smooth departure."

"Too kind! So considerate!" exclaimed Mrs. Bottler.

"Not at all," said Lord Cardiff with a smile. He glanced back, his eyes full of laughter, as he ushered Mr. and Mrs. Bottler ahead of him and exited the room.

"Toad-eaters," Henry said with a curl of his lip.

"But useful in the end," said Chastity. "They brought Dru among us, after all."

"Yes, there is that," Henry agreed. "But our acquaintance

with them is completely at an end. Dru, you will not go back to that house."

"But where shall I go, then?" asked Miss Paige helplessly. "I have my friends in Bath, but they do not have much room for a long-term guest."

"You will remain here, of course," Henry said.

"That will not look at all well in the eyes of the world. She will do better to go home with me," said Lady Mackleby. "I will take her round to the shops so that she may acquire a proper trousseau. I will also introduce her to all of my friends. She will thus acquire a bit of town bronze before the wedding and become acquainted with some of the better circles. I imagine that I can do better by her than did Mrs. Dabney!"

Miss Paige looked rather alarmed at this program, and she sent a glance of appeal to Henry and Chastity. Henry appeared disinclined to accept Lady Mackleby's suggestion, but before he could utter his opinion, Chastity made known her own thoughts.

"It really is for the best. And do not deny it, Henry. You do not wish the least hint of scandal to attach itself to dear Dru, and you know that Lady Mackleby is just the one to establish her credibly and bring her out," said Chastity.

Henry frowned, obviously not liking it. However, he finally acquiesced. He raised his prospective bride's hand to his lips. "I will not be able to bear to be apart from you for long, my dear one. I promise that I will come up to London as soon as I can to be with you."

Miss Paige smiled, though her lips trembled slightly. "Then I really have nothing to fear, my lord." She turned to Lady Mackleby. "I accept your kind invitation with gratitude, my lady."

Lady Mackleby snorted. "I daresay. You've fallen into high grass, my girl, and you seem to have the sense to know it! Aye, you may color up all you wish. It becomes you. I wish Chastity had had just a tenth of your shyness. She might have been credibly established now, rather than becoming a maiden aunt!"

With that salvo, Lady Mackleby drew Miss Paige off with

her, expressing the intention to begin their packing. "There is not a moment to be lost. The weather could change at any time, and I do not wish to be caught fast at Chester by a snowstorm. My stay here has been extremely trying to my constitution."

Chapter Twenty-one

Chastity and Henry were left standing alone in the drawing room. He threw himself down in a wing chair and thrust his hands into his breeches pockets. "I am quite worn down with all of the excitement," he drawled. "It has made me hungry as a bear, too."

"I am not at all surprised. You have been up to your neck playing dangerous games and conducting a hidden romance!" retorted Chastity, sitting down opposite her brother.

Henry laughed. "I apologize, Chastity. I have used you abominably, haven't I?"

"Oh, no, it is all very amusing! Why, we have all participated in a grand charade from start to finish. I doubt that we ever have such a house party again," said Chastity, dropping her chin into her hand.

"I devoutly trust that we do not!" Henry said.

The door was flung open. Chastity and her brother looked around, equally startled. Regina rushed into the room, her eyes narrowed in a whitened face. When she saw Chastity, she exclaimed, "You are just the one I most particularly wish to see!"

Chastity was at once contrite. "I am sorry, Regina! I should not have upended the water vase over your head."

"I thought it rather a good notion."

"Shush, Henry. Can you not perceive that Regina is overset?" asked Chastity.

"Shall I find another vase of flowers?" asked Henry irreverently.

"I will thank you to stay out of this, my lord!" Regina uttered.

Henry's brows scaled upwards. "My lord! Am I no longer dear Henry to you, Regina?"

Archie abruptly came into the drawing room. He was breathing quickly, as though he had run downstairs. "Regina! This is not well done, believe me."

Regina paid no heed. She had eyes only for Chastity. "You knew! You knew that whey-faced nonentity was throwing her cap at Henry, didn't you?"

Henry straightened abruptly. "Regina, I warn you that I will not tolerate—"

Chastity waved him back. In a very cool voice, she said, "If you are speaking about Miss Paige, no, I did not. I did not realize that there was anything developing between her and Henry."

Regina glared at her sister-in-law. "Pray do not lie to me, Chastity! Such duplicity scarcely becomes you! Of course you knew. You are always in Henry's confidence. Everyone knows that. And you never gave a hint to me of what was in the wind."

Archie tried to stem his wife's hostile words. "Regina, this is not the time nor the place!"

She turned on him. "I will never be mistress of Chester, now that Henry is going to be wed! Don't you realize that?"

Henry leaned back in his chair, rather amused. "My dear Regina, I had no notion that you took such possessive pride in my holdings. Your ambitions on Archie's behalf are admirable, but rather misdirected, don't you think?"

Regina stomped her foot. "I want to leave immediately, Archie! Do you understand? Immediately!"

"Very well, Regina. We will do so, for you have put me to the blush once too often," Archie said. He turned to his brother, his eyes searching Henry's face. "However, we shall return for the wedding, if Henry and Drusilla will have us."

Henry stood up and reached out affectionately to clap his

brother on the back. "Archie, old fellow! I would not wish it any other way. You are to be my best man, you know."

Archie said in a rather choked voice, "Thank you, Henry. I will be honored, to say the least."

"Well, I shall not be at the wedding!" Regina declared.

Archie's expression suddenly hardened. Very coolly, he said, "Then you may remain in London, if that is your wish, Regina. But I shall come down for my brother's wedding day."

Regina stared at her husband, for once speechless. High spots of angry color flew into her cheeks. Archie took hold of her elbow and urged her toward the door. "Now let us go upstairs and ready ourselves for the journey, Regina," he said quietly.

"Unhand me at once!" Regina exclaimed in a furious voice.

"I think not, dear wife," said Archie, exiting with her out of the room.

Chastity watched them disappear, then turned an astonished expression to her other brother. "Henry! Did my eyes and ears deceive me? What just happened?"

Henry laughed. "I suspect that Archie is beginning to discover that he has a backbone, after all. I only hope that he is able to stick to his guns."

"Oh, so do I! Wouldn't it be marvelous if Archie did not let her bear-lead him anymore?" said Chastity. "I think that they would both be so much happier."

Henry looked at his sister curiously. "And what about you, Chastity? Are you made unhappy by my decision to wed?"

"Of course not! Dru is such a dear. Now, if it had been Mrs. Dabney, I would have expressed myself much the same as Regina," said Chastity.

Henry laughed.

There was a knock on the door, and they looked around. Lord Cardiff stood on the threshold. "Forgive me, my lord, Miss Cummings. I don't wish to intrude."

"Nonsense. You are always welcome, Cardiff. You should know that by now," Henry said. "In fact, I would like you to consider Chester as your second home anytime that you are able to visit."

"Thank you, my lord," said Cardiff. He advanced into the room, glancing in Chastity's direction. "My lord, would you mind if I had a few words alone with Miss Cummings?"

Henry threw a look at his sister. She was sitting quite still, smiling across at Lord Cardiff. A sudden light went on in his lordship's mind. He immediately stood up and started toward the door. "Not at all, Cardiff. I was just about to go up to speak to Lady Mackleby and Miss Paige about their departure. Perhaps I can persuade them to stay for luncheon." He left the room, shutting the door behind him.

Lord Cardiff had watched Lord Cummings exit and now turned back toward Chastity. "I hope that you are not annoyed that I have asked for this interview, Miss Cummings."

"Not at all, my lord," said Chastity quietly. She gestured to the wing chair near her. "Won't you be seated?"

Lord Cardiff sat down. For a moment he was silent. Then he said, "Miss Cummings, I believe that you understand that my true reason for coming to Chester at all was to play out the little drama that we had devised for Mrs. Dabney."

"Yes, it occurred to me when Mrs. Dabney's activities were brought to light," said Chastity.

Lord Cardiff looked around slowly. "Strange. I have come to feel quite at home at Chester, as though it has become in some way my own house."

"You will be leaving, of course. Where will you go?" asked Chastity curiously.

Lord Cardiff looked at her. He did not deny her statement. "I will return to London to report to my superiors the satisfactory end to this business. Then I will either return to Spain or spend the remainder of my leave with some friends or with my family."

"Pray remain with us here at Chester. You have become a very good friend in this short time, my lord," said Chastity.

Lord Cardiff smiled. "I will regret leaving Chester, Miss

Cummings. This place, and you, will always have a place in my heart."

"Thank you, my lord. I will remember you, too, very favorably." Chastity smiled at him.

She understood him rather well, she thought. He was a man not easily held or swayed by anything other than his own desires. His was a restless nature, which at present thrived on excitement. Chastity knew that with the thrill of international intrigue gone, Chester had become naught but a quiet country house.

Chastity studied his imperturbable face. "You take your leave too suddenly, my lord. I had hoped that you meant to stay a few days longer. We shall naturally have questions put to us when the neighborhood becomes aware of your departure. In fact, of the departure of so many of our number."

"My plans have of necessity been changed. Henry shall undoubtedly offer a suitable explanation if anyone expresses curiosity," said Lord Cardiff with a faint smile.

"You will certainly be missed, my lord," said Chastity sincerely.

He reached out to take her hand. Lifting it to his lips, he kissed her fingers. Retaining her hand for just a moment longer, he said quietly, "Good-bye, Miss Cummings."

"Good-bye, Lord Cardiff," said Chastity, equally quiet, but with a faint smile.

There was an expression almost of regret in his penetrating blue eyes. But Lord Cardiff did not say anything else. He merely smiled down at her for a long moment.

The door opened, and Mrs. Webster came in. She stopped short when she saw Chastity and Lord Cardiff. "Oh! I seem to make a habit of intruding upon you at the most inopportune times, dear Chastity," she said with a dismayed expression.

Lord Cardiff turned his head to smile at Mrs. Webster. "I was just going, ma'am." He bowed to Chastity and once more raised her hand to his lips. "Your servant, Miss Cummings," he said quietly. He nodded to Mrs. Webster and strode out.

Mrs. Webster turned a stricken face toward her niece. "I am

sorry, Chastity! I have run off another one of your gentle-men!"

"It is not of the least consequence, dear Aunt," said Chastity, rising. She tucked her hand into her aunt's elbow. "Now, what is that you wanted, Aunt?"

"Why, I was looking for the bone that I had given one of my dogs. I was certain that she was gnawing on it in here," said Mrs. Webster, peering around. "She wants it and is quite de-pressed that she hasn't got it anymore."

Chastity cleared her throat, covering up her impulse to laugh. "Indeed, Aunt? Well, I shall help you hunt for it. Per-haps it is under the settee?"

"You are such a very dear girl, Chastity. I do wish that you would tell me in advance when you are going to be entertain-ing a gentleman, for I would make certain then that I did not interrupt your tête-à-tête," said Mrs. Webster, watching as her niece got down on her knees to peer under the settee.

"You are quite right, Aunt Serena. It is simple thoughtless-ness on my side," said Chastity. She held up a small object. "Here it is! I trust that your dog will be considerably cheered to have it back."

"I am certain of it, my dear. She is so very sensitive, you know," said Mrs. Webster, happily taking possession of the sliver of bone.

Mrs. Webster left the drawing room. Chastity did not fol-low her, but instead went to the window and looked out. Below her, a private chaise stood on the graveled drive. As she watched, Lord Cardiff emerged from the manor. He was dressed for travel in a beaver and caped greatcoat. Chastity felt a tinge of regret at the departure of the handsome lord, but it was a surprisingly mild emotion. He paused on the front steps while he adjusted his gloves. As though he felt himself to be under observation, he glanced up at the window. Chastity did not draw back. She raised her hand in farewell.

Lord Cardiff sketched her a short bow. With an amiable nod, he bounded lightly down the steps. The gravel crunched under his boots as he strode rapidly to the waiting carriage. He climbed up into it and closed the door after himself.

Chastity did not wait to watch the carriage roll away down the drive. She left the drawing room and went downstairs to the dining room.

As she had half expected, Mr. Halston was serving himself at the sideboard. He glanced around to see who had entered, and his eyes lit up when he saw her. His expression warmed Chastity's heart. "All of this excitement makes one all the more hungry," he remarked.

"Yes, so Henry said," agreed Chastity.

She closed the door behind her. Without turning to look, she turned the key in the lock. At the grating sound, Mr. Halston's brows shot up.

"What are you about, Chastity?" he asked.

Chastity left the door and walked toward him. "I am compromising you, Jeffrey."

"Are you?" he asked, interested.

Chastity reached him. She took the plate from him and set it down on the sideboard. "Oh, yes. I most assuredly am," she assured him. She slipped her hands around his neck and stood on tiptoe to press her lips against his.

His arms came around her quickly, and suddenly it was he who was kissing her. Chastity melted into his tight embrace. When Mr. Halston raised his head, he was breathing rather quickly. There was a warm, astonished light in his eyes. "You have surprised me profoundly, Chastity."

"Do you dislike it?" she asked, tilting her head and looking up into his eyes.

"No! Oh, no, I do not dislike it," he said, and bent his head to kiss her again.

There was a rattling of the handle and a muffled banging on the dining room door, to which neither of them paid attention. At last, when she was able, Chastity remarked, "That must be Henry. He said that he was hungry as a bear."

"If I unlocked that door, we would certainly be compromised in the eyes of the world," said Mr. Halston musingly.

"How unfortunate. Would I be forced to marry you?" asked Chastity with intense curiosity.

"Yes, you would," said Mr. Halston firmly. There was a very warm expression in his eyes.

"Dearest Jeffrey! Open the door quickly!" said Chastity. "I should like to be compromised as soon as possible!"